CALLED UPON

Jason Swiney

Jim & Sandy,

Enjoy the adventure!

Jason

Colossians 3:17

Scripture quotations are from the Holy Bible, King James Version.

Copyright © 2014 by Jason Swiney

ISBN-13: 978-0692223680
ISBN-10: 0692223681

www.calledupon.com

To contact the author:
calleduponnovel@gmail.com

To Katie
My wife and best friend,
By my side through every adventure,
May God forever guide us,
Always Yours,
J

1

The man watched his prey from the diner's parking lot, where the darkness was aided by a current of gray clouds drowning out the summer moon and a neighboring gas station that had long closed for the night. Besides the light that spilled through the open blinds of the diner's large windows, only a single lamp post from the nearby gas station battled the darkness. But this very darkness, along with the interstate, descending from the mountain, within twenty seconds of pressing the accelerator, was precisely why the place had been chosen.

The man knew his territory.

Red numbers on the vehicle's clock reminded the man of how long he had waited, much longer than he had planned. But as he watched his prey move toward the cashier in the silent world behind the glass, the man readied his mind for the approaching moment. He exhaled slowly, methodically recited the rules, and felt the primal strength building and coursing within. Despite one unforeseen circumstance, which the man now convinced himself was fortune's gift, tonight's strike was inevitable. He had fallen behind and the chosen prey would feel his venom.

He quietly opened the van's door. The disabled interior light remained dark. Keys remained in the ignition. Other supplies waited neatly in the back.

He focused on his prey. No hesitation.

Strikes were about speed and timing.

Especially this one.

Yes, the man thought, especially this one.

2

G asping, I drew in the cool air forced downward by a churning ceiling fan. Sweat chilled my face and neck. Dull pains pulsed from my forehead and beneath the muscles of my left shoulder, but the sharpest pain, the one that frightened me most, ran along the edge of my left wrist. *Idiot.* I couldn't afford another fracture. Not now.

With unsteady eyes I surveyed my surroundings. A thick quilt stretched to my feet. The top of a plastic wastebasket rose above the cushions of an unfamiliar plaid couch that had apparently served as my bed. Afraid to move my left arm and wrist, I used my right hand to swipe my moist eyes and forehead. My palm burned immediately and I saw the loose bandage that dangled from the heel of my hand, exposing raw, scraped skin.

Where was I? I closed my eyes to search my memory but found only broken images of a dream that had tortured my sleep for weeks.

A lake, cold and dark...blanketed by fog...treading the frigid, choppy water...no shoreline...exhaustion...drowning.

I swallowed more air and opened my eyes for reassurance, but pain and guilt and nausea engulfed me. I had broken my word...and probably my wrist as well.

But where was I? And who had taken care of me?

I shifted tenderly onto my aching shoulder to peer into the wastebasket. Clean. But that was in sudden danger of changing as the room began to tilt, ricocheting the pain in my skull front to back, temple to temple. The repulsive taste of last night's drinks crawled up my throat.

I am better than this, I told myself, knowing months of training were potentially wasted. I grasped the wastebasket as the walls swayed. I lowered one foot to the floor to help hold the room still. Inhaling deep, closing my eyes, I counted silently as I exhaled. But the dream's bleak images returned.

The dark waters of the lake reemerged and pooled behind my closed eyelids. I exhaled slowly and continued counting as fog rolled across the water. As I braced for more images from my always fatal nightmare, the waters of the lake quickly receded and a new image emerged. A face. A teary-eyed female looked down on me, holding my own face in her soft, reassuring hands. She mouthed indistinguishable words. I shook at the unexpected image, my eyes wide, heart pounding. The lady's face was familiar and real. *Too real.*

My head was a mess.

I released a slow, extended breath and gradually sat, making sure the room held firm and my stomach held its contents. Water. My mouth and body yearned for it. As the room settled I glanced around for an entry to a kitchen or bathroom, savagely craving to stick my face under a faucet. But my unknown caretaker was a step ahead. On the coffee table, within arm's reach, a glass of water glistened on a coaster. Beside it waited a bottle of Tylenol, more bandages, and a tube of ointment. At least I had plummeted into the home of an angel.

I reached for the glass with my left arm to test the throbbing wrist but my hand trembled with the weight of the water. I cursed and switched the glass to my right. With one long drink I emptied it. The Tylenol could wait until I found more water, but first I needed to get my bearings.

Light filtered in through three high windows. A rock fireplace dominated most of the main wall. Pictures and candles lined a thick wooden mantle. A dark, polished piano sat in one corner. Placing the empty glass back on the coaster I noticed the light blue stationery under the bottle of pills.

Bradley,

There are muffins on the kitchen counter if you're hungry. Help yourself. I have your keys and wallet, so please don't call anyone to pick you up. If you leave I will track you down within hours. So just call this number when you're ready.

282-7723

Mark

5

3

I crumpled the note against my raw palm, grabbed the Tylenol bottle, and stood from the couch. The room wobbled but I kept moving, aiming for the row of pictures above the fireplace. The pain in my shoulder and wrist flared again as I reached for the mantle.

Strangers stared from the pictures. Behind one slightly dusty pane, a family of four posed after sunset on an immaculate white beach. Two smiling sisters sat back to back on the sand in front of their kneeling parents. All were barefoot and wore khaki colored shorts and dark blue tops of various styles.

A nice-looking family…a nice looking family that I didn't know.

I brought the picture closer. My mom would have killed for such a moment. The thought caused me to smirk, knowing she would have literally had to strangle my older brothers to make it happen.

The father in the picture, with the sleeves of his navy dress shirt rolled midway up his forearms, shared the dark hair and dark skin of his oldest daughter. A thick mustache hid part of his smile. Mark, I assumed, but I couldn't place him. Nor did I know the girls. The oldest, in that middle school stage of awkwardly cute, grinned tightly, as if trying to hide a mouthful of braces. The youngest sported pink-rimmed glasses and showed more teeth than a crocodile in a smile that stretched across her face.

I didn't know these people…but I was in their home.

Slender with lighter hair, I wondered if perhaps the mother in the picture was connected to the college. Her face seemed familiar. *Was she the lady I had just envisioned hovering over me, holding my own face in her hands? Perhaps.* Or perhaps they were all strangers who simply found me on their doorstep. I cleaned the glass of dust and fingerprints with the front of my shirt and returned the picture to the mantle.

And then it struck me.

This Mark had left the note, but where was his family?

"Hello?" I called toward a dimly lit hallway leading from the den. I moved closer, picking up the empty water glass from the coffee table along the way. "Hello?" I called again, louder. Nothing.

Had these people simply left me in their home?

My head and throat sent sharp reminders of pain and thirst, both wrestling to be acknowledged first. A few steps into the dim hallway I found the kitchen. On a black granite counter sat a basket draped with a green kitchen towel. A smell assuring salvation from hunger seeped from under-neath. *Blueberry muffins.*

A cordless phone waited near the basket. I devoured a muffin, washed down two Tylenol, and attempted to sum-mon the courage to dial the number on the crumpled note. What choice did I have? I reached for the phone.

Think. Think. What happened last night? The party was the last thing I remembered, but how did I-

The sudden shrill ring of the phone in my hand startled me. As my pounding heart began to settle, the ring contin-ued to echo painfully within my skull. *Private number* glowed across the phone's Caller ID screen. I waited for the caller to give up.

Where was I? And what had I gotten myself into?

I wanted to do exactly what the paper instructed me not to do. I wanted to run. I wanted to go out the front door and call someone to pick me up…to find me…wherever I was. But it was summer session, meaning all of my teammates and the majority of my friends were away from campus. The few I did know had been at the same party and were probably in similar shape.

And I wasn't calling Coach Glynn. *Coach*. He always said to call him in any situation, but we knew better. I studied the numbers on the note. "Face your fear," I said aloud, mocking my coach's gruff voice. I dialed.

"Hello?" answered a quick, solemn voice after one ring.

"Umm…yes…is this Mark?"

"Is this the young man who slept on my couch last night?" the man asked.

"Yes sir, I'm sorry about…I'm not sure how I…um… sir, do I know you?"

"Bradley, do you make a habit of waking up in strangers' homes?"

"No sir, this is not a usual-"

"Listen Bradley, it is *Bradley* right?" he asked. "Bradley Curran Morrow it says on the driver's license I'm holding, or do you go by Brad?"

"Brad was my father's name, I go by *BC* actually."

"Well *BC*, make yourself at home. See you in five minutes." The man abruptly ended the conversation. I put the phone on its cradle and finished off a second and third blueberry muffin. Still hungry enough to devour the only remaining muffin, I folded the green cloth over it instead.

Five minutes.

Passing a mirror in the hallway I encountered my horrid reflection. Bloodshot eyes. Wild hair. I must have slept hard on one side and never moved. The left side of my hair was matted to my head while the right flared toward the ceiling like the angling spray of a slaloming water skier. I needed my hat.

I searched around the couch before realizing it must be in my car. *My car? Where was my car?* I grabbed my shoes, un-laced and placed neatly by the couch, hurried outside to a neighborhood street I didn't recognize, and found my aging Honda sitting alone in the driveway. I checked it for any new signs of damage before reaching for the handle. No obvious dents or scrapes, but…locked.

And this *Mark* had my keys.

Back inside I quickly found a bathroom and tried to tame my hair. As I finger brushed my teeth with borrowed tooth-paste, the thud of a shutting car door sounded outside. I hur-ried into the living room and halted ten feet or so from the door. Steps sounded along the front porch. Sweat beaded again on my forehead. Uneasiness grew in my gut.

Should I open the door for the man to his own home?

Should I take a seat…should I just stand here?

Was there any possible way to play this cool?

In front of the couch, beside the wastebasket, the quilt which had covered me lay crumpled in the floor. I grabbed it and began folding as keys rattled in the lock. My heart pounded and my stomach swirled as the door opened. I met Mark's eyes as he appeared in the doorway, but my "Hello" never came. Instead, I instinctively grabbed the plastic wastebasket as a wave of blueberry mush and red liquor exploded from my mouth. Doubled over, I kept my face in the plastic container. A second wave followed.

"Well good morning," I heard Mark say. "You sounded much better on the phone."

4

I scanned the road that ran in front of Mark's house wishing once again to just take off, flee, high-tail it down the road and not look back. But I didn't even know which direction to run. Without much choice, I tossed the trash bag into the roadside bin, glanced at my locked car beside Mark's Ford Explorer, and headed back inside the house.

Mark was in the kitchen when I returned. Lowering my eyes, I took a seat at the breakfast table where a canned Coke and a damp washrag already waited. Mark remained silent on the opposite side of the counter, but his stare burrowed into my skull. I wiped my hands and face with the cool, wet rag.

"Well, *BC Morrow*, I'm Mark Boone," he finally said. "It's nice to meet you face to face and conscious. Why don't you try sipping on that Coke? It always settles my stomach, not that I ever find myself in your situation."

"Thanks," I managed. Head down, I focused on a lone ladybug making its way atop the intricate floor tiles until I once again became dizzy.

"How about a blueberry muffin?"

"I'll pass," I answered, holding my stomach. I popped the Coke lid for a cautious drink. The cold can felt soothing against my scraped palm. I stole a quick glance at Mark Boone as he peeled back the green towel and took the remaining blueberry muffin. He was definitely the man from the picture. He appeared to be in his early forties, thin but solid, like he still knew his way around a weight room. The thick mustache was gone, replaced by a short, well-groomed goatee. His eyes were purposeful and uninviting. I quickly looked back down to the swirling tiles.

"So BC, what do you remember about last night?" Mark got straight to the point and the question startled me. I had hoped for answers, not questions.

"Not much sir," I said. "Well, not anything really. Have I done something stupid?"

"Besides waking up hung over in a stranger's home? Son, you're lucky to even be alive. Are you hurting anywhere?"

Lucky to be alive? What does he mean by-

"Are you hurting anywhere?" he repeated.

"I hurt everywhere." I placed the cold Coke against my forehead. "But mainly my left side, especially my wrist." I held my left arm in the air and squeezed my hand several times, trying to compare the pain to the previous breaks. The first time it was fractured, in a bike wreck at fourteen, it had been crooked, ugly, and obvious. The second break, a mere six months ago, was a lingering pain until verified by x-ray. A pain much like this one. A pain that required a cast and then weeks of rehabbing, weeks I couldn't afford right now.

"And where were you drinking last night?" Mark continued.

I did know that answer. I assumed Mark did too, so no use in lying. "A house at Eagle Cliffs. Some freshman's family has a summer home on a bluff. I really didn't know a lot of people there, but-"

"*Eagle Cliffs*? Drinking with those gated-community ritzy folks, huh? And then trying to drive all the way back to campus?"

I hung my head, "Apparently so." I had avoided such wild social gatherings for months. I had even avoided the infamous marathon of graduation parties for my older, senior buddies at the end of the school year. I had set a goal, made a commitment, and stuck to it. I had even signed a contract that I had written for myself. And then, for reasons I couldn't explain, I had allowed myself to drift back to old habits.

"Why is a college boy still here during the summer anyway?" Mark asked. "Did you fail some classes?"

"No sir…just working." *And training*, I thought, but saying it didn't seem appropriate in my present condition. I rubbed my temples and hoped the interview would soon be over.

"So, just partying, working, and trying to stay out of Dalton, huh?" asked Mark.

"How did you-" I looked up to see Mark displaying my open wallet and driver's license.

"Bradley Curran Morrow. Six feet and one inch tall, one hundred and eighty-five pounds, from Dalton, Georgia. Twenty-one years old." Mark tossed the wallet onto the counter in front of him. Beside it he placed a folded five-dollar bill and my cell phone.

"These were in your pockets too," he said. "But I'll keep your keys for now."

I had suddenly had enough of this conversation.

"Look, sir, I'm not sure about anything this morning. I am very sorry for whatever trouble I have put you and your family through, but I need to get going. I hope I haven't done anything stupid...or harmful. But I was hoping you would tell me how I...."

Mark's faint grin vanished and his eyes narrowed.

"BC, does it feel good to not remember the things you've done?"

"No sir, I-"

"Do you think it's safe for severely intoxicated college boys to be operating vehicles when they can't even control their own mind and body?"

"No sir."

Mark started around the counter. I straightened, suddenly fearing what I may have done to this man, or worse, to his family. And then I saw the gun. A black pistol holstered on the approaching man's hip. Beside the weapon shimmered a bronze badge.

"You're a police officer?"

"I'm a captain and detective with the Halston County Sheriff's Department, so now do you understand why I don't condone the late night actions of Bradley Curran Morrow?"

"Yes sir." *Good grief*, I thought, *how did I end up in a police officer's home?*

Mark stopped on the opposite side of the breakfast table. Lean muscles flexed throughout his forearms as he gripped and squeezed the top of an empty chair. His forceful, penetrating eyes were locked on mine.

"Am I going to jail?" I asked, the words stumbling from my mouth.

"BC, there's only one reason you're not in jail, but we'll get to that. First, I need to know what you remember after leaving this party."

"Nothing sir, I'm sorry. I know I shouldn't have tried to drive-"

"But you did, BC. You-"

"Did I hurt someone?" I pleaded. "Please tell me, did I hurt anybody?"

Captain Mark Boone of the Halston County Sheriff's Department didn't answer. Without breaking his stare, he spun the chair, placed a black combat-style boot in the seat and leaned toward me. "Son, I'm not going to tell you what you did last night. I don't want to plant any false memories in your head. But I need you to remember as much as you can on your own. Do you understand?"

I knew nothing. My mind was a mess.

"Do you understand?" Mark repeated louder.

"Yes sir, I think so...do I need a lawyer or something?"

Mark seemed to ponder the question. "Son, let's take a ride." He turned toward the door. I quickly grabbed my wallet, cash, and cell phone from the counter and followed the detective out of his kitchen, wondering if my next destination was the Halston County jail. Once outside, Captain Mark Boone opened the passenger door of his unmarked, charcoal-colored Explorer and pulled out his radio.

"Captain Boone sir...did I drive here last night?" I asked.

"Not even close, BC. Are you staying on campus?"

I gave the detective the address of the place I had just found for rent a week earlier, which I only remembered due to its odd name and numbering. Mark radioed in.

"This is two-seven, go ahead nine," responded a static-filled voice on the radio.

"Two-seven, I will be in need of a ten-twenty-five in approximately ten minutes at 333 Burning Maple, you available?"

"10-4, meet you there Capt'," came the reply. So the police station *wasn't* my next stop. Regardless, with my

15

current landlord, being brought home by a cop probably meant once again looking for another place to stay.

Mark moved toward my car and motioned for me to get in the passenger side. As soon as he unlocked the doors I scanned the backseat and floorboard for my faded green Boston Celtics hat. No luck, but a dirty maroon cap lay at my feet. *Yonah State Park,* a place I had never heard of, arched in tan stitching across the front. The hat, filthy and smelling of campfire, had apparently been left by one of my recent passengers. I thought of my horrid reflection and hair in Mark's mirror, adjusted the back strap, and shoved the dirty hat on anyway.

I had expected Mark to pop the trunk or skim through the junk piled in the backseat, but the car was in reverse two seconds after the engine cranked. Mark, I assumed, had already made himself familiar with my car's contents. We exited the driveway and within three turns traveled a road I finally recognized.

We were in Andrews, an interstate town between campus and last night's party. Although the entire area was considered part of the same mountain, the two-lane highway from Andrews ascended even higher as it snaked toward Cohutta College.

My five-speed quickly hit fifth gear, and Captain Mark Boone only seemed to be missing some blue lights, a siren, and a criminal to pursue. I usually enjoyed the mountain drive toward campus, but my stomach swirled as Mark attacked the curves. I put both feet flat on the floorboard and closed my eyes. *One...two...three...exhale...*

"Just a few more miles," said Mark, shifting down then quickly back to fifth. "I haven't driven a stick in a while...I miss this."

I finally quit counting. The spinning-room trick to combat hangovers had no chance on winding asphalt at high speed, and neither did I. "Mark, I'm not feeling so well, you may need to slow-"

"It's your car, puke all you want."

I lowered the window and tilted my face against the rush of the warm June morning.

"So Mr. BC Morrow, you don't live on campus. Are you renting a house?"

I placed both hands on the dashboard, inhaled deep, and exhaled slowly. "I'm renting an upstairs from an older guy," I finally managed. More curves loomed ahead.

"What's his name? If he lives this close to Andrews, I'll know him."

I thought for a moment, trying to get my landlord's name correct in my head. "Mr. Giles...*Eli* I believe is his first name."

Mark grinned. "You don't say. I know *Mister* Giles quite well. But the real question is how well do you know him?" Not well at all, I thought, but well enough to know that showing up hung over with a police escort was a problem. My stomach churned.

"I only found the place a week ago," I said. "It's cheap, and I may just need it for a couple more weeks. I slept on a friend's couch in the dorms at the beginning of summer session but-"

"But the college kicked you out because you weren't taking classes."

"Something like that."

"And then you found my couch last night," Mark responded. "Well, BC, that may have actually worked in your favor."

17

I assumed I knew what Mark was implying but I waited silently for clarification, my head and stomach still battling the winding road.

"Eli Giles is a good man," Mark continued, "but you would have been looking for another friend's couch if you had stumbled into Eli's home in your condition last night. I can get Eli's home number, but I'll need your cell number."

The turn onto Burning Maple, Mr. Giles' road, was finally in sight, but my nausea was worsening. "Can I write it when we stop?"

Mark laughed. I fully expected Mark's parking display in Mr. Giles' gravel driveway to include a screeching 180-degree slide that would make a stunt driver jealous.

"Captain Boone, you said there was a reason I wasn't...um, in jail?"

"I said we'd get to that."

"Well, can you tell me how I ended up at your house?"

"BC, let's just say you had a very eventful night, and as I said, I would first like for you to try and remember as much as possible on your own. It's important, very important. But I'll be in contact soon, probably within the next few hours. Take a shower. Clean yourself up. You may have to come back to town to get that wrist checked anyway. But keep your cell phone close."

As we pulled into the gravel drive I locked eyes with a silver-haired patrolman already waiting in his car between a row of thick Leyland Cyprus and the roadside. He gave a quick nod to Mark and followed us toward the house. I was relieved to see that my landlord's black, weathered truck wasn't in the driveway. Mark parked without any stunt maneuvers, raised the windows, and turned off the ignition. He handed me two business cards and a pen.

"Keep one, write your cell number on the other. You mentioned working on campus, so give me that number as well."

I hesitated. "It won't come directly to me."

"Will they know where to find you?"

I hesitated again, too long to answer *no*.

"And where are you working on campus?" Mark asked.

I wanted to lie but couldn't pull the trigger. "I work for the athletic department," I finally admitted. "Mowing fields, painting, cleaning storage rooms...summer grunt work mostly."

"Sounds like a cushy job. How did you end up with that?" Mark asked.

I knew it was time to lie. I hadn't been taken to jail. Captain Mark Boone didn't seem interested in speaking with Eli Giles, my anti-alcohol, anti-partying landlord of less than a week. But this is where the truth could prove fatal. I just needed to keep basketball and Coach Glynn and the chance of a lifetime, which I may have already ruined, out of the conversation.

"Captain Boone, did you say you were calling me, or I was to call you?"

"I didn't, I asked if you played a sport on campus. I'm not sure you're thick enough to be a football player, even at a small college like Cohutta. So I'm saying baseball, shortstop or outfield. Am I right?"

I reached for the handle.

Captain Mark Boone jingled my keys. "If you want these just answer my question."

"I play basketball, sir. Point guard. I'll be a senior this up-coming season," I blurted. Mark didn't react, but his stare said keep talking. "I've been on campus training for an all-conference team that will be playing exhibition games in Europe in early August. The final try-out is less than two weeks away in Nashville. But I may have just ended that dream last night." As I spoke I felt the pain flaring again across my injured wrist. I hated to say anything more, but now I couldn't leave the car without knowing one answer. "Captain Boone, will you be speaking with my coach for any reason?"

Detective Mark Boone squared my direction and his eyes locked on mine.

"BC, that is yet to be determined, nor is that my main concern right now. What *is* a definite at the moment is that I need to shake your hand." Mark extended his right hand. I waited for the punch line to some sarcastic police joke, but Mark's eyes were genuine, his expression serious. I glanced oddly at Mark's outstretched hand and reached my own toward the detective.

The same detective who was driving my car because I got liquor drunk off some college-style punch, did who knows what, ended up on the man's couch, and threw up in his trashcan. Of course he would want to shake my hand.

Mark's grip was extremely tight. "BC Morrow," he said. "Thank you…" Before he could continue his jaw quivered. The detective quickly swiped a building wetness in his eye with the back of his left hand. He took in a long, deep breath. "Thank you BC for saving my daughters last night. I can't repay you for what you did, but I'll try. Son…I thank you more than you'll ever know…now get to remembering. *We've* got work to do."

Mark bolted from the car and was pulling out with the deputy by the time I could process all he had said.

"Thank you for saving my daughters?"

What *did* happen last night?

My mind was an absolute mess.

I leaned the passenger seat back and stared at the ceiling. I pulled the dirty maroon hat that smelled of campfire down over my face and closed my eyes, trying with all my might to recall the events of the previous evening.

Within minutes I was back asleep.

5

The man squatted, his bare back resting against the rough bark of a pine tree. He had been there for hours, watching the path, long before the sun had started warming the forest. Sweat beaded and slithered down the man's chest and arms. The sweat, he knew, was not only from the heat, but from the pain. He breathed in spurts, fighting the pain from ribs he assumed were cracked, battling the weakness, keeping his attention toward the descending path and the forest below.

Except for the knife blade he spun slowly against his palm, the man remained still. He replayed the events in his mind, enraged that he never thought to pull the blade from his belt during the intruder's attack. It would have ended the disruption. It would have ended the transgressor. He would have gotten his prey.

He dug the blade's tip into his palm and watched the deep red blood bubble forth and drip to the ground. He exhaled slowly, beating back the weakness, defeating the pain.

The unexpected encounter, he knew, had changed the game. And now there would be consequences…for him…and for others.

The man watched one last drop of red disappear into the dirt before turning his eyes back to the path. The summer foliage was too dense for him to see the van he had left beneath the trees somewhere far below. But he waited and listened intently for sirens...for searchers...for more transgressors. Let them come, the man thought. Let them chase. Let them feel the strike of a true predator.

Except for the slow turns of the blade, the man remained motionless. He narrowed his eyes and controlled his breathing.

Coiled, watching, waiting.

6

"Boy, you alright?"

"Huh?"

"You alright?"

Curious eyes and a weathered face hovered over me as the world came into focus. My face and arms glistened in perspiration and my mind clung to a fading dream, where once again reality had been replaced by a dark lake, a dense fog, and my own drowning. The taste attacking my mouth was nothing short of awful. It was as if I had once again started the day in the same miserable condition. I needed more water. I needed more Tylenol.

Instead, I had Mr. Eli Giles studying me as if I was unidentified road kill.

"Sorry to open up the door and startle you," said Mr. Giles. "But you weren't quite responding to knocks on the window. I was just making sure you hadn't gone belly up on me."

"I'm okay Mr. Giles…didn't mean to sleep out here. I guess I need to get moving." I leaned forward and cradled my head in my hands. Again I felt the stinging scrapes along the heels of my palms and the throbbing of my left wrist and shoulder.

"You sure you're okay?"

"I'm good Mr. Giles, just tired."

"And how'd you end up on the passenger side of your own car anyway, you waiting on your chauffeur?" The old man laughed at his little joke.

"Long story, but I'm not waiting. I'm coming inside."

By my guess Eli Giles was somewhere in his seventies, maybe even eighty. Even in early June the old man wore a long-sleeve collared shirt beneath faded overalls and a worn blue cap of the local high school atop his lanky frame. The only feature that ruined his farmer-meets-mountain-man ensemble was the off-brand, grey sneakers with the Velcro straps.

"Boy, a man has got the right to sleep where he chooses, even the passenger seat of his little car if he wants. But it looked to me like you were about to wither like a dried corn stalk in there. At least turn the air on while you sleep, or pull under a shade tree."

"I appreciate that Mr. Giles."

I checked my watch. Twelve forty-five. I had slept for nearly an hour.

Mr. Giles had already turned and was carrying a lawn chair to the shade of a large poplar tree. Every few steps he turned and said something in my direction, as if he was debating the mental state of his new renter. I admired how easily Eli moved for his age, while the college athlete who had been training for months struggled to get out of a car. Pulling my left elbow across my chest to stretch my knotted shoulder muscles, I instead caught a whiff of my own stench. *The old man had gotten right in my face*, I thought. Surely he recognized the smell of alcohol oozing through an idiot's pores. But Mr. Giles hadn't mentioned it, and that made my guilt even worse.

I slowly made my way onto the stone porch and inside the two-story farm-style house. The home had more space and character on the inside than could be detected from a casual exterior glance. My section was upstairs, the entire upstairs, made up of three rooms and a central hallway. There were two bedrooms, one of which had been converted into a small den, and a snug bathroom. Two of the bedroom windows looked toward the back of Mr. Giles' property. The old man had a half-acre garden bordered on the far end by a series of large, gray rocks protruding like whale backs rolling out of a green sea. Beyond the rocks, the mountain sloped quickly into forested ridges before melting into the valley. The amount of living space, the view, the cheap rent, and the fact that I could no longer be a squatter in the dorms had made it impossible to turn down.

I simply had to abide by Mr. Giles three rules: No drinking, no girls, and no loud music. That was fair enough, and besides, I had told him, I wasn't on campus this summer for those things. I was here to save some spending money and to train. At least I had been. On a wall in my new room was tacked the all-conference try-out invitation and my training calendar. For further motivation a mint, unstamped passport waited on the desktop below. Only thirteen days remained until the two-day try-out for rising seniors from our eight-team conference. Twenty-two senior players had been invited, only twelve would be chosen. Those selected for the team would play games in six different European countries over two weeks in early August before the Fall semester started.

And I was on a mission to make that team.

I studied my training calendar. I had planned for two hours of my Saturday to be spent at the campus athletic center, the Joe-MAC, but that wasn't going to happen. With a black marker I crossed out everything written beside the *13* and wrote "WASTED". Then, beside the *12* on Sunday I wrote "Triple Everything". If the left wrist wasn't in a cast by tomorrow I'd just have to make up the missed work. One morning session. One lunch session. One evening session. I had plans for Europe.

I intended to take a quick shower, but the steamy water was rejuvenating, and aches and pains loosened from my body and swirled down the drain. But not the wrist. It throbbed and felt weak. If it wasn't significantly better by morning I would call Whitman, the team trainer, and have him look at it. Closing my eyes against the spray, arms extended against the shower wall, I suddenly shook at the unexpected vision of falling forward with outstretched hands toward a dark, asphalt ground.

Without warning, the first memory of my missing night had arrived.

Between the invigorating shower and the sporadic flashes of forgotten events, I lost track of time. When the water finally became a jolting, freezing downpour, I toweled off and grabbed a notepad from my room. As I scribbled I remembered more, like the dam holding back a river of lost images was crumbling in slow, random chunks.

And suddenly the faces of two frightened girls emerged before me. *Was I actually remembering them or simply seeing the faces from Mark's family picture?* This had to be real. They were older, much older...scared...and yelling. *Their names? What were their names?*

Mark never mentioned his daughters by name and if they had told me it was still lost within my head. I closed my eyes and clearly recalled the panic in their faces.

27

"Thank you for saving my daughters," the detective had said.

From what?

From *who?*

And then the third figure emerged. A man. Tall, lean, but quick and strong. He had no face, at least not one my memory could recreate. He had moved toward the girls in the parking lot. He had...

How could I have forgotten this?

I jotted down a few more notes before my memory ran dry. I dug semi-clean clothes from my bags and took two granola bars from the snack pile on my desk. My body welcomed the simple nourishment. I chewed quickly and again studied the training chart tacked to the wall, wondering how long these injuries and this mess with Mark Boone's daughters would keep me away from the court. I looked at my scraped palm as the vision of falling against an asphalt ground flashed before me once again.

How had I gotten myself involved with something like this?

I decided to drive back to Andrews, find some actual food, and be closer to the police station in case Captain Mark Boone called. I grabbed the notepad, hurried down the wooden stairs and out onto the porch. The screen door's creaking caught the attention of my landlord sitting across the yard in the shade. Mr. Giles' feet were propped on an overturned half-barrel and he held a Mason jar of tea.

"Taking off again?" Eli yelled. "Well tonight you're more than welcome to sleep upstairs in that room *you're renting.* No need to sleep in the woods...or in your car...or wherever you took refuge last night."

"I think I'll take you up on that offer."

Eli grinned, gave a quick two-finger wave with his free hand, and went back to watching the world exist.

7

I was hungry. Hungry enough that I nearly finished off a large, thick-crusted pepperoni pizza with green peppers and onions at Miss Celia's Pizzeria. I leaned back to stretch out my stomach and threw the white napkin of surrender onto the last remaining slice. "Defeated," I said to no one in particular. One slice away from victory but I couldn't do it. With the lunch crowd long gone and the supper patrons yet to arrive, I mostly had the place to myself. I found the aging juke box on the wall and played four songs for a dollar: Johnny Cash, CCR, Counting Crows and a Bruce Spring-steen from the Nebraska album. Nothing wrong with some old stuff.

I returned to my table and skimmed the randomness scribbled on my notepad.

...left the party...sitting behind the dumpster...
...man in a dark van...did something to the tire...
...two girls...man approached...quick...
...I tried to yell...

Other pieces of the lost night floated in my mind but I struggled as to where they fit in the evolving puzzle. I tore off the sheet, started over, and attempted to put the events in order. Halfway through the new draft my cell phone rang.

Private number.

"Hello Captain Boone," I answered.

"You skipped town yet?"

"Halfway to Mexico," I countered.

"You got anything for me?"

"Actually I do, sir, and I'm in town already. Do I come to the sheriff's office or to your house?" I asked.

"The sheriff's office," replied the detective. "Report to the front desk and they'll send you through."

"To your office or to my concrete cell?"

Mark laughed. "How soon can you be here?"

"Five minutes, and I know where it is."

"Why's that? Have you been an overnight guest with us before?"

"No sir. I've never spent time in the Halston County jail."

"Well, BC, the day's not over," the detective said before hanging up.

* * *

The Halston County Correctional Center was a massive complex. It sat on one of the many ridges extending south of Andrews. From the outside one could tell it was a divided facility. One portion had large windows, immaculate land-scaping, and a wide parking area. The other section, three stories tall, had narrow windows which I assumed didn't open and was surrounded by a double row of high fencing topped with coiled razor wire. It was obvious which half a person wanted to visit.

Inside the lobby, framed pictures of former sheriffs and previous Halston County jails lined the walls. The oldest pic-ture, which depicted a one-story wooden structure with iron-barred windows, seemed to be taken directly from an old Western.

"BC Morrow?" asked one of two female deputies from behind a thick-glassed reception area as soon as I entered. I nodded as she pointed toward a black metal door to my right. The door buzzed and unlocked as I reached for it. "First hallway on the left, third door on the right. Captain Boone is expecting you," she said.

Following her directions, I found Captain Mark Boone and another man in a clean, spacious office seated at a conference table. Both stood as I entered.

"BC, this is Detective Trent Ingle. Trent, this is Mr. BC Morrow, star basketball player and senior at the college."

"Is that right?" asked Detective Trent Ingle. "Star player, huh?"

"Not quite," I answered, shaking the detective's hand and taking a seat.

"I've always been more of a football guy myself," said the younger detective. Trent Ingle looked to be in his late twenties. He had a cropped, military-style haircut and wore khaki cargo pants that perhaps fit better in earlier years. Both men wore black Polo-style shirts with an embroidered *Halston County Investigative Division* insignia.

"How is that memory doing?" Mark asked.

"Better, much better. I think I may be able to help some." I tapped on the notepad and dropped it to the table. Detective Ingle made a slight fist pump of approval. "But Captain Boone, I can't make out the man's face. I'm not sure that I ever really saw it, and I assume a description is what you want from me."

"It would be nice," said Mark. "But at least you remembered that there *was* a man. I was becoming a little worried after you couldn't remember anything this morning. I started thinking you may have suffered a concussion to go along with that hangover. But maybe more will come back to you as we go through it."

"Let's take a look at what you've got," said the younger detective. I slid the notepad across the table. It felt strange hearing my memory read aloud in Detective Ingle's voice.

"I left the party at Eagle Cliffs and drove back through Andrews. I must have realized that I didn't need to be driving because I pulled into the Waffle Shack parking lot to rest. I got out of my car to walk around or puke, I can't remember, but I ended up behind the dumpster sitting against a fence…"

"So you first saw the suspect while you were behind the dumpster?" Mark asked.

"Yes, sir. I think so anyway."

"How close were you to his van?" Detective Ingle asked.

"I don't know. Not very far. Thirty feet or so. I remember hiding from the headlights as he pulled in. I really didn't want to be seen at the time, you know? But I guess I got curious after I never heard his door open. He just sat, parked near the dumpster, facing the restaurant. I just hoped that he would leave before I was ready to go back to my car. I guess I just assumed he was waiting on his wife or girlfriend to get off work. I must have peeked out when I finally heard his door open. I remember him walking toward the car parked between his and the restaurant…your daughter's car…and messing with the tire."

"How did you not see his face when he turned to walk back?" Detective Ingle asked. His tone made me feel less like the witness and more like the criminal.

"I just didn't…I probably ducked back behind the dumpster when he turned around, I'm not sure. But I do remember hearing the van's side door being slid open."

"Hearing it but not seeing it?" Detective Ingle asked.

"Let's get back to cutting the tire," Mark said. "What I am trying to figure out is how he knew to cut *their* tire. How did he know that two young females would be in that car?"

"I don't know. As I said, I think their car was already there."

"So he didn't follow them into the parking lot?" asked Captain Boone.

"He could have, but I really don't think-"

"Perhaps he didn't expect *two* girls," said Detective Ingle. "Perhaps that threw him off."

"But the monster still went after them both," said Mark.

The younger detective nodded toward me. "Well, the guy definitely didn't expect our drunk-dumpster hero to come running out of nowhere."

And that was the last thing I could remember, running toward a figure who had grabbed two girls from behind. *But hero?* I hadn't thought about that. Probably because I didn't quite feel like one, and besides, the description was dripping with sarcasm as it spilled from Detective Ingle's mouth.

"Is this going to be on the news?" I asked.

Captain Mark Boone leaned forward and rested both elbows on the table. His dark eyes narrowed. He rubbed his chin with his trigger finger. "You need a little fame, do you?" he asked.

"No sir, not at all," I replied. "That's not what I meant. I was…I was hoping to avoid being known as…" I looked back toward Detective Ingle. "As the *drunk-dumpster hero*."

"Then I would avoid getting drunk," Mark stated.

"Yes sir, I know…I just-"

"For now, it will not be on the news, BC. My girls didn't even call the police, it seems they panicked and headed home as fast as they could. Laurie, my oldest, got you and Maggie into your car and just drove. Laurie couldn't find her cell phone in the confusion. She thought she lost it in the parking lot, so she never even attempted to call 911."

"I don't remember any of that," I mumbled.

"I know you don't," Mark said. "Detective Ingle, will you continue reading for us what BC Morrow *does* remember." Mark leaned back in his chair and clasped his hands behind his head. Detective Trent Ingle read the remainder of what I had written. When he finished both men waited for several seconds before peppering me with more questions:

"Did the man have any tattoos or distinguishing marks?"

"Did you ever look at his license plate while squatting behind the dumpster?"

"Is this the best you can tell us about his van? Dark color, dark windows?"

"What about the…Did you notice any…Do you remember…"

I felt exhausted at the end of the questioning. I hoped both detectives knew I was trying to help, but with each smirk or sarcastic jab I was starting to care less and less about what Detective Ingle thought. Both were obviously frustrated attempting to deal with a witness who wasn't of sound mind during the attack, but then again, my condition was the very reason I was crouched behind that dumpster in the first place.

Thankfully, Detective Ingle left first. He shook my hand but not as eagerly as before. I didn't know if Captain Boone was finished with me, but I wasn't budging from the chair, much less leaving, until he dismissed me. Although I had been at the right place at the right time to save two lives, I had clearly admitted to driving while intoxicated to two officers of the law.

"BC, we have to get a better description of that vehicle," Mark finally said. "Laurie was able to help us some with the guy's description. She saw him as he fled, but it is such a dark area and he had his cap pulled low. But she swears his cap had a small emblem on the back, like a club."

"A *club*?"

"Like on a playing card…she saw a symbol she thought resembled a club, but white."

He paused and I could see the wheels turning behind his eyes. Mark looked comfortable in deep thought, and from my brief time with him I got the impression he was a solid investigator. But how did Mark stay so calm working a case that was obviously so personal? And was that even policy to work a case that involved your own kids? From the cop shows I watched, that's when a detective would have been removed from the case due to a *conflict of interest*.

"BC, do you remember anything about this hat…any words…images…the color?"

"Sorry, but no," I replied. "I wish I could help you more, Captain Boone."

He peered at me strangely.

"Well BC, you can. You can actually help me in two ways."

I straightened in my chair giving Mark my full attention.

"First of all, I need you to keep quiet for a while about what took place. My girls have been instructed to do the same. We're working with the TBI on this and-"

"TBI?"

"Tennessee Bureau of Investigation…and they want to see if enough evidence can be collected to identify this predator quickly. They believe going straight to the media with a generic description might send this guy into hiding before we can catch him. They want him to think he's in the clear, which he is for the moment, and resume his day to day activities while we try to ID this creep. Believe it or not, there are only a small number of law enforcement personnel who know that the intended victims were my daughters. And I don't know if Laurie and Maggie were attacked randomly or if they were targeted, but I'm checking all my past cases for anyone who may be out for some revenge. But either way, I don't want their names in the media, so I need you to keep quiet." Mark took a pair of handcuffs from his belt and placed them on the table.

"I haven't spoken a word to anyone," I assured him.

"And the second way you can help is by not having plans for lunch tomorrow." Mark's odd request had my attention. "My wife and girls want you to eat with us at the house after church. So you can help me by showing up and making my wife happy." Mark's eyes dared me to say anything other than *yes*. As did the handcuffs on the table.

"What time do I need to be there?"

"We will be home from church a little after noon. So let's say one o'clock. Is that too late?"

Mark picked up the cuffs and slammed the metal loop against his palm, causing it to spin through the clasp and reopen.

"One o'clock sounds perfect."

I stood as Mark stood, shook his hand once again, and started toward the door. "And BC, one more thing," said the detective. "There is another reason we are trying to keep names, especially yours, out of the news while we work this investigation. It is the same reason I decided against taking you to the hospital to get checked out last night."

"What's that?" I asked.

"You just disrupted the intentions of an individual whose plan was to kidnap two young girls, and then do...something terrible with them." Mark's face tensed at the sound of his own words. "We don't know who we are dealing with, but I can guess at the type of person he is. And I can assure you that you have severely ticked him off. If your name hits the news as being a hero, he may just decide to come after you."

8

I hurried through the detention center parking lot, locked my car doors, and checked my cell phone. I had a new voicemail and a new text message to answer, but first I wanted to get out of Andrews. What if the criminal was a local? What if he was watching the police station to identify witnesses? I probably couldn't recognize the man if I passed him in the aisle at the grocery store, but what if the attacker could recognize me? I figured he was either in hiding or he was looking for revenge against the punk that spoiled his plans. And I didn't like the 50/50 odds.

On the outskirts of Andrews, before the long wooded stretch that led toward campus, I pulled the car into a weed-infested, vacated gas station and checked the rearview mirror to see if anyone seemed to be following. A small red pick-up hesitated, probably making sure I wasn't going to pull back onto the highway, and continued past me toward the college. Cell phone coverage was decent in Andrews and higher up the mountain on campus, but it was practically non-existent in between, including at Eli's house. The voicemail had been from Kit Hendrix, a teammate at home in Nashville for the summer, and the text message was from Payne.

It simply read, "U Going?"

I had to think where I was supposed to be *going*.

Brody Payne was *Mr. College.* A former soccer player, the fun-loving, fifth-year student had evolved into *the* frat boy of Cohutta College frat boys. A born salesman, it was often difficult to turn down his wild suggestions. He had invited me to the previous night's party at Eagle Cliffs and even handed me a drink thirty seconds after I arrived. His text was a reminder that a group was going to Chattanooga tonight for minor league baseball and bar hopping. His text also reminded me of the current mess I was in.

I didn't even send a reply.

* * *

When I arrived back at Mr. Giles' house a note was taped to the screen door.

> *BC,*
> *Call Coach Glynn.*
> *Eli*

I removed the note and crumpled it in my fist, instantly frustrated at everything. Two weeks from the try-outs and I had slipped. And now Coach Glynn was looking for me. *Why had I ever mentioned to Mark Boone that I played basketball?*

I couldn't avoid calling Coach Glynn, but I first needed to interrogate my landlord. I checked the living area and kitchen. As I moved toward Mr. Giles' bedroom door, debating whether or not it would be rude to knock, I saw movement through the dining room window. The old man was intently working on something in the shade of the back porch. As I opened the screen door to join him, Eli grinned and pointed across the weather-beaten picnic table.

"Pull up a seat college boy."

I slid a green plastic chair to the table. Eli dropped a piece of folded sandpaper onto the table top, where a newly crafted wooden birdhouse lay on its back.

"Working hard?" I asked.

"Just getting this ready to paint. I didn't expect you back so early. You get my note?"

"Yes sir. Did Coach Glynn say what it was about by any chance?"

"Nope, but he just called a few minutes ago. Said he couldn't reach your cell phone, but wanted you to call him as soon as you could…said it was important. He didn't leave a number…said you would have it."

I had it. All the players had it. And Coach Glynn had all of ours. I intentionally hadn't given Coach the number to Mr. Giles' place and I wondered who he had called to track me down. And then I remembered…*Captain Mark Boone had surely spoken with him.* I took out my cell, but as I expected, the antennae symbol on the screen had only empty space beside it. *No reception.*

"Mr. Giles, would you mind if I used your phone? My cell won't work out here."

"Go right ahead, there's one in the kitchen. I need to put one upstairs for you…or you can try walking out there." Eli pointed to the rocks at the far end of his property. "When my boy Joseph is here he goes out there to do his talking. I don't guess I'll get one of those cell phones if you have to go stand on the edge of a mountain to make it work. But you're more than welcome to use my real phone."

Curiosity and the possibility of privacy sent me toward the rocks. Roughly fifteen yards beyond Eli's garden a dozen or so various sized chunks of mountain began protruding from the ground. The three largest rocks rose from the surrounding yard to nearly shoulder height, with the middle slab sloping gently enough for an easy four-step ascent to the top. Sure enough, one bar indicating reception appeared on my cell and a hesitant second bar faded in and out. I sat on the smooth stone and looked out across the valley. Eli Giles' property definitely came with a beautiful view. At least I'd be in a heavenly setting while Coach Glynn scolded me like the devil.

Honestly, I hoped for a scolding because the fear quickly gaining traction in my mind was that Coach may just decide to end my playing career altogether. I had clearly broken Rule #1 of the team code I knew so well – *No Cohutta College basketball player shall be involved in activities detrimental to himself, his teammates, or his school.* I was guilty as charged. Again.

I took a deep breath, attempted to calm my thoughts, and desperately hoped to get Coach Glynn's voicemail so I could put off the inevitable. But I had no such luck.

"This is Coach Glynn, Cohutta College Basketball."

"Hey Coach, this is BC," I said dejectedly.

"Yeah...hey, BC, listen, we need to talk." He sounded preoccupied, agitated. "We've got some things we need to discuss, but now is not good. Let's meet tomorrow...early."

"Yes sir, I'm actually eating with Capt...um, some people...down in Andrews tomorrow around one o'clock."

"How about ten o'clock in my office? Any problem with that? You don't have church do you?"

"No...I mean yes, sir. *No* to the church part. *Yes* to the time. I'll be there at ten."

I should have known Coach Glynn wouldn't handle the matter over the phone. He dealt with issues face to face and in his office. Twice last year Coach Glynn had called me in for disciplinary meetings. After avoiding serious trouble my freshman and sophomore years, I found enough arrogance and alcohol as a junior to make a fool of myself on campus more than once. Not only did I find myself in front of Dean McAllister, perhaps the loudest and most heartless man on earth, but I also learned that Coach Glynn had many sets of eyes around campus. On my second trip to his office he point blank informed me that I was not representing the program in the appropriate manner and was in danger of being removed from the team. He did suspend me for the first three games of the season, which put me in his dog house and cost me playing time when I did return. And just a few games after I finally reclaimed the starting point guard position, I broke my wrist diving for a ball during a Christmas tournament in Memphis. Season over, just like that.

The more I thought about it, the more I feared my Sunday meeting with Coach Glynn. Initially, when I saw the note taped to Eli's door, I expected another scolding or perhaps a second small suspension. But while sitting on the rocks, the thought that kept returning was that I was the only upcoming senior for an expected rebuilding season. *Why not just remove me from the roster and concentrate on the younger players? I would.*

My mind tried to rationalize my defense. I was twenty one. Legally I could drink.

However, I knew it was the driving after the drinking part that was the major issue. A DUI was reason enough for Coach Glynn to end my basketball career. And being kicked off my college team would be an automatic disqualifier for the all-conference squad traveling to Europe.

I fought back the wetness forming in my eyes.

Had I just ruined everything I worked so hard for?

It didn't appear that Mark planned to charge me, but maybe as an officer he felt he had to do something, like call my coach. I stayed on the rocks a while longer trying to get my story straight for tomorrow's meeting. *Coach knows how hard I've been working*, I thought, *perhaps he'll take that into consideration*. I pondered calling Captain Boone, just to verify what I was walking into with Coach Glynn in the morning, but cowardice conquered that idea. I had no choice but to wait it out, let it gnaw on me all night, and face Coach Glynn in his office. I would just have to convince him that I was good for Cohutta College basketball and that my actions from the previous night would never happen again. *Never.*

Eli was still on the back porch when I returned. Two Mason jars and a pitcher of sweet tea had appeared on the table. I welcomed his invitation. We sat and talked for a while, mostly about his son. Joseph, I learned, lived in Atlanta and was in real estate. He was successful, married, and had a five-year old boy named Tucker. Eli rotated the unpainted bird house on the table. *To Tucker, From Papa E* was etched into the back.

"So those big city birds can have a good home," Eli said.

"Do you get to see them much?"

"They stay busy."

I scanned the mountain-top view from Eli's porch. "Surely Joseph can't go too long without seeing this place. It's beautiful here."

"I think so. Maybe it will be an easy sale for him once I pass away."

"I could live here, not that I could ever afford it. But if I could..."

That was all the prompting Eli needed to delve into the history of the house and the property. "My daddy bought this property from A.W. Wilbanks, and we started building this house in the evenings. I was twelve. And working with my dad on this place is still one of the greatest memories of my life…" As Eli reminisced I gladly listened, welcoming the distraction. At one point Eli mentioned the year he and his wife moved in, but that was all he said about her. I had seen pictures of her throughout the house. One in particular, of a dark headed girl with a youthful smile sitting on a wooden pier, ankles crossed, always caught my eye.

Eventually the mosquitoes drove us inside. I carried the pitcher of tea to the fridge but not before pouring another glass to take to my room. Eli made great sweet tea. It wasn't what usually filled my glass on a Saturday night, but it was good. Upstairs, I knew my television only picked up three channels, and none clearly, so I rummaged through a stack of books on a closet shelf looking for something to occupy my thoughts.

I didn't want to think about the man who attacked Laurie and Maggie Boone, still out there somewhere, perhaps hunting for more victims…or for revenge. Nor did I want to think about the stubborn pain in my left wrist or tomorrow morning's meeting with Coach Glynn, either of which could end my quest to play basketball in Europe. A book wasn't my first choice, but I needed something, so I finally chose one by its cover.

Lying in bed, I checked my watch. It was a little past nine o'clock but it felt later. I stared at the maroon *Yonah State Park* cap hanging on the bedpost and wondered again which pal would have left it in my car. I thought of Brody Payne and his crew forty miles away in Chattanooga, being obnoxious, pestering girls, and downing drinks. And I was actually glad I wasn't with them. I sipped my sweet tea, adjusted the pillows behind my head, and opened the book to page one.

"I'm a nerd," I muttered to myself.

With a soft lamp lighting my way, I devoured more than fifty pages before my eyelids gave in to several hours of exhausted peace. But sometime after midnight, I once again found myself swimming toward a distant shoreline, hoping to reach land before the billowing fog enveloped everything and the water pulled me under. I heard myself shouting for help. I felt the shivering of my hands and muscles. I tasted the water as it slid past my gasping lips.

It was the dream I couldn't stop.

And it was another night of sinking to the bottom of a cold, dark lake.

9

Thunder sounded in the distance. The rain was coming.

The man needed to hurry.

He found a fallen branch along the ground, as round as a young girl's arm, he thought, and snapped it easily with his boot. The man wrapped his shirt around the broken branch, dousing it with the remainder of the fuel. The torch illuminated his chest in the darkness, flickering against the inked serpent that ran along the inside of his arm, across his chest, and down his other arm. Its tail and rattles wrapped around his left wrist. He remembered the pain of the needle as the serpent was created. He had welcomed the feeling of a lost strength being awakened.

More thunder.

No one had followed him. He had waited nearly twenty-four hours. Always ready to strike. Always ready to eliminate any threat that entered his territory. But he would not play the role of a cornered animal. He would not wait for intruders to desecrate his territory. The man knew what needed to be done.

The first drops of rain teased his skin in the heat of the fire. The man moved toward the van, ribs igniting in pain as he flung the torch through the opened side door. He nearly reached for his ribs but pushed the weak thought aside.

Yes, the unseen young man had hit him hard. But he welcomed the pain. It was a constant reminder of a quest that must be completed.

He watched the flames within the van grow and dance and destroy. He moved toward the van, arms held wide, letting the serpent running across his chest and arms bask in the sweltering heat.

Pain would never stop him.

No, he thought to himself as moved even closer to the flames, it would take much more than pain to ever stop the Rattler.

10

I awoke early Sunday morning to the drumming of a heavy rain. The book I had started the night before lay beside me on the bed. It was a strange story, unlike anything I had ever read. I assumed it belonged to Eli's son, Joseph. I couldn't see Eli reading of battles between conniving demons and warrior angels with Earth and its residents as its battlefield. The novel had taken my mind off several unpleasant thoughts, but even as vivid and suspenseful as it was, it couldn't hold off the reoccurring dream of drowning that forced its way inside my head once again.

The morning rain continued for nearly an hour more and I lazily enjoyed the rhythm of the thick drops slapping the metal roof, still trying to not think about my impending meeting with Coach Glynn, and trying to make up for yet another restless night. As the rain slowed to a drizzle, I rolled from my bed and searched for gym clothes in my *Cohutta College Basketball* travel bags. After a week at Eli's I still hadn't put my belongings in any of the drawers. I checked my watch. I could easily get to campus and knock out an hour's worth of court time before the meeting. *Perhaps a sweaty look would remind Coach Glynn of my dedication to the program.*

* * *

By the time I arrived on campus the sun was reclaiming the skies. I pulled into the gym parking area and saw no sign of Coach Glynn's truck, which meant the gym's doors were locked. I dug my MP3 player from my glove box and settled for a campus run. My body, especially my left shoulder and wrist, ached as I began. Ancient oaks spread throughout shielded most of the sidewalks from the rising summer sun, and I slowly circled the main quad and the sprawling stone academic buildings before stopping for a better stretch. *Twelve days left*, I told myself, blocking the impending meeting with Coach from my mind, *twelve days until I earn my ticket to Europe.*

On my second start I turned up the music, quickened my pace down steep Cannon Lane and eventually onto a well-kept nature trail that meandered for a mile like a mulched stream around hardwoods, stone benches, and flower beds. Besides the aches from my recent battle wounds, I was in the best shape of my life and I felt it in my lungs and legs. I exited the trail onto a narrow campus side street where I was forced to run along the curb. No sidewalk, just a continuous row of ranch style homes occupied by professors. A horn sounded above the band jamming in my head and a streaking dark blur moved around me.

A large van. Navy blue. Tinted windows. I shuddered for an instant before reading *Cohutta College Campus Security* on the back door. I knew the driver was probably the young guy who installed and repaired security cameras around campus and would often rebound for me whenever he saw me shooting basketball alone in the gym.

49

As I regained my stride my mind returned to the Waffle Shack parking lot.

I wondered if the man who tried to abduct Laurie and Maggie Boone had thrown other girls into his dark van. Had there been previous victims, and would there be future ones?

I picked up my pace. *12 days for Europe. 12 days.*

I gained ground on a female jogger. Blonde hair bounced in a ponytail, athletic calves flexed with each step. Chelsea Simms, no doubt, and it was hard not to stare. Staying in shape for soccer, keeping pace with the song playing through her ear buds, she climbed the steep road in front of me. I hadn't realized she was attending summer session, but we had a history, and since she hadn't noticed me jogging behind her I changed direction and veered onto a gravel road that ran behind the campus golf course. A half-mile later the road dead-ended at a scenic bluff overlooking the Tennessee countryside. I sprinted the final hundred yards, ending my run by splitting between two wooden benches which faced the magnificent view.

I raised my hands in the air like a champion and released a ridiculous, victorious yell over the bluff. Then I quickly looked around to make sure no one was present to witness my spontaneous lunacy.

All alone. Just me and the mountain.

I walked closer to the cliff's edge, taking in the view while replenishing my lungs with pure mountain oxygen. The rains had left behind a beautiful day. Far below, the divided crops of farmers resembled quilted patches of various greens and browns. Silos, barns, homes and ponds were sprinkled throughout. A highway cut through the landscape, running beside several miniature buildings and a pristine white country church. At least two dozen vehicles, seeming like toy trucks and SUVs, filled the church's rectangular parking area. A tiny hatchback made its way along the highway, slowed, and turned into the church lot in search of a vacant space. Within seconds, an indistinguishable, antlike family appeared and moved hurriedly toward the white building's front doors.

Good, you made it, said the sarcastic voice in my head to the ant people far below. *Now don't disturb anyone while you slide into the back row, and don't forget to pray for BC's meeting with Coach Glynn...he needs it.*

I wondered if this was what God felt like, minus the sarcasm, while sitting high above and checking in on the inhabitants of earth.

* * *

As soon as I entered the stairwell leading to the athletic offices my nerves went into overdrive. *This could be my last day as a Cohutta College basketball player.* The thought made me sick. With each step I lost more of the words I had prepared for Coach, but I was drawn like a hooked fish toward his open door. Coach Glynn was behind his desk, squinting at his computer screen, finger pecking his keyboard.

"Hey BC, come on in. How is everything?" he asked in his deep, gruff voice. He was either testing my honesty or he had no knowledge of my drunken encounter with an at-large criminal. If it was the first, I intended to fail miserably.

"I'm good Coach, how are you?" *Keep it simple. Wait and see what he knows, BC.*

"I've been better. My truck is in the shop...timing belt, my cell phone screen is frozen...can't tell who is calling me, and my kids won't listen...just like their momma." Coach

Glynn never cracked a smile or diverted his eyes from the computer, where I hoped he remained. His six-foot-five frame was less intimidating in a chair.

"Sorry about all that," I said. *So far, so good.*

Coach Glynn clicked the mouse furiously, slapped the side of the monitor, and then turned all his attention toward me. "BC," he said in a much more serious tone. "I seem to have put my trust in some people lately who have let me down, and I just don't like that feeling."

"I understand Coach," I said, my heart sinking. *The man knew everything.* I was at his mercy. I suddenly felt sick again.

"BC, you are our only senior, our leader by default, so you do understand what is expected of a team captain, don't you?" My throat went dry and I could only nod in response. "Good then. As captain, I think there are some things you need to know. Coach Tomlinson is leaving, he told me yesterday."

Wait…is this not about me?

"He's been offered a head coaching job at a private high school in North Carolina. Personally, I think he's made a hasty decision, but now I have to find and teach our system to another assistant, which I hate doing."

Coach Tomlinson, or *Coach T*, as the players called him, had been the assistant since I had been at Cohutta College. He was the steady target of player jokes and impersonations, but overall, he did a solid job. Coach T took his role seriously, a little too seriously sometimes, which is why we made fun of him.

"I hate to hear that," I said.

"Just listen," ordered Coach Glynn. "Thad Tatum from Madisonville, the six-eight red-headed recruit we had signed, won't be joining us. He's had two underage drinking charges this summer. One from a senior trip in Panama City and another last week while driving in Madisonville. I simply told him we no longer had a spot for him. I'm tired of dealing with that kind of junk."

"I understand, but I hate to lose his height on our-"

"Just listen BC." Coach's expression grew more severe. "And lastly, Bender won't be coming back to school."

It took a moment for Coach Glynn's words to sink in.

"Bender? Why not?"

"He called on Friday to say he's burnt out on basketball and transferring to a bigger school. He's going to Georgia Southern...and some crap about us not having the major he wanted. Personally, I think he's chasing a girl down there, but anyway, he's not coming back. At least he had the guts to call me on the phone."

I didn't know a great deal about hiring a new assistant coach, and the red-headed giant we expected to join the team may have turned out to be an uncoordinated goof, but losing Bender wasn't good. It wasn't good at all. Bender was a *player*.

"Coach...we need Bender," I said. His smirk told me I was stating the obvious.

"Well, we don't have him, and our young team just got younger...and smaller. You're our only senior, your buddy Kit is our only junior, and then there's a horde of freshmen and sophomores. I've never had a roster like this one."

"Kit is going to have to step up and play big," I said. "Everyone will, but especially Kit." Coach looked at me as if I had announced that I could create chicken salad out of chicken manure.

"Well BC, this is obviously putting more responsibility on you. Depending on who we hire as an assistant, you're probably going to do some teaching to the younger guys. You may even be running some practice drills when we split into groups."

I nodded. Coach continued. "This is by far the youngest team I've ever had, so I'm counting on you to set the example...on and off the court. That crap you pulled last year better be done with. You need to demonstrate what being in this program is all about."

In other words...don't drink from the spiked punch bowl, drive around town, puke behind a dumpster, and then wake up on a local detective's couch.

"I understand Coach, you can count on me." And I meant it. At least I hoped so.

"Good, here's your first assignment." Coach Glynn tossed me a thick brown envelope. "That packet has team stationery, envelopes, plenty of stamps and a sheet listing everybody's home address. You need to write each player. This is something Coach Tomlinson usually did, so it's a good thing you decided to stay on campus this summer."

"So what am I writing?"

"Inform them that *you* expect them to be working hard to make our team better. Remind them that they are representing Cohutta College basketball with their actions, even while off campus during the summer. And by the way, when do you report to Nashville for the all-conference try-outs?"

"Twelve days, a week from this Friday."

"Are you ready?" he asked. I flexed my wrist to judge the pain.

"I think so. I've trained hard for this Coach."

"I know you have, and you should be on that team. You may have missed the second half of last season, but you're the best senior point guard in this conference. I truly believe that. And don't think I haven't called and emailed the selection committee to let them know."

"Thanks Coach."

"No problem, traveling around Europe for a couple weeks playing basketball is a once-in-a-lifetime experience."

"I hope to find out."

"And I hope you get to. So represent us well at the tryouts," he added before pointing again to the packet. "And as for the letters, don't forget to put the dates for our preseason meeting and the start of on-campus conditioning."

"So *when* are the dates for those...the meeting and the conditioning?" I asked.

Coach Glynn shrugged his shoulders.

"That is up to you, *captain*."

11

Even though I had been an overnight guest at the Boone home, I had to call Mark for directions. I expected a solid dose of sarcasm, but he politely told me the way and even reminded me to be careful driving over. After leaving Coach's office, I had stopped by Eli's to spruce up. Hoping to make a better second impression, and knowing the Boones were returning from church, I pressed over a long-sleeve collared shirt and snipped the frayed threads from the bottom of some khaki pants. My dress shoes were scuffed, but as my late grandmother would have said, this outfit was currently my "Sunday best."

I found the Boone home easily, but before I could knock, the front door swung open and I was greeted by a burst of human energy. "Hey BC," she yelled, grabbed my elbow, and pulled me inside. "Come on in buddy, folks are in the kitchen, Laurie's not here yet, how are you?" I assumed this was Maggie, Mark's youngest daughter. Before I had time to answer her first question she fired a second. "All dressed up, huh? Didn't have time to change after church? Well, kick your shoes off and stay awhile." Maggie wore lengthy white shorts, no shoes, and a green tank top. Her hair was pulled back tight and her wide smile seemed to defy the boundaries of her narrow face.

Mark appeared from the hallway holding a stack of plates. "Hey BC, glad you found the place," said the detective. "But you didn't have to get dressed up for us. That's my fault. I should have told you that the Boones get comfortable as soon as we hit the door after church." Mark wore shorts and a red t-shirt that read *Constructors For Christ* in faded lettering. "I see you've met Maggie again, come on in the kitchen and meet my wife."

Maggie secured my elbow and escorted me behind her father toward the kitchen. "Met me *again*?" she asked. "BC, do you not remember me from the other night?"

"It wasn't a good night for me," I admitted as we entered the kitchen. Mark's wife stood at the sink rinsing her hands.

"I agree...you looked rough," continued Maggie. "You convinced me to never drink."

"Enough Maggie Boone," came her mother's voice in my defense. Turning from the sink, Mark's wife wiped her hands with a dish towel and eyeballed Maggie.

"Sorry BC," chirped Maggie as she hopped onto a kitchen stool. "But I have to admit, you do clean up very well."

"BC, this is my wife Donna," said Mark.

Donna stood nearly as tall as her husband. Slender, athletic, she resembled a runner, and it was easy to see Maggie's resemblance in her face.

I offered my hand as Donna approached but quickly realized she wasn't settling for a handshake. She wrapped her arms around me and squeezed tight. After a lengthy embrace, Donna grabbed my shoulders and stared directly into my eyes. "It's nice to meet you again, BC. Thank you for saving my girls." Donna's face tightened and tears welled in her eyes.

"You're welcome, Mrs. Boone, I just happened to be in the right place."

"It's *Donna*...and God put you in the right place. Don't you *ever* forget that, because we won't."

"Yes ma'am," I responded. She hugged me again.

"And now that you've done your part, BC," Donna Boone announced loudly, "we need Captain Boone and his boys to put that wicked man behind bars where he belongs."

"Working on it," grunted Mark from the dining room.

"So BC doesn't even remember the big event?" giggled Maggie.

Donna jumped to my defense once again. "That doesn't matter now, Miss Maggie. You're here with us today because of what BC did, whether he remembers all the details or not." Donna nodded her head in Maggie's direction. "BC, you'll have to forgive our youngest daughter, she takes after her father's side of the family."

Maggie laughed and Mark shot back with "I heard that" as he hurried through the kitchen and out a sliding glass door leading to a back deck. Less than a minute later Mark was back in the doorway, platter in hand. "Burgers are done," he announced. "They were cooking fast, the Lord knew we were hungry."

The charcoal-grilled burgers smelled delicious. We followed Mark into the dining area. Mark took one end of the table and Donna the other. Just as Mark asked his wife if she wanted to start eating or wait on Laurie, the closing thud of a car door sounded outside.

"Just in time," he said.

"Laurie, our oldest daughter, dates a boy whose parents attend another church," Donna said. "She went with his family today and their service gets out a little later." I nodded, not that it mattered much to me. Maggie, sitting directly opposite me, quickly added spice to the story.

"Yeah, Laurie may be a little grumpy. She had planned to eat with Dylan's family and head to the lake, but mom made her come home since we had company."

"Maggie, act like you have some manners please," Mark responded. "Dylan has been invited to eat with us, too. So no snide comments. Let's make this a pleasant meal and I won't ground you for two unpleasant weeks."

Maggie's demeanor changed instantly. She apologized to both her parents and then to me. The genuineness of her apology caught me off guard.

"You didn't offend me, Maggie," I reassured her. She released a wide, gorgeous smile at my response, as if she had won my acceptance.

And then Laurie Boone entered the room.

She was and was not the same young girl from the family picture I had studied on the mantle.

Slender, confident, she wore a black, sleeveless dress that fell just above her knees. Laurie Boone had her father's dark complexion, noticeably green eyes, and deep brown curly hair that fell just beyond her shoulders. Her smile was natural and contagious. If she was upset for having to change her plans, she didn't show it. "Hey guys," she said as she placed her pocket book on the counter and stepped out of her shoes.

I tried not to stare, but Laurie Boone was a beautiful girl. A very beautiful girl.

A wide-shouldered boy with long hair sweeping across one eye stood behind her. A backpack was slung over one massive shoulder. He waved, mumbled a greeting to everyone, and then disappeared down the hallway.

"Hey BC, nice to see you under better circumstances," Laurie Boone said. A perplexed look lingered in her eyes, as if I wasn't what she expected.

"He cleans up well, doesn't he?" shot Maggie.

"It's nice to see you too," I finally managed, standing as she rounded my side of the table. Laurie shook my hand and smiled. "I'm just glad no one got seriously hurt," I added, not knowing exactly what to say, but not wanting to release her soft hand.

"We thank the Lord for that," responded Donna.

Laurie took the open chair beside me. Part of me wanted her to sit on the opposite side of the table, beside Maggie, where it would be easier and less obvious to steal glances.

"Laurie, are you keeping your dress on to eat burgers?" Maggie asked.

"It takes too long to change, and I'm starving."

"Me too," agreed Mark. "But let's wait on Dylan, then bless this meal and eat." When Dylan returned he had changed into camouflage shorts and a tight blue shirt proclaiming *HCHS Cougar Football*. The poor stud stood confused for a long second before sliding into the vacant seat beside Maggie. I noticed the subtle roll of her eyes.

Laurie made a quick introduction. Dylan reached across the table and shook my hand, making sure to let me feel the intensity of his grip.

"You've already met Dylan's oldest brother," added Mark. "Detective Ingle from my office."

I nodded and glanced toward Dylan. "Are you planning on going into law enforcement too?"

"Don't think so."

"Let's pray," said Mark.

I was familiar with bowing heads during a blessing, but the Boone family immediately reached around the table to join hands. I followed their lead. Mark's strong grip held my left hand and Laurie's slender hand slipped into my right.

Mark gave the blessing.

He thanked the Lord for his family, for the blessings bestowed on them, for the opportunity to fellowship with guests, and for keeping Laurie, Maggie, and me safe in the midst of danger. Laurie squeezed my hand when her father mentioned my name. A soft electricity ran throughout my body. As Mark continued to speak to the Lord, I peeked at the faces around the table. Only one other pair of eyes weren't humbly closed.

Dylan stared directly at my and Laurie's interlocked hands. I wondered if he had noticed her gentle squeeze. Our glares met for a brief moment before the big lad shut his eyes. Even then, he just couldn't seem to remove the disgust from his face.

12

The Boones served a wonderful meal.

By the end I had stuffed myself with two of Mark's burgers and a slice of Donna's apple cobbler. I had also answered seven million questions, mostly from Maggie, and laughed continuously. Donna wanted to know about my family, Mark wondered what I planned to do after college, and Maggie asked about everything. Even Dylan lightened up and asked me a few questions about playing college basketball.

I learned that Maggie was about to be a sophomore in high school, Laurie planned to study music at a small Christian college in northeast Georgia, and that the Boone family was still debating whether to join an annual church-building mission trip quickly approaching in mid-June.

I also learned, mostly from Mark, that all the Boone women were musically talented. Donna and Laurie were pianists, while fifteen-year-old Maggie played guitar. According to Mark, all three of *his* girls could sing, and did so from time to time at church. He tried to convince Laurie to entertain us on the piano, but the confident young lady who sauntered in earlier became a blushing girl at her father's request. Besides that moment, Laurie Boone carried herself more like she was in her final year of college rather than someone who had just finished high school.

Maggie wasn't nearly so shy about her music. "You're more than welcome to come hear me play tonight, BC." Donna quickly explained that Maggie was leading the music at the evening's youth service at church.

"She's really good," Laurie said.

"She's right, I am," Maggie added.

Mark threw a crumpled napkin which bounced off Maggie's forehead. "Okay, Miss Humble."

"I just thought BC might want to bring his girlfriend to a free concert. Or do you *have* a girlfriend?"

"Don't you need to rehearse or get some rest?" Mark asked.

Maggie picked the balled napkin from the floor and fired it back at Mark. "You mean *go downstairs and leave BC alone.*"

"Something like that."

"I do have some chords to perfect," said Maggie. "May I be excused?"

"Absolutely," Donna answered.

The rest of us moved to the living room. Mark settled in the recliner, Donna leaned against pillows in front of the fireplace, I took the love seat, and Dylan sat too close to Laurie on the couch. Our discussion quickly turned to the event that brought us all together.

"BC, did you wake up sore Saturday morning?" Laurie asked. "That was a hard spill you took Friday night." Laurie nestled back into the cushions of the very couch I had slept on. I wondered if the entire family had passed by me that morning as I lay ragged and unaware. I also wondered if it irritated Mark to have Dylan still shifting closer to his beautiful daughter. I had known Dylan for less than an hour and it irritated me.

"Honestly Laurie, I don't remember much after running at the man, but yes, I felt awful Saturday morning."

"But that had nothing to do with hitting the ground, right?" remarked Dylan, taking a swig of an imaginary bottle to clarify his point. Mark shot a quick disapproving glare, surely the same he used during interrogations.

"Laurie, do you mind telling the story again?" Mark asked, "BC's memory needs some filling in, and maybe one of you will remember something new."

Laurie's mesmerizing green eyes focused on me. She leaned forward, rested her elbows on her knees, clasped her hands, and intertwined her long, slender fingers. Dylan reached forward and rubbed her shoulder.

"Well, as you may or may not know," Laurie began, "Maggie and I had double dated with Dylan and this boy Maggie likes. I drove since Dylan's Jeep was in the shop. After the movie we dropped the boys off. Dylan lives out near Bazelwood so we had to come back through town anyway. Maggie and I had a late-night craving for pecan pie so we stopped at the Waffle Shack."

"It was the first time I had let Maggie stay out that late," stated Mark.

"And the last," Donna added.

"I just wanted the girls to spend some time together before Laurie went off to college," said Mark.

Laurie continued. "We got inside and realized we had forgotten to call and let them know where we were, so I went to the car to get my cell phone."

"Unless he followed them into the parking lot, I think that must have been when he found his target," Mark said.

"And we praise God the man didn't take Laurie then," added Donna.

Laurie took a deep breath, Dylan shifted closer. "I went to the driver's side to look for the phone. If he was watching at that point he probably assumed I was alone, would be an easy target, and cut the rear, passenger-side tire after I went back inside."

I looked toward Mark. "But I heard him slide open the van door? So what was the point of cutting a tire the driver was unlikely to see if he intended to abduct her right there in the parking lot?"

"Not sure," Mark said, "but my theory is that he wanted a second opportunity in case *Plan A* wasn't available. If witnesses appeared, or he got spooked, I think *Plan B* would be somewhere down the road when Laurie realized she had a flat tire."

"So he could be there to *offer his assistance*," added Dylan.

Donna, her eyes pink and moist, sighed heavily. "But he went after both of my girls. Just an arrogant monster...right there in that parking lot," she said.

Dylan's comforting arm was now around Laurie and his hand moved from elbow to shoulder along her tanned, bare arm. *Laurie Boone, you can do so much better*, I thought, *so much better.* "I think it was because Maggie noticed the tire when we came out to leave," continued Laurie, "I think Maggie ticked him off by spotting the tire."

"Perhaps," Mark said. "But if this guy is arrogant enough to think he could abduct two girls at once-"

"And he would have," said Donna.

"Then he has abducted before," Mark finished. His comment hung heavily in the room until Laurie spoke again.

"But it was such a dark parking lot, practically empty without all the college students around, and Wimpy's gas station next door was closed and dark as well. I think the guy just decided he had a good opportunity and took it. The problem was he didn't know about our dumpster hero ready to burst out and save the day." Everyone laughed except Dylan.

"And just to let it be known," I said, "I was not *in* the dumpster. I was behind it."

"Yes you were," said Donna, eyes closed prayerfully, smiling. "Yes you were."

"Anyway," continued Laurie, "I was already on the driver's side when Maggie noticed the tire. I walked around and squatted down beside her…and that's when…that's when…"

For the first time in the story her voice became hesitant. Dylan placed his strong hand of support on Laurie's thigh. I suddenly hoped Captain Mark Boone would shoot him. Laurie casually guided Dylan's hand back to his own knee as she continued speaking.

"I never saw the man and I never heard him, but all of a sudden his hands were-"

A quick knock sounded on the front door. Donna rose from the floor and wiped the streaking tears from her cheeks as she moved toward the kitchen. "I'll let one of you answer that," she said. Mark, already headed that direction, opened the door to two teenage girls. Laurie bounced up from the couch and made quick introductions. Five seconds later I had forgotten which friend was Kayla and which was Kristen. Both were obviously puzzled at how I fit into the dynamics of those gathered in the Boone's living room. I assumed, on Mark's orders, that these girls had no clue about the attempted abduction of Laurie and Maggie. Story time was abruptly over.

"Where's Wallace?" asked Dylan.

"He said he'd meet us at the lake," replied one of the girls.

"We'll be back in a minute, I need to pack a bag," Laurie said. She grabbed an arm from each girl and led them down the hallway toward her room.

"Who's the guy?" I heard one ask in a loud whisper.

As I turned back from watching Laurie walk away, I noticed that only Dylan and I remained in the Boone's living room. *Wonderful*, I thought, *Mark had deserted me.* Dylan laced his fingers behind his head and leaned back on the couch, his t-shirt fighting against his large biceps. "I guess that's the end of the story."

"I guess so," I answered.

"We're heading to the lake in my brother's boat."

"The detective?"

"No man, my other brother Colby. He's got a sweet ski boat."

"Sounds fun."

Surely Mark hadn't just abandoned me.

"Yep," Dylan continued. "Wakeboarding, tubing, girls in bikinis…nothing beats that." An eruption of female laughter escaped from a distant bedroom. "You see, there's something about the lake and the sun and a fast boat that just gets girls excited."

"I'll have to remember that."

Dylan smirked.

"So you're not worried about this guy who just attacked Laurie and Maggie two nights ago?" I asked.

"I'll be right beside her if any punk tries-"

"BC," came Mark's saving voice. He stepped into the room holding a battered pair of running shoes. "You got time to shoot some hoops? You can wear these old things. I've got a goal out back that barely gets used. How about it?"

I was off the small couch before Mark Boone finished the question. As far as I was concerned, Dylan could entertain himself.

13

*A*ll strikes are quick. All strikes are unseen. All strikes are fatal.

The Rattler mouthed the rules repeatedly as he made his way up the steep, wooded ridge. He had struck quickly, he thought, perhaps even quicker than the previous time. But he had been seen, and the strike had not been fatal. Breaking one rule breaks them all, and he had broken two.

All strikes are quick. All strikes are unseen. All strikes are fatal.

A rock jutting from the dense slope snagged his side. Pain. The constant reminder of his carelessness. He breathed deep and pushed the pain from his ribs back into his soul. But the fact that it was still there angered him more.

And anger made him think of the young intruder. The unseen opponent had taken the prey right from his grasp. The Rattler pulled himself onto the crest of the ridge, pausing to catch his breath and to visualize his next encounter with the intruder.

He flicked his forked tongue to taste the air of his territory. Pain, yes, he knew real pain. And he knew its strength.

A scalpel, one he held to a torch until it glowed orange, had split the tongue. He had made the incision himself, piercing the middle of his tongue, then pulling it forward toward the tip. The scalpel burned so hot it cauterized the tongue as it sliced through.

No bleeding. Only burns and pain.

Real pain. Real strength.

The man stroked the split tips of his tongue and recited the rules. All strikes are quick. All strikes are unseen. All strikes are –

A stick snapped in the forest below.

The Rattler quickly crouched behind a large, fallen tree. No one should be here, he thought, knowing there were no trails nearby and still three ridges to cross before the first homes appeared.

Perhaps it was an animal.

Or perhaps they had found him. He listened to the distant rustling of leaves, to another stick breaking under the weight of a step, and then...singing.

The man drank in the young, female voice that awakened his senses. He listened closely. The tune and lyrics were unrecognizable to his ears.

His narrowed eyes found the flash of movement and color through the trees in the ravine below.

The Rattler slid the six inch blade from its leather case along his belt and recited the rules.

14

Mark Boone had a terrible shot. His form was nearly worse than the result. I tried not to say anything, but after chasing down several line-drives ricocheting wildly off the rim, I couldn't contain my laughter.

"What's so funny?" Mark asked. "I know you're not making fun of my basketball skills." Mark's attempt to hold a serious expression kept me laughing.

"I hope you're more accurate with your pistol."

"Keep laughing, BC, and you'll find out. But alright, *Mr. Basketball*, let's see what you've got." Mark fired the ball into my hands. I instinctively flinched expecting pain to flare from my wounded left wrist, but the only sting was from the long asphalt scrapes still healing along my palm.

For some reason Mark had spent serious time and money creating a basketball half-court in his backyard, pouring a large concrete slab complete with a painted lane and foul line. The absence of a three-point line gave the court an "old-school" feel, and I liked it. I took my first shot from behind the foul line. It circled the rim and popped out.

"You may need to scoot in a little," said Mark. I took off my dress shirt and hung it over a nearby gate. Underneath, I wore a *Boston Celtics* t-shirt with a faded print of the leprechaun mascot spinning a ball on one finger.

"Oh, he's getting serious now," said the detective.

"You bet." I readjusted my toes in the borrowed Nikes. When I had crammed my feet in the shoes earlier while sitting on the Boone's back deck, Donna came out to say good-bye, give me another hug, and let me know that I was welcome anytime I needed a home-cooked meal. After she left, Mark informed me that Donna's aunt had lung cancer and on most Sunday afternoons Donna took her mother on the hour drive to visit. So he had started using the basketball court again, especially since Laurie and Maggie were both starting to have their own plans.

"You're not working on the investigation today?" I asked him.

"The TBI is involved and I'm in constant contact with them," Mark answered. "They're trying to link this to other abductions...and there are good agents working on it as we speak. But honestly, it is killing me not being at the office right now, but I need to give my family some normalcy."

Mark rifled me the ball with a two hand-pass toward my chest. This time I felt absolutely no pain from the wrist. *12 days to earn my ticket to Europe*, I thought, my confidence returning. I took the next shot from a few feet farther back than my first. *Swish*. I moved around the area where the three-point line should have been. I made my next four shots.

"It just takes a shot or two to get adjusted," I boasted.

Mark continued to feed me passes until I missed. We shot and talked about the investigation until Dylan opened the back sliding glass door and made his way down the wooden steps. Mark quickly suggested playing one on one.

"First to ten baskets wins," he declared.

"I'll play the winner," announced Dylan. He sat in a blue plastic chair just off the court.

I beat Mark, but only on the score. He beat me on my body, my arms, my wrists, everywhere. After my ninth basket I missed a couple easy shots and dribbled it off my foot twice just to prolong having to play Dylan. Thankfully, Maggie appeared carrying a tray with watermelon slices and two large glasses of water.

"I thought I'd bring these out before Dad croaked," she said. We took our time-out on a picnic table that resided in the shade of the house. Maggie retreated back inside and Dylan was on the court dribbling and shooting, warming up for the next game. He obviously lacked skill, but I got the impression he just wanted to knock me around the court for his own enjoyment.

"So, what inspired you to build this court?" I asked Mark.

"Laurie."

"She plays basketball?"

"Nope," Mark said, shaking his head. "But she did when she was eight. She played one year and had a blast. So I built her this court. When basketball season rolled around again, she wanted to take dance or gymnastics instead, I can't even remember. After that it was mainly used for bike riding and sidewalk chalk."

The sound of the glass door sliding open took our attention. Laurie shielded her eyes from the sun as she appeared on the deck. She had changed from her dress into sky blue shorts and a t-shirt. Her curly, deep brown hair was pulled back into a ponytail. Still smiling. Still beautiful.

"Speak of the devil," Mark said loud enough for her to hear.

"Angel," Laurie corrected. "And just letting you know we're headed to the lake."

"And which bathing-"

"The one-piece, as always," Laurie interrupted.

"Thank you," replied Mark. "Are you sure you feel like going?"

"I need to Daddy. I can't hide at home forever."

"*Forever*? It's been two days."

"She'll be fine Mr. Boone," said Dylan, sounding like a bodyguard. He slammed the ball between his hands, dropped it to the court, and sprinted up the wooden stairs as if training on the steps of the high school football stadium.

"Laurie, keep your cell phone on and be back before dark," Mark said.

"I will, I promise. It was good to see you again, BC, take it easy on my dad please," Laurie yelled, but before I could formulate any words she disappeared back inside with Dylan. I was instantly disappointed that Mark hadn't forbidden her to go.

"You're okay with Dylan being her bodyguard today?" I asked.

"I'm one step ahead of them," Mark responded. "I have another set of eyes working at the lake today, she'll never have a clue. And I'll be with Maggie at the church, so both my girls are covered."

I took another swig of water. "Do you think they were targeted or that the attack was just random?" I asked.

Mark shook his head. "I still don't know, but I'm leaning toward random. I've dealt with some real scum, but not any that I could see being out for revenge like this. It could be someone I arrested who changed for the worse while being locked away, but I'm more inclined to think my girls were the random victims of a man I haven't met yet." Mark balled his fist. "And I can't wait to introduce myself."

"Well, Captain Boone, I hope you get your chance very soon. And please call me when you do." I finished off the cool water in my glass and sat it on the tray. "But I should probably get going. I'm sure you have plenty-"

"Why? I thought you were in training?" Before I could answer Mark tossed the ball into my stomach and strutted back toward the court.

* * *

It was after four when we finally called it quits. Mark couldn't dribble or shoot, but besides being a brutal defender, he was in great shape. Like two boxers who had gone twelve rounds, we limped painfully around the house to my car. Mark pretended to peek in my windows.

"Any six packs in there?" he asked.

"No, I finished them on the way and threw the empties into your bushes." I nodded toward the immaculate shrubbery and flowers surrounding his mailbox.

"Seriously BC, be careful with that stuff. I thank you again for being there for my girls, they wouldn't be here without you. But I worry about a guy who would be in that condition and get behind the wheel. None of us are invincible."

I lowered my head, studying the cracks in the driveway. "I know sir, I-"

"I'm not trying to make you feel bad, I...*we*...just want you to be safe. I've worked too many accidents, BC. I've had to deliver news to moms in the middle of the night...it's awful. It's a phone call you don't want your mother to receive. But I'll quit preaching." He reached out and shook my hand again. "If you happen to remember anything else about the other night..." Mark went silent and studied my shirt. "The club."

"Huh?"

"Laurie said it looked like a white club on the back of the man's hat. But what if it was a clover or a shamrock... like those." Mark pointed at my shirt.

I looked down at the three-leaf clovers which covered the vest and hat of the pipe-smoking Celtic's leprechaun. "You think the guy was wearing a Celtic's hat?"

"Maybe-"

Maggie suddenly appeared at the front door calling for Mark. She held his cell phone high in the air and scampered down the steps. "It's Detective Ingle, he needs to talk with you, said it was urgent," she yelled.

My heart sank. *Was Detective Ingle the one watching Laurie? Was she okay?*

Mark took the phone and moved into the yard. I tried to study his face for an answer. The youngest Boone daughter marched toward me, placing a hand on her hip and wrinkling her brow.

"Was that about Laurie?" I asked Maggie.

"I don't think so, but I *know* you weren't leaving without telling me goodbye?" she scolded.

"We were just on our way back inside," I lied. "But now that you're here, *goodbye Maggie Boone*, I enjoyed hanging out with you and your family." I moved toward my car door and waved to Mark pacing in the yard. Still on the phone, he held up one finger indicating that I should wait. Maggie hurried to my side.

"BC, I know you're a little sweaty and my mom already hugged all over you, but I'm getting one too. You saved my life. That calls for a mandatory hug. Actually, I'll give you two…one is for Laurie. I don't see her squeezing on you with Dylan around."

Mark closed his phone and started toward my car just as Maggie wrapped her skinny arms around me. For a moment I wondered if Mark's expression had to do with the recent call or with his fifteen-year-old daughter embracing a good-timing college boy.

"Maggie, we've got an issue, I need to leave right now," said Mark.

"Will you be back in time to take me to the church?"

"You're not staying here alone, Mag. You'll just have to go with me for now. I'll try to get someone to take you-"

"But I'm playing tonight, everybody's counting on me."

"I know Mag. I'm sorry, but-"

"Mark, I can take Maggie and drop her off, whatever you need me to do." The offer shot from my mouth before my mind had time to deflect it.

Maggie bounced and brought her hands up prayerfully beneath her chin. "Please dad, can BC take me? Please." Mark checked his watch and then glanced toward me.

"BC, I really hate to ask, but there's a situation and I-"

"It's no problem, Mark, really, I don't have plans."

Mark turned toward his pleading daughter. "Maggie, you'll just have to get there early. Go inside, get everything you need. Try not to keep BC waiting." Maggie turned and skipped toward the front door.

Concern covered Mark's face.

"Is it Laurie?" I asked.

77

"No, that wasn't about Laurie. But BC, I really need to go. I didn't want to say this in front of Maggie, but Detective Ingle said a nineteen-year-old girl from just across the county line was reported missing this afternoon. And with the current situation we're not waiting the normal period to begin searching for any females that are reported missing. So if you don't mind, when you get to the church make sure one of the youth leaders is there before you leave. You don't have to stay, either a deputy or I will pick her up."

"No problem Mark…really…get going if you need to."

He paused after starting toward the house. "And BC, I'd appreciate two more favors."

"Anything."

"First, wait out here until Maggie comes back out, we don't allow boys in the house while we're gone. But you may be sitting out here a while, getting ready quickly and being a fifteen-year-old girl is incompatible."

"It's no problem, Mark, really."

"And secondly, please scan the church parking lot when you get there. If any vehicle or person seems suspicious, just keep Maggie with you and call me immediately."

Mark turned and hurried back inside. I sat in my car, turned the air conditioning to full blast, and cleared Maggie a place to sit by tossing the empty fast-food bags and Coach's packet of team stationery from the passenger seat to the back. I looked again for my own green Celtics hat hoping to show Mark the white shamrock symbol on the back. It had to be in the car somewhere. I knew I had worn it to the party at Eagle Cliffs and I had searched for it Saturday morning when Mark had driven me home, but…*wait…surely not…*

My hat wasn't in my car. After my parking lot encounter with Laurie and Maggie's attacker, my hat never made it back to my car.

But another hat did.

As I put the pieces together, and thought back to Laurie's description of the man's hat, Mark reappeared running down the steps wearing jeans and a new shirt. In one hand he carried a small duffle bag and in the other hand was his holstered pistol. Mark nodded my direction, hopped into his Explorer, and speedily backed out the driveway. I bolted from my car and waved him down before he shifted into drive.

He lowered his passenger side window.

"Mark, the man *was* wearing a Celtics hat."

"How do you know?"

"Because it was mine."

Mark shifted the Explorer into park. "Do what?"

"And I've got his. It's maroon with the name of some state park written on it. I've got the man's hat. Our hats must have been knocked off when we fell to the ground. He grabbed mine as he ran for his van. It's a green fitted Celtics hat with a small white shamrock on the back."

"Where's his hat?"

I started for my car but realized the attacker's hat was on the bed post in my room at Eli's. I told Mark.

"Okay…don't touch it anymore. I'll contact the TBI. It may be later tonight but someone will be by to get it. I'll call you." Mark shifted into gear. I watched the Explorer disappear down the neighborhood road. *Go find that missing girl Mark*, I thought. I retreated to my own car to calm down and cool off. I couldn't believe I had the fugitive's hat. I couldn't believe I had *worn* this man's hat, the hat of a deranged predator…*or perhaps murderer*, if indeed this man had other victims as Mark speculated.

I leaned my seat back and closed my eyes. I shuddered as I pictured the filthy maroon hat hanging above my head last night while I slept.

I had the monster's hat. A man who wore it when he...*oh, no, no, no*...a man who now had my hat...and not just my favorite Celtics cap, but the one with my name written on the inside.

The monster knew my name.

15

*T*respassers. Hikers. Unprepared and lost.

The young man had appeared a few seconds behind his singing girlfriend, paused briefly, and flung a silver drinking can to the forest floor. They had continued through the trackless ravine below, heads down, concentrating on their steps, never looking onto the ridge as they passed.

And the Ratter, knife in hand, watched them.

Crouched. Coiled. Ready to strike.

It was his territory. And he had a decision to make.

All strikes are quick. All strikes are unseen. All strikes are fatal.

He wondered from where they had come. There were no marked trails within miles. Perhaps they had boat trouble in a cove on the wilderness side of the lake. But who would decide to walk out straight through this expanse of forest? He hated their ignorance, but the man knew the hikers would find their way out if they maintained their current direction, eventually stumbling upon dirt roads and outlying mobile homes. But it was the same direction he needed to be going.

Yes, he had a decision to make.

He envisioned the strike. The distance was too great to go unnoticed. There were too many dead leaves and fallen branches to move silently. He would simply go straight for the young man, eliminating him quickly, knowing that the girl would either react in one of two ways. She would become frozen with fear, perhaps screaming, as her boyfriend lay crumpled on the forest floor and the Rattler calmly moved toward her. Or she would flee, with panic and fear causing her to become even more disoriented within his territory.

Either way, she would belong to the Rattler.

All strikes are fatal, the man thought, but not immediately fatal. Prey can be kept for as long as necessary. Hours. Days. Even longer.

The Rattler sat back against a tree and removed his hat. He listened to the footsteps and voices gradually move farther away. He had time to track them down if he so decided. But they had not noticed him, and for now, that had saved their lives. The Rattler studied the letters inside the green Boston Celtics hat. He traced the curves of the two letters with his finger.

"But who are you BC?" the man whispered. "And did you see enough to lead others to me?"

The Rattler flicked his serpent-like tongue against the letters. He tasted the hat's scent. He envisioned his prey.

"Either way BC," the Rattler said aloud, "I'm coming for you either way."

16

*A*re you not coming in?"

Maggie had my passenger side door open and one foot on the pavement. I reread the bright blue banner stretched between two columns of Harmony Grove Baptist Church's original brick sanctuary.

Catch The Wave – 5:42 Every Sunday.

"What's with the odd starting time?" I asked.

Maggie put her foot back inside the car and closed the door. "The 5:42? It's scriptural…from the book of Acts. I don't have it memorized but it's our theme this summer for *Wave.* "

"And *Wave* is?"

"What we call our youth service."

"So this building is just for the youth?"

"This building is now the *Harbor.* They put us noisy kids as far away from the main church as possible. But it's been totally remodeled on the inside. My dad helped with a lot of the construction…come inside and check it out."

From my view the building still appeared to be an old fashioned sanctuary, only absent a steeple and dwarfed by a nearby octagonal structure of stone and glass. The two contrasting buildings were separated by a large parking area lined with holly bushes and young dogwood trees. Besides my car, the only other vehicle in the lot was a green Toyota Camry parked two spaces away. No sinister van or villain to be found.

"BC, are you afraid to come inside?"

I was actually afraid of several things at the moment. I was afraid of my feelings for a recent high school graduate that I had just met. I was afraid knowing a wanted criminal I had ticked off had my hat with my name written inside. And I hated to admit it, but I was indeed slightly afraid of hanging out with the local Christian youth at Harmony Grove Baptist Church.

"I think I'm a little too old for *Wave*. But whose Camry is that?"

"It's Mac's, she's helping our youth pastor for the summer. You probably know her, she goes to the college. She's pretty, dark headed-."

"*She*?...And her name is *Mac*?"

"Her last name is MacDowell or something, we just call her *Mac*. Her first name is Julie, but we already have a million girls at Wave with 'J' names, so we call her *Mac*."

"I don't think I know her."

"Well, she's inside setting up so come say hello. You told my dad you didn't have any plans. Just come in, listen to the music, and then leave when you want. We do the worship music first, then the message...and then the snake handling." Maggie laughed at herself and punched me in the arm. "C'mon, BC, I'll dedicate a song to you."

I checked my watch. Seventeen minutes past five. I had no desire to hang out with middle schoolers while making small talk with some *Julie* girl from campus who I didn't know. Volunteering with a church youth group meant we obviously ran with different crowds. I wanted to leave, but I had no good reason to decline Maggie's offer. I was a little curious to hear Maggie play, and I thought staying might win me some points with her big sister. Laurie Boone had moved Dylan's hand off her thigh for a reason, so perhaps all wasn't well with the local lovebirds.

Maggie reached into the backseat and pulled her guitar case to the front. "Well BC, what's it going to be?" she asked.

"I'll come in if you promise *not* to dedicate a song to me." Her big smile returned. "But I'll drive around a bit first and then be back before it starts."

"Sounds good, but you better keep your word." She slid out the door and headed toward the building. I waited to make sure the front doors were unlocked. Suddenly, Maggie sat the guitar case down on the steps and sprinted back to my car. I rolled down the window.

"Here BC, I almost forgot. I still had your cell phone."

"Thief."

Maggie laughed. "It was my Plan B to get you to come back. Don't forget to call my dad and let him know we made it."

When Maggie had finally exited her house, dressed in jeans and a black shirt declaring *Pick Jesus* on an image of a guitar pick, she had slung her guitar case in the back seat, patted the dash and said, "Alright college boy, let's see what this baby can do." On the entire ride to Harmony Grove my passenger never ceased talking or asking questions. And after describing both her dream car and the clunker her dad would no doubt buy her when she turned sixteen, she had spotted my cell phone near the gear shift.

"Cool phone, can I look at it?"

"I guess," I had said, not knowing that within five seconds she would be scrolling through my phone contacts and questioning every name listed.

"Who's Allison? A girlfriend?"

"Who's Bender? That's a funny name. Is he cute?"

"Coach...let's call coach and see what he's doing. I'll tell him that you whipped my forty-three year old dad today in a game of one-on-one and that I definitely think you should start next year."

Before arriving at the church Maggie entered Mark's cell number in my phone, which was fine since I had already misplaced the business card Mark had given me in Mr. Giles' driveway. Although he never told me, Maggie insisted that Mark wanted me to call after I had dropped her off safely at the church. She reminded me twice more after returning my phone. "Just call him," she said.

I thought of Mark speeding off to investigate the missing girl. "I think your dad is quite busy."

"Well, leave him a message." Maggie grinned slyly and headed toward the old sanctuary. I waited until she was safely inside before leaving.

* * *

Before returning to Harmony Grove, I wasted nearly twenty minutes exploring several back roads of Halston County. I scanned dozens of driveways for the attacker's dark van, but by the time I returned to the church I was even more confused about the van's possible make and model. I couldn't be sure if the van had been black, a dark green, or maybe even a deep blue like the one I followed back into the Harmony Grove parking lot. The dark Dodge pulled near the youth building and spilled out six kids, none of which appeared to have seen their first day of high school.

And I was about to hang out with them.

"Becoming cooler by the day, BC," I sarcastically told myself as I parked and waited for the adolescent crew to go inside.

It was strangely quiet when I finally entered the building, and as I picked up on one soft voice resonating from the front, I realized that everyone was praying. I slid into the back row of folding chairs and took in my surroundings. It was not what I expected. First, it was actually crowded. From what I could tell most of the forty or so present seemed to be even younger than Maggie, which explained the lack of cars. However, several taller figures scattered throughout the crowd appeared to be older high school students.

There was no traditional pulpit. Instead, an elaborate wooden structure extended toward the crowd and stretched nearly the entire width of the narrow building, leaving just enough space on each side to access doors leading backstage.

Large wooden columns held the raised platform several feet above the floor. Thickly braided ropes, oars, and circular life preservers added to the effect. An oval sign hung from the ceiling directly over the stage. Its bright green paint indicated that the former sanctuary was now *The Harbor*.

The long side walls of the sanctuary were covered in Christian fish symbols like those I'd seen on the backs of cars. There were hundreds, all painted in various shapes, sizes and colors. Some were larger fish with names and dates painted inside. On the wall near me, an orange fish with oversized red lips, green eyelashes and a cross-shaped earring had *Elizabeth 9/7/12* painted on its belly. I wondered about the holy fish induction process and if anyone would be joining the wall tonight.

The unseen girl toward the front finished her prayer and a multitude of "amens" and claps filled the room. The lights dimmed and the projected image of crashing waves appeared high on the wall to the left of the stage. Maggie emerged from the front row and ascended the platform. She retrieved her guitar from the back of *The Harbor's* stage, walked toward a lone microphone stand, and without a word, began strumming. No one sat and no one sang. As the lights dimmed even more and an overhead stage light gave Maggie a lavender glow, the whole room simply soaked in the soothing chords flowing out like gentle ripples from her guitar.

Softly, Maggie began to sing and the youth took their cue to join in. It was the only church song I would have recognized.

> *Amazing Grace, how sweet the sound*
> *That saved a wretch like me...*
> *I once was lost, but now I'm found*
> *Was blind but now I see...*

The words projected onto the front wall and I realized I had never known more than the first few lines. I read along as Maggie and the youth continued.

> *T'was Grace that taught...*
> *my heart to fear.*
> *And Grace, my fears relieved.*
> *How precious did that Grace appear...*
> *the hour I first believed.*

I had to be the only individual in the room not singing. I had expected a gathering of immature kids, but that wasn't what was taking place. Two students near me had their eyes closed, others had hands raised high into the air, but all were engaged in the music. And they were singing like they believed every word. I, on the other hand, felt like an imposter who had infiltrated a secret meeting. I thought back to my friends from middle and high school and tried to picture them participating in such a gathering.

It never would have happened.

Gradually, the music and Maggie's prayerful voice brought chills along my arm.

As soon as she played the last note of "Amazing Grace", a white-haired young boy I hadn't noticed behind her went wild on a drum set. Another boy, skinny with head tilted, hair hanging completely over one eye and ending at the corner of his lip, took his position on stage and held his bass guitar low as if it was made of concrete. After cotton-top finished his wicked assault on the drums, Maggie stepped back up to the microphone. "Let's make some waves," she said.

I wouldn't have recognized the next two songs anyway, but I knew they weren't to be found in a hymnal. These were rocking, righteous songs which had my head nodding and my feet tapping. Maggie Boone was talented, very talented.

I finally slipped out at the end of the third song, giving Maggie a discrete wave just as she instructed the youth to "greet one another in fellowship." After a few minutes on the road I realized that I had turned down my radio and was humming the last song Maggie's band had played. The song's chorus and upbeat tune were stuck in my head, but I'm quite sure I butchered the few lyrics I did try to sing.

From Harmony Grove I drove back through Andrews on my way to Eli's. Thirsty and needing gas, I pulled into Wimpy's Gas & Go, the small, family-owned convenience store which neighbored the Waffle Shack. While my car filled up, my eyes caught sight of the infamous dumpster in the parking lot next door.

The scene of the crime, I thought. There was no yellow police tape sectioning off the parking area like in the movies. Through Mark I knew that law enforcement had already searched the area, but it had been quick and as inconspicuous as possible.

Curiosity sent me through the withering, litter-filled bushes that separated Wimpy's from the Waffle Shack. Behind the dumpster, beneath a rusty, beaten chain-link fence ran a two-foot high concrete retaining wall. I soon realized why I had lingered in that spot for so long Friday night. Taking a seat on the wall, I leaned back against the fence, which gave in just enough before holding firm. It was rough, too close to the dumpster's stench, but hidden from view and surprisingly comfortable. *A drunk man's recliner*, I thought. I held my nose and studied the area hoping something would spark another lost memory.

It seemed ages since the attack, not a mere forty something hours. I spun my key chain on my finger as I tried to recreate the events of that night in my mind.

But just as the stench and the flies were claiming their territory, my key chain snapped and sent several keys clanging against the broken asphalt below. I reached down to pick up the first key and spotted the familiar markings on the wall beneath me. *Surely not?*

I studied the faint scratch marks as if they were ancient hieroglyphics. They were crude, barely visible, and upside down, but there was no mistaking what they were. I said them aloud until I had them burned in my memory. *I hadn't remembered writing these until just now...until seeing them myself.*

I shouted, leapt over the bushes and sprinted back to my car. I searched wildly for Mark's business card. I emptied the glove box and my wallet.

Call Mark...call Mark...I was supposed to call him anyway to tell him I had dropped off Maggie....Maggie...she put his number in my phone! I've got his number in my phone!

I found my cell, scrolled to Mark's name and hit SEND. On the first ring I remembered that he was probably in the midst of searching for the missing girl. It didn't matter, he needed this information now.

Pick up Mark...pick up...

"Hello?" said a pleasant, familiar sounding female voice.

Mark's secretary?...The female officer from the front lobby?

"Yes...I'm trying to reach Captain Mark Boone, it's an emergency. I have-"

"This is his daughter, Laurie...is this BC?"

"Laurie?" I could hear voices and laughter in the background.

"I'm at the lake, BC, do you need something?"

"Sorry, I thought I called your dad's phone."

"No, this is my phone. How did you get my number?"

Maggie...either Maggie entered the wrong number or she...slick one Maggie.

"Laurie, I need to get in touch with your dad, but I've got good news, real good news. I'm at the Waffle Shack and I found-"

"Did you see the guy again?" she asked. I quickly scanned the parking lot and the motel across the street. I hadn't once thought of the possibility of the man being nearby.

"No…no. But I'm at the dumpster. There's a concrete wall that I sat on Friday night and get this…I wrote down his license plate number. It's scratched into the wall with a rock beneath where I was sitting. I almost missed it behind some weeds. Six crooked letters and numbers. I think I did it after I saw him slash the tire, I don't know, but we've got him!"

Laurie didn't respond. For a moment I thought I had lost the signal and had been speaking to air. "Laurie?"

Dylan's voice sounded in the background. "I'm talking with BC," I heard her say. "Dylan, I'll tell you in a minute, just calm down."

Just leave the lake Laurie, let's celebrate. I'll take you anywhere you want-

"BC, call my dad right now. Hang up and call him right now."

I had no desire to disconnect from her voice. But either Laurie hung up without another word or Dylan did it for her. I sat in my car for a moment allowing my adrenaline to settle. I wondered if Mark would still need the man's hat. Even with a license plate number, I wanted the hat out of my room, and I shook thinking about it hanging over my bed as I slept. As I held my phone preparing to call Mark, two very different thoughts entered my mind. First, I now had the attacker's hat and license plate number, but he still knew my name. I suppressed a wave of panic hoping Mark and law enforcement could find him quickly.

And then I delighted in my second realization. I still didn't have Mark's number.

Sorry Dylan. I had no choice but to call Laurie back.

17

The Rattler lifted the discarded beer can from the forest floor as night slowly crept over the forest. No wonder the hikers had been lost, he thought, crushing the can into his fist.

The Rattler despised alcohol. He had lived with it long ago. It blurred the senses. It gave a false sense of empowerment...of strength. But it wasn't real strength. It was for the weak. And he would never be weak again. Never.

The smell from the can reminded him once again of his carelessness...of the night this BC hit him so hard he couldn't breathe, so hard he couldn't keep hold of his prey. The man's blood boiled as he remembered the smell of this BC's breath upon his face as they fell and wrestled on the asphalt.

But this BC had lost his strength.

He couldn't contain the Rattler for long. He was un-disciplined...weak. Too weak to cut the head off the Rattler. Too weak to finish what he had started. He had his chance and he had failed.

But the man knew that he, not the weak BC, had been the one to panic. The strong had fled from the weak. "I will never be weak again," the Rattler said *aloud, slamming the can against the trunk of a large hickory tree. He continued his trek toward the next ridge, toward the dirt road and the houses and the people.*

It was time to come out of hiding.

It was time to see what the world now knew about the Rattler. He removed his shirt to let the serpent breathe, his senses awakening as night fell further upon the forest. It was time to reclaim his territory. It was time to hunt.

He had announced his dominion with the first strike, with the girl no one seemed to miss, and his territory had expanded since. He studied its terrain, its people, and its routes. Even, perhaps especially, in the dark, he knew the desolate highways between the small towns, exits from neighborhoods, the mountain campus of Cohutta College, and lost dirt roads that seldom saw a visitor. His territory was becoming vast and they would know it. They would respect it. They would fear the Rattler.

The man stopped to catch his breath at the bottom of the last ridge. Darkness had completely settled. He inhaled the air of his territory and held it in his lungs. He had no desire to leave it. But that, he knew, would now be up for discussion. The man climbed the final ridge, finding the crest before pulling the flashlight from the cargo pocket on his thigh.

He aimed it into the darkness and flashed twice.

In the distance headlights pierced the night, flashing twice in response.

"Right on time," thought the man…"Right on time."

18

D oes he have a name?"
I watched Mark hold the plastic bag at eye level and study the hat. "He sure does," Mark said. I took a bite of a peanut butter granola bar and followed Mark off Eli's front porch toward the cars. In the grass, the darkened spots of Mark's arriving footprints were still evident in the morning dew. "We're ninety-nine percent certain the van's owner is the suspect. He fits the description, has a criminal history, and-"

"But you're not going to tell me his name."

"And why would you want to know?"

"I just want a name to put with the image in my mind."

"I can't release that yet, BC, but if we don't have him by Friday it's going to be all over the news."

"Four days? You're going to make me wait four days to know his name?"

Mark placed his oversized convenience-store coffee on the Explorer's roof while he opened the door and tossed the sealed evidence bag inside. "The TBI is still hoping he'll assume all is safe and decide to reappear at some point this week. But if not, his name and face hit the media Friday morning."

"Before the sicko gets another weekend to prowl for young girls?" I asked.

"Exactly."

My fist covered an escaping yawn. "Well, should I go to work?"

"Go to work. Keep your normal routine. The man's address is about an hour away, but I wouldn't consider it local. And neither is his last known place of employment."

"What about my hat?"

"You sure it was just your initials and not your name?"

"Just *BC*."

"I could be wrong, BC, but I don't see someone in this man's situation looking for instant revenge. He's either on the run or lying low to see what he's stirred up. And even if he noticed your initials, he probably thinks the 'C' is for your last name and nothing about the hat associates you with the college." Mark's casual answer eased my own fears, at least for the moment.

I pointed to where Mark had tossed the evidence. "I guess his hat isn't that big a deal now?"

"Every piece counts," Mark responded. "If we can use it to link our suspect to the scene, then it's a huge deal. Maybe it even helps link him to other attacks." He slid into the driver's seat and reached for the open door.

"Well, Mark, just let me know when you're ready for the stake out."

"Do what?" asked Mark, looking puzzled.

"*I* stopped him in the parking lot. *I* ended up with his hat. *I* found the license plate number that *I* wrote down at the crime scene. I figured you might as well use me for a stake out."

Mark grinned. "That's a great idea, BC, I'll even provide you a stake-out partner...Dylan." The detective's sarcastic laugh was quickly silenced by the closing of his door and the Explorer's cranking engine. Mark Boone was a master at getting in the last word.

Even in the early morning, which I wouldn't expect to be anyone's best time of day, I noticed a difference in Mark. He hadn't yet caught the suspect, but having a name and a piece of evidence seemed to remove some of the unease from Mark's face. Perhaps it was a cop thing. Perhaps he knew it was now only a matter of time.

Mark had been ecstatic when I finally reached him Sunday evening from Wimpy's convenience store. He had me stay at the dumpster until a TBI agent arrived to take digital pictures of my caveman-style etchings.

During our Sunday evening conversation I also learned that the missing nineteen-year-old girl Mark had sped off to find had indeed been found safe. What Detective Ingle first thought to be another abduction turned out to be an upset girl, mad at her father, who left home to meet a guy she had befriended in an Internet chat room.

* * *

After he stopped by Eli's Monday morning to get the suspect's hat, I didn't hear from Mark again until Wednesday afternoon. He called as I left work just to give me an update. Mark said the attacker had not returned home and the TBI assumed he was on the run, but something was hesitant in his voice.

"And what are you not telling me?" I asked.

"Nothing BC, just touching base with you and keeping you informed. But you may see a few Halston County deputies as you go about your day. Where are you right now?"

I told him I was headed to the gym and I even invited Mark to join me for another round of one on one. He declined, saying it wouldn't be right for him to embarrass a star athlete on campus. And then he hung up.

As I pulled into a parking space at the athletic center, my phone buzzed with a text message from Kit Hendrix, my friend and teammate who lived just south of Nashville.

Heading your way this weekend, will u b on campus?

Yep, at the gym probably, I replied, and waited for Kit's response. His text came quickly.

It's summer dude, get a life.

* * *

At the court I reminded myself that nine was the new magic number.

Nine days until tryouts. Nine days to earn my spot to Europe.

And then I ran sprints. I worked on ball handling drills. I did some quickness drills and jumped rope, which I usually hated in practice. I shot free throws and followed any misses with a punishment sprint to the far baseline and ten push-ups. And then, with a grin I couldn't contain as I envisioned Paris and Frankfurt and Vienna, I just shot basketball.

Growing up I could spend hours at the goal in my driveway, just shooting. It simply became my escape. When I argued with my mom or was upset with my brothers, which was often, I shot basketball. When Pepper, my black lab, got ran over, I shot basketball. When Leslie Collinsworth dumped me in ninth grade for a senior, I shot basketball.

Since the day I started driving I always kept a ball in my car in case an open gym beckoned me. While I enjoyed pickup games with friends or the epic, sometimes bloody battles against my older brothers, what I liked best was simply having a gym to myself. The rhythmic echo of a dribble, the squeak of my shoes on the hardwood, and the swishing of the net after a perfectly released ball were always soothing. And the main reason I chose to attend the small but prestigious Cohutta College, besides the fact Coach Glynn recruited me to play basketball, was because of the Joseph Emerson Mountain Athletic Center, better known as the Joe-MAC.

At Cohutta I quickly became a regular at the courts. The Joe-MAC became my new refuge. Besides the main gymnasium used for varsity basketball and volleyball, the Joe-MAC had three practice courts, a weight room, an indoor track, and an indoor pool. Best of all, it stayed open late.

My freshman year had been a constant series of floundering academically and socially. I was drowning in a world I didn't understand. High school classes had come easy for me, and suddenly I had to learn how to study. I couldn't relate to the guys in my dorm or the girls that caught my eye. Most were products of private schools, which I was not. Most had money, which I did not. And most had parents or older siblings who had attended Cohutta College or a similar prestigious institution, while I initially just hoped to make it through one full year of classes. That way I'd at least have bragging rights against my older brothers.

The basketball team at that time was loaded with upper classman. Only one other incoming freshman was on campus for basketball. He was my roommate when school started, but he went home on the second weekend and never returned. So I began migrating alone to the courts at the

Joe-MAC. While some on campus studied and the majority spent their weekends swilling beers, pursuing the opposite sex at local fraternity houses, or road tripping to some rich kid's lake house, I shot basketball.

It wasn't that I was opposed to those things, but I was usually short on cash and clumsy on conversation. The gym was simply my familiar friend.

After my first full season playing basketball and getting to know my older teammates, my college life began to change. Guys invited me places, some pretty girls knew my name, and a few of my professors even discussed our recent basketball games after class. I managed a grade point average that allowed me to keep my academic scholarship and went from being miserable to looking forward to coming back. And by my sophomore year I knew to complete my studying and get my shooting in at the Joe-MAC long before the parties started.

I had new friends waiting for me.

19

As I left my Wednesday workout, Coach Glynn stood in the gym lobby chatting with what I assumed were the parents of a recruit. The high school boy, oddly standing at the glass exit door staring at the parking lot, was several inches shorter than me. A point guard, I assumed, and perhaps my future replacement. Even with his back to me I could see that the boy's blonde hair stood high above his forehead, the collar of his shirt pointed upwards, and he wore trendy sandals. He was already dressed for the frat houses.

Coach called me over. "Looks like you were working quite hard in there."

"Europe," I replied.

He slapped me on the shoulder as the recruit's parents stared my direction. "This is our senior captain, BC Morrow. BC will be a member of the all-conference team traveling overseas in August."

"Hopefully," I interjected.

The recruit's mom wished me luck. The father mumbled and turned his attention to a glass case against the wall filled with pictures of past glory and nets cut down from ancient championships. Their spiked-hair son finally spun from the door, an odd expression on his face. "Did you all see that man that just walked out?" he asked. I hadn't seen anyone.

"You mean the delivery guy?" answered Coach Glynn.

"He took something off that desk," the boy answered, pointing to the Joe-MAC reception area that stayed unattended for most of the summer. "He reached across, took something, and headed quickly for the door."

Coach Glynn walked toward the reception desk. "Nothing valuable should be up here, he must have left something and came back for it." The spiked-hair recruit didn't look convinced and turned back toward the glass door. But Coach Glynn continued. "BC, this is Will Sharp and his parents. Will plays at the Woodland Academy near Nashville."

"The Woodland Academy? Isn't that where Kit Hendrix played?" I asked.

"He sure did," answered Will Sharp's mother. "Will was a freshman when Kit was a senior, so he didn't get to play with Kit on the varsity."

"He should have," said Mr. Sharp, never taking his eyes from the glass trophy case.

"Kit was awesome to watch," said the mother.

"Until clutch time," the father responded. He turned from the trophy case, arms crossed, the gold bracelet on his left wrist as thick as the gold watch on his right. "Has he gotten any tougher during his two years of college?" This guy did know Kit.

"Kit is going to be a big part of our team this season," answered Coach Glynn. That was one thing I always respected about Coach Glynn. He might talk to us players like dogs at times, and the whole team knew what he thought about Kit, but he always backed his players to anyone who wasn't part of the program. This included the ridiculously wealthy and arrogant fathers of recruits.

"Kit and BC will be the battle-tested leaders of this year's squad. We'll be counting on them heavily." I thought the recruit's mother was about to clap. The father nodded unimpressed. Coach slapped my shoulder once again. "Speaking of…have you sent those letters to the players yet?"

"Just a couple left," I lied.

I edged toward the exit and told the Sharps it was nice to meet them. The father walked without response toward the main gym, but surprisingly, Will Sharp extended his hand. "It was nice to meet you, BC. Tell Kit I said hello when you see him." Perhaps the apple didn't land directly under the tree.

"Let me show you all the rest of the Joe-MAC," I heard Coach Glynn say as I slid out the door. After grabbing some food on campus, I drove back to Eli's. I took Coach's large brown envelope from my back seat and headed for the backyard boulders to write and make a few cell phone calls. I needed to let my mom hear my voice. I needed to text Kit about his plan to visit and my recent encounter with the Sharps. But mainly, I wanted to call Laurie.

Since her story about the night our lives intersected had been interrupted when her friends arrived, I still wasn't clear about what happened between me and the attacker. Not knowing the details gnawed at me. I could have asked Mark, but I needed another reason to speak with Laurie. I just needed to summon the nerve to call her.

A strong evening breeze convinced me that trying to hold papers and write near the mountain's edge wasn't practical, so I returned to a rocker on the front porch without making the first phone call.

Cohutta College Basketball was written in an eye-catching font across Coach's horizontal folding stationery. Inside, Coach Glynn's contact information was printed in the upper right corner. Beneath it, former Assistant Coach Tomlinson's information was struck through with a black marker. *Real classy Coach Glynn*, I thought. At the bottom of the card, when opened, hunter green letters trimmed in gold proclaimed "Go Mountaineers! Focus, Fight, and Finish Strong!" Above the team motto, which contained the only f-words Coach allowed his players to use, the expanse of white was waiting for my words of wisdom. And I had no clue what to write.

I skipped the first few names on the roster and started with Kit.

> *Kit,*
>
> *I hope you're enjoying your summer and still making time for the off-season work outs. You are going to be a big part of what we accomplish this season. FYI – We'll meet with Coach Glynn the Sunday night before classes begin and conditioning will start the last week of August. And I suggest adding a skull tattoo to the bulging biceps you've made during the off-season.*
>
> *BC*

I felt nerdy writing to my teammates so I tried ending with a little sarcasm. Kit was six-foot-four, but maybe weighed a hundred and seventy pounds soaking wet. Coach Glynn often announced to the team that Kit must be allergic to the weight room. Besides the personalized final line, the cards for returning players all carried identical messages. For the four incoming freshman I dropped the sarcasm. I didn't know them and they didn't know me.

As I completed the last card, Eli staggered rear first through his creaking screen door. His odd entrance, I realized after I failed to offer any assistance, was to protect the tray of food and drinks he carried. The screen door released from his hip and slammed loudly against the house.

"You up for a little company?" he asked.

"It's your house Mr. Giles, I'm your company."

The old man leaned toward me with the tray. I lightened his load by taking a glass of tea and a saucer topped with pecan pie. He lowered himself into a rocking chair and rested the tray in his lap. Eli wore his usual outfit. Overalls. Plaid shirt. Tennis shoes. Blue cap. I noticed the hat had *Cougars* stitched in grey across the front.

"Cougars, huh?"

"Yep," Eli said. "The Halston County Cougars. I enjoy those high school football games." I suddenly remembered Dylan's blue *HCHS Football* shirt from the Boone family dinner.

"Do you happen to know a player named Dylan Ingle?" I hated the question as soon as I asked it.

"Heck of a linebacker. He really knocked the stew out of folks. Is he a buddy of yours?"

"Not really," I responded.

"You're not in any trouble I need to know about are you?" the old man asked.

"No sir, Mr. Giles, why do you ask?"

"I've had two police cars turn around in my driveway today, and one that keeps moving slowly along the road out yonder."

Mark, I thought, *working behind the scenes.*

"Mr. Giles, I can assure you they're not after me." I wanted to tell the old man who they were looking for, but I didn't want him to worry. I had also promised Mark to keep quiet about what was taking place.

"Son, you need to start calling me *Eli*, Mr. Giles makes me sound old." He winked as he clarified. A strange chirping caught my attention. A squirrel poised on a nearby limb alerted its comrades of our presence. Eli took a pinch of his pecan pie and threw it out toward the base of the tree. "Let's see if this will keep you quiet for a while." We watched as the squirrel cautiously spiraled down the thick trunk and claimed Eli's offering.

"So BC, you mentioned before that you played ball at the college?"

"Yes sir, basketball. This will be my last year though."

"Time goes quick, doesn't it?"

"Yes sir."

"Can't say I've ever been to a basketball game over at the college. My son and I used to go watch some football games when he was younger. Those were fun."

"When was the last time Joseph visited?" I asked.

"Have I told you about Joseph?"

"Yes sir, the other night, when you were working on your grandson's birdhouse."

"That's right. Oh, they come up from Atlanta every other month or so. You said you're from Georgia, didn't you?"

"Yes sir, Dalton, just south of Chattanooga."

"Oh, I know Dalton. I preached a few revivals down that way…many moons ago."

"You were a preacher?"

"For over forty years. And I still fill in at a couple small churches around here from time to time."

How did I not realize that I was renting from a holy man?

While I savored my last bite of pie I pondered the irony of a college student like myself renting a room from a preacher. Perhaps God simply had a sense of humor.

"I really enjoyed those Dalton revivals," Eli said, reminiscing. "Those people were some good, hard-working folks who always had a hunger for God's word. A preacher friend of mine from Dalton also worked at one of those big carpet mills." Eli flicked another piece of pecan pie toward the squirrel.

"More carpet mills there than any place in the world supposedly," I said. "And honestly, that is why I stayed here for the summer. My oldest brother is a shift supervisor so he always has a job lined up for me when I get home. It's a good job, but I just don't think I'm made for the monotonous work of a carpet mill."

Eli nodded. "I understand. My wife and I moved up to Michigan right after getting married. We lived in Pontiac, and I worked on the assembly line installing car seats for nearly six years."

"What brought you back from Michigan?"

"Five Michigan winters and the pulpit. My grandfather was a preacher. My daddy was a preacher. It was just a matter of time before I picked up the family business. My daddy had a stroke, which was the main reason we came back. I filled in the week I got home and kept at it for a few decades. BC, what does your dad do for a living?"

The question didn't bother me anymore.

"Sir, he doesn't do anything…he's not living. He drowned somewhere in Oklahoma when I was six. But I really didn't know him. It was always just my brothers and my mom."

Eli laid his fork and empty plate on the tray.

"Son, I'm sorry to hear that, and since my foot in my mouth doesn't taste too good, I'll switch subjects. How is our basketball team looking?" We both had a laugh before he asked again.

"I'm serious, how's your team going to be this year?"

I tried to sound optimistic. "We should be okay. We lost four solid seniors, but we have some young talent and a junior who could help if we can get his head on straight."

"What's wrong with the boy?"

I shook my head thinking about my buddy Kit. "Well sir, he's got too much confidence off the court and not enough when he's on it. He's tall, extremely athletic, has some skill, but just doesn't play aggressive enough. He just has so much potential that it's frustrating. But who knows? Maybe he'll be an animal for us on the court this year."

"What's the boy's name?" Eli asked.

"Kit…Kit Hendrix."

Eli shook his head. "*Kit?* Well right there's his problem. His momma probably called him *Kitty* half his life. That boy needs a new name."

"If only his parents had named him Duke or Roy," I said, thinking of tough cowboy names. "But then he may have ended up playing at a major university."

"I'm serious. You're the senior on this team aren't you? If this boy can help you win during your final season you need to do something about it, don't you? Well, give this Kit a new name."

"I think it will take more than a nickname to make Kit a beast on the court."

"It worked for Peter."

"Who?"

"Son, do you know your Bible?" The look on my face gave Eli his answer, so he just continued. "Listen, a disciple named Simon had the talent but no consistency. Up one minute and down the next. So Jesus gave him a new name...*Peter*, which meant *Rock*. That is what Jesus knew he could be. That is what Jesus *needed* him to be. So here was Simon, who was following and wanting to please Jesus, and along their journey Jesus sometimes called him Peter, and other times called him Simon. When Peter was acting foolish, or falling asleep when he was supposed to be praying, Jesus would call him Simon."

Eli took a quick swig of tea and then jumped back into the lesson.

"But Simon wanted to be Jesus' *Rock*. And over time that is who he became. It didn't happen overnight, but it happened. After Jesus ascended into Heaven, Peter became a force to be reckoned with. He stood up to Jewish religious leaders, preached a Pentecost sermon that saved three thousand souls, wrote letters of scripture, and did plenty more. He lived up to the name Jesus gave him. Your boy needs a new name."

"*Rock?*"

"No, but something better than *Kitty*." We both laughed again.

Perhaps Eli Giles was on to something. A napkin blew off Eli's tray and as he leaned toward me to pick it up, I saw Kit's new name atop the old man's head. It had been in front of me the entire time. It was a name suitable for turning a *Kitty* into a beast. I went through the brown envelope of player letters and removed Kit's. I rewrote the card and addressed a new envelope to the ferocious, aggressive junior I planned to create.

I held the new name toward Eli for his approval. He touched his cap.

"From a kitten to a *Cougar*...I like it," Eli said.

As we laughed a Halston County patrol car could be seen moving slowly along the road. It paused at Eli's driveway for a few moments before moving on. The old man cut his eyes in my direction.

"Boy, are you sure you're not in trouble?"

20

The Rattler carved the letters deep into the planks of the old barn.

ALL STRIKES...

He had agreed to wait, but now, on the third day, the Rattler was growing impatient. As he carved, the sound of an approaching engine grew louder. He moved to a slit between the planks and peered at the vehicle moving slowly over the ruts in the washed out road. Finally. The Rattler finished carving the final two words and drove the knife deep into the wood in exclamation.

ARE FATAL

The barn door opened. The Rattler eyed the man who could have passed for his brother. They were blood after all.

"Anything?" asked the Rattler.

"Your house seemed quiet. I made one pass, nothing more. I will go by again tomorrow."

"How about the radio or newspapers?"

The man tossed the newspaper and a thin white book at the Rattler. "Still nothing, you can check the paper yourself. But I thought the book might interest you."

The Rattler flicked through its pages. "And where did you find this? What is a Joe-MAC?"

"I made a little stop on the campus, following your hunch." The man closed and latched the barn door. "But the ride gave me time to finalize my decision."

The Rattler closed the thin book. "And what have you decided?"

The man unbuttoned his shirt and moved to the center of the barn. The Rattler eyed the impressive serpent that ran along the inside of the man's arms and across his chest. The man had known the pain too, the pain that generated strength and clarity and purpose. Yes, thought the Rattler, in a sense we are brothers. More than brothers.

"I have made my decision," said the man with the copperhead tattoo. "It is time to move on. Whether you were seen or not, you broke the rules and your carelessness has tainted this territory, for you and for me. It will now only be a matter of time."

"It will always be a matter of time," shouted the Rattler. "We will always be hunted."

The man pointed his finger toward the Rattler. "Your greed and foolishness have cost you the right to decide," he yelled. "You asked me to consider your proposal and I did. But we are leaving. This weekend we begin our search for a new territory."

The Rattler calmly removed his own shirt and stepped toward the man at the center of the barn. The man was slightly older and significantly thicker. But the

Rattler never flinched, never hesitated. He had been weak before, but he would never be weak again.

Never.

"Then why did you stop by the campus?" asked the Rattler.

"Curiosity, nothing more. But my decision has been made."

"I challenge your decision," hissed the Rattler, shaking out his hands then balling his fists as his knuckles popped. He flicked his forked tongue toward his opponent.

"I assumed you would," replied the Copperhead. "I assumed you would."

The two serpents circled each other for a few brief seconds. Eyes narrowed. Fangs ready.

The strike was simultaneous and vicious.

21

Thursday began peacefully.

It was painting day. My work assignment was to repaint four concrete dugouts at the college's baseball and softball fields. All four would be forest green, top to bottom, inside and out. I had arrived before seven at the Joe-MAC, shot hoops for an hour, grabbed the needed supplies, and drove to the fields to get the bulk done before the heat of the day. The fields were practically side-by-side, separated only by a wide gravel parking area.

Without a partner for conversation, I listened to my MP3 and painted at a steady pace while my mind meandered through the events of the past few days. *I had saved two lives...I had been interrogated at a police station...I had met a local girl I couldn't stop thinking about...and I was eight days away from earning a trip to Europe.*

But I couldn't shake a growing feeling that something major was brewing.

Maybe it was due to the day's idyllic peacefulness, but I felt like I was literally idling in the calm before the storm. Perhaps it was the looming try-outs. Perhaps it was because the man who attacked Laurie and Maggie still hadn't been captured. Or perhaps it was Laurie herself, the girl with the green eyes, curly brown hair, and a boyfriend. I still planned to call Laurie and find out exactly what had happened after I rushed out from behind that dumpster.

Perhaps today was the day.

For most of the morning I had the world to myself. The only signs of life had been a small pack of cyclists who glided silently down the road, a small red pick-up truck that turned around in the gravel parking lot, and a fun-looking burnt orange Jeep Wrangler that sped by.

After moving my supplies from the freshly painted softball dugouts, I had just refilled the paint tray at the baseball field when my cell phone vibrated in my pocket. I checked the caller ID and stared in disbelief. Even though it displayed *Mark Boone*, I knew I had yet to correct that number in my phone.

"Hello?"

"Hey BC, it's Laurie, you busy today?"

I must be living right, I thought, breaking into a two-second dance of happiness, knowing no one was around to witness.

"A little busy…just working at the baseball field."

"Are you alone or do you have help?"

"Just me today, why?"

"Well, I just called to warn you. Dylan didn't like the fact that you called me twice at the lake the other night. He's got a temper, BC, a *bad* temper, and I guess it's just been brewing. But he called a while ago and said he's on his way to settle some things with you."

"Are you serious?" I asked, practically laughing.

"Very serious, BC, he gets in these rages and there is not much anyone can do. And he'll probably have his punk brother with him."

"Detective Ingle?"

"No, Colby, the other one. He's a very bad influence on Dylan."

"So a high school boy and his brother are on their way to beat me up because I called his girlfriend?"

"Yes, and Dylan's not a high school boy, he graduated two years ago."

Really, so you don't mind dating older guys?

"Laurie, I was calling your dad, not you. Maggie put your number under your dad's name in my cell, remember, I was just trying to get in touch with your dad."

"So you didn't want to speak with me?"

"That is not what I meant," I protested.

"Just be on the lookout, BC. There is no telling what he'll do if he finds you. And just to let you know, Dylan usually carries a baseball bat in the back of his Jeep."

An engine revved behind me as she spoke. Turning, my eyes locked on the orange Jeep that had passed by earlier. It idled at the far end of the parking lot, facing my direction. I hadn't heard it pull onto the gravel. The morning sun reflected off the windshield.

"Did you say a Jeep?"

"Yeah, a little beat up, orange, with a hard top. Why?"

"I think Dylan's here."

The Jeep Wrangler accelerated quickly, spewing gravel across the parking area and heading directly toward me. My brain and feet remained frozen in a fog of disbelief and confusion as the speeding vehicle devoured the distance between us. I dropped my phone and backpedaled as the Jeep slid to an angry stop less than ten yards from where I stood.

This was bad. Very bad. I raised my wet paint roller in defense, expecting Dylan to emerge on a rampage from the driver's side. Instead, the figure rushing toward me was slender and attractive and giggling. *Laurie*. Wearing a baseball cap pulled low and large sunglasses, Laurie held her cell phone like a dagger and chuckled at my expense.

"Gotcha!" she yelled.

"Where's Dylan?"

She continued to laugh. "You should have seen the look on your face."

"How did you know where-"

"I went by the athletic offices and some guys in there told me where to find you. Then I spotted you out here lost in your own little world and I made the most of it. Sorry."

"Is that really Dylan's Jeep?"

"Sure is, but with no Dylan. We swapped cars for the day. I can tell you all about it on the way. Are you up for an adventure?" she asked.

I peered at the work I had left. "Well-"

"I had hoped to borrow you for a couple hours," Laurie pleaded. She looked at the paint supplies spread out around the dugout. "Unless you're too busy."

"I need to have this finished today. Can you give me an hour? I'll hurry."

Laurie stepped toward the supplies and picked up my spare paint roller. "I don't have an hour," she said. "Let's get to work."

* * *

Laurie confidently shifted gears in her boyfriend's Jeep as we left campus and headed for the highway. Dylan, I learned, worked as a lifeguard during the summers and would be protecting swimmers at Lake Halston Beach for the majority of the day.

"Who taught you to drive a five-speed, your dad?" I asked.

"Nope, Dylan," she responded, so again I changed the subject.

"So tell me about this adventure I've been recruited for."

"We're going undercover," she pointed to the cap and big sunglasses on her face. Laurie had me grab a hat from my own car before we left. I had just bought a new Cohutta College hat from the campus bookstore to replace my lost Celtics hat, so I placed it in the back seat beside a large t-shirt and a pair of Dylan's cleats. I wondered why he had cleats in his car if he had graduated two years ago. Perhaps he still had college football dreams or played church league softball. I didn't ask Laurie. There was no need for further Dylan discussions.

"Undercover, huh? Sounds serious."

"Yep, and I needed an undercover car, *he* knows what mine looks like."

Laurie built the suspense perfectly, and would have waited forever to make me ask the question.

"Who is *he*?" I finally offered.

"Joe Vaughn Burrell." She pulled a few sheets of paper from the visor above. "Joe Vaughn Burrell is the man who attacked me and Maggie."

Laurie handed me the papers. The first page had a handwritten name and address. The second and third pages were Internet directions and a map to an address in Belford, Tennessee.

"You're not kidding are you?"

"I saw a notepad with info about the investigation on my dad's desk last night. I couldn't help it, I had to look. And then there was no way I could sit around all day after I knew

118

his name and where he lived. So I Googled the directions and printed them off." She glanced my way but I couldn't see her eyes through the dark sunglasses. I tried to wrap my mind around everything Laurie had just told me.

"Are you sure-"

"Do I need to take you back?" she asked.

I looked at the map. *Belford, Tennessee. 49.4 miles away.*

The estimated travel time on the driving directions said an hour and two minutes one way. That would mean that I would spend two, perhaps three hours with Laurie.

"I just don't want you to get in trouble Laurie. I take it you didn't tell anyone what you were doing."

"My parents think I'm at the lake."

"With Dylan?"

"Yes, but I didn't specify which lake, so we need to stop by Nickajack so I won't be a total liar. And the officer who has been trailing me is out of town today, I heard my dad speaking on the phone to him last night. My dad told the guy not to worry about it and that I would be with a group at the lake."

"And instead you're with me?"

"My dad trusts you."

"He did."

"BC, I'm not turning around."

And I didn't want her to.

***

A portion of the journey required us to travel on Interstate 24 toward Chattanooga.

"Let's kill two birds with one stop," I mentioned after a green interstate exit sign displayed a boating symbol and some local eateries. "I'll pay for lunch, and we can eat by the lake."

Laurie agreed. We pulled off the exit and had a choice of two fast food places. We ordered drive-through tacos and then spent ten minutes following dilapidated signs to a boat ramp. Nickajack was a wide, beautiful lake, but we obviously had not discovered the main public access area. Tall weeds surrounded an apparently seldom-used boat ramp. Two rough picnic tables waited in the nearby shade.

Facing the lake, we sat on top of the sturdiest table and kept our feet on the bench, away from the calf-high grass. Dozens of names were carved into its faded wood.

"Look," Laurie said laughing, "*Peanut* loves Tina forever."

"Well," I responded, pointing to my side of the table. "We might have a problem, *Shane* loves Tina too, it's carved right here."

22

Barefooted, Laurie walked out on the sloping concrete boat ramp until the water lapped at her knees. She flipped the bottom of her khaki shorts up twice so she could take another step into the lake. I watched from the picnic table until she dared me to follow. Like a little boy, I picked up a few flat stones on my way to skip along the lake's smooth surface. My first fling took one immaculate skip before being swallowed by the water, never coming close to a second ricochet.

"Impressive," Laurie said with heavy sarcasm.

My mind had followed the drowning rock.

"I dream about lakes," I said aloud, surprising myself.

Laurie wanted to know more, but I didn't feel like whining about my nightmare to the very girl I wanted to impress. But Laurie was persistent, and beautiful, and I gave in. It felt good to actually tell someone, especially Laurie. I described how the dream began with me in the lake, a thick fog approaching, and without any knowledge of how I got there or in which direction I might find the shore. I told how each dream seemed to be slightly different, but ended virtually the same way. In each I would swim for my life until being utterly overwhelmed by fatigue and the pull of the water.

"So it always ends with you drowning?" asked Laurie.

"So far."

Honest concern filled her eyes. "How often have you had this dream?"

"It started a couple months ago, but more often lately."

"Does it scare you?"

"Well, I'm always glad to wake up, if that means anything."

"Maybe the dream itself means something. Or like in scripture, maybe it's God speaking to you." She looked toward my feet only inches from the water's edge. "You may want to stay out of the water."

"I'm not sure God, if he is up there, has much to say to me." As soon as I spoke I could see the grimace flash across her face. Still thigh deep in the lake, Laurie looked me directly in the eyes.

"What do you mean?" she asked.

"Laurie, I didn't mean to offend you. You obviously have a very Christian family."

"But?"

"But I just wasn't raised like you were. I had a grandmother that went to church, but my family, well…we just didn't."

Laurie moved toward me, the water revealing more of her wet, glistening legs with each step. "BC, I don't believe in God because my family does. I believe in God because of what I know, what I've seen, and what is in my heart." She picked up a stone, turned, and side-armed it out toward the water. On the fourth skip I quit counting.

"Show off."

"And you didn't offend me. It would take much more than that. But since we're not offending each other, can I ask you a question?"

"Sure, ask away."

"What *do* you believe?"

It seemed such a simple question.

I tried to form an intellectual sounding response, but the answer just wasn't there. I mumbled a few sentences about God that I didn't even understand and then moved along the shore looking for more rocks. After I pathetically skipped three more stones, Laurie threw me a life preserver.

"We probably need to get going, BC," she said. "We still have a mission to accomplish."

* * *

The Internet directions proved amazingly accurate. After entering Belford, a town neither of us knew, we were on Joe Vaughn Burrell's road in four quick turns. We counted the mailbox numbers aloud as we drove slowly through an older neighborhood containing one brick ranch home after the next.

"Laurie, I never have heard exactly what happened Friday night after this guy, Joe Vaughn Burrell, grabbed you and Maggie."

"You're kidding, and you and my dad are such buddies."

"Buddies?"

"He's never asked Dylan to shoot hoops with him in the backyard."

Laurie slowed and read the number on the approaching mailbox. We were still several houses away. "Well, Burrell grabbed us from behind as we squatted beside the tire. One hand covered my mouth and one covered Maggie's. He was strong, very strong, and he pulled us backwards. We were practically back pedaling not to fall down, but that is exactly what we should have done. He would have had a hard time dragging us to his van."

Laurie took a deep breath. "He only said *scream and I'll kill you*. He said it twice and I think he meant it. His hands were pressed so tight we couldn't scream anyway. Then all of a sudden it was like we ran into a wall." She took her hand from the gear shift and playfully slapped my chest. "Maggie and I fell to the ground and the man flew forward."

"Because of me?"

"You rammed him from behind. The side of my head was pressed so tight to his chest that I could hear the *umph* come from his throat when you hit him. I think you knocked the breath out of him. Everything from there just happened in a blur. I grabbed Maggie to check on her but I remember you diving on the guy again. He was on his hands and knees, I think trying to catch his breath, and you did this all-out ugly flop on his back."

Laurie laughed at the memory. She had a laugh that was simple and pure and made my soul feel better. I tried to re-call grappling with Joe Vaughn Burrell in the parking lot. "How did-"

"There it is." Laurie pointed forward. We both fell silent and Laurie tapped the brakes. The four numbers we had both memorized shimmered in silver stickers on a rusting black mailbox. I took in the predator's lair as we passed.

Brick…ranch style…shrubs…birdbath…empty carport…rusted swing set.

A swing set? The thought of this man having children knotted my stomach.

"Do you think he has a family? Surely he doesn't have kids," Laurie responded. She had noticed it too. Laurie pulled the Jeep onto a side road and found a cul-de-sac that made for an easy turn around. Two older boys picked up their skateboards and stood beside their homemade wooden ramp as we interrupted their stunts. An older lady sweeping her driveway waved like she knew us. Joe Vaughn Burrell lived in a small-town, all-American neighborhood.

"This is not what I was expecting," Laurie said.

"Me either, it's not evil enough."

Laurie turned left and headed back toward Burrell's small brick home. I had forgotten about Laurie's story until she picked up where she had left off. "You and Burrell fell like two pancakes stacked on top of each other. Somehow he got out from under you and took off toward his car. I could still hear him breathing funny. I got a brief look at his face as he adjusted his hat-"

"My hat."

"That's right, your hat. But I didn't watch him. We ran toward you. We didn't know who you were or where you came from, but our instincts said go to you. You were struggling to stand, but you pointed toward your car and all three of us piled inside it. Maggie was in the back screaming and you were in the driver's seat trying to make your key fit into the ignition. That's when I realized you were in bad shape."

"That's a nice way of putting it."

"I'm a nice girl. But anyway, you weren't making much sense. I first thought you had a concussion, but then I smelled your breath."

"Sorry about that." We were nearing Burrell's residence again. Laurie slowed the Jeep but talked faster, trying to finish the story.

"But I wasn't getting out of your car. The doors were locked and staying locked. Somehow Maggie and I pulled you into the passenger seat and I crawled over you to drive.

If you don't remember, you kind of ended up with your head in the floorboard and your legs going between the seats to the back. You looked quite uncomfortable. Well, honestly, you looked dead. You were unresponsive the rest of the way."

I didn't respond. My focus shifted again to the brick house out the driver's side window. As we passed, Laurie practically stopped for an extended look before accelerating quickly. *So much for being inconspicuous.*

"I could have ended up in there," she said.

I scanned the road and the neighbors' homes. "I wonder why there is no law enforcement around?"

"I don't know, but they obviously know more than we do. Maybe they've given up on this place. Or maybe Joe Vaughn Burrell is halfway to Mexico by now."

We came to the first stop sign past the suspect's house.

"Let's go by once more," Laurie suggested. "I want to see it one more time."

"We did drive all the way down here."

We turned around in an empty driveway and prepared for another pass. As we approached, I wondered what his neighbors called him. *Joe?...Vaughn?...Mr. Burrell?.* Or was he the neighbor that no one really knew and rarely ventured outside? On this pass I focused on the backyard.

Rusted, broken swing set...dogwood trees...storage building...low stack of firewood. Joe Vaughn Burrell was living, or at least pretending to live, a normal man's life.

Laurie shifted gears to speed up as a truck pulled close behind.

"I'll turn around and we'll get out of Belford," she said. As Laurie continued to fill in the missing gaps from Friday night, she turned left on the first road that appeared. In the side mirror I saw the trailing vehicle make the same turn. It was a dark blue truck with deeply tinted windows.

"So after we ran inside the house screaming, dad rushed out to the car to check on the strange boy-"

"Laurie, you may want to hold off on that story," I said.

Laurie followed my gaze and adjusted the rear-view mirror to see for herself. Without indicating the next turn with her blinker, she took a sudden right on a narrow neighborhood road. I turned in my seat to see the blue truck make an aggressive turn and accelerate, erasing the gap Laurie had created between the vehicles. I grabbed the overhead roll bar when it appeared the truck was going to ram the Jeep from behind.

And I cursed loudly.

It was ugly and unexpected and offensive. It came without thought, from the worst part of my gut, the part where even using God's name in vain wasn't off limits.

My heart sank as I kept my eyes on the approaching vehicle. Flashing blue lights exploded from its dash and grill. A short siren burst filled the air. Laurie gradually pulled the Jeep to a stop on the roadside. When I finally faced forward, Laurie's head was lowered and her hands tightly squeezed the steering wheel.

The blue lights continued to reflect inside the Jeep.

"Laurie I'm sorry, that just slipped…"

She gave no response. I stared through the windshield. My heart felt black and heavy. In the distance a man stopped his riding lawnmower to check out the action. Movement flashed in the passenger side mirror. A booming female voice ordered that I put both hands on the dash. And then she appeared to my right, holding her distance from the vehicle. She also held a pistol.

A second officer appeared outside Laurie's window. The bullet proof vest over his t-shirt read TBI. *Tennessee Bureau of Investigation*. These weren't local officers, these were agents. It was apparent from the man's posture that his right hand gripped an unseen weapon. His face was stoic, his eyes hidden behind mirrored sunglasses.

"You folks lost?" he asked in a heavily Southern accent. Lies and guilt swirled in my mind, but Laurie responded first.

"No sir," she answered. "Just ready to get home."

The officer asked for Laurie's license. Her hands trembled as she extended it through the open window. He studied it for several minutes. "Laurie Elizabeth Boone from Andrews, you wouldn't happen to have the same address as a Captain Mark Boone of Andrews, would you?"

"Yes sir, I would," Laurie answered.

"I am trying to make sense of this coincidence," the agent responded. He scanned the inside of the Jeep as he spoke. "You wouldn't happen to have gotten your hands on some inside information to a current investigation, an investigation that pertains to a young girl fitting your description being attacked in the town of Andrews, would you?"

Tears flowed steadily from behind Laurie's sunglasses.

"Yes sir...yes sir, I did."

"I bet it's also safe to assume that you would not like Captain Mark Boone to know about your current whereabouts or current activity?"

"No sir, I would not," she managed through heavy sobs. The agent handed Laurie's license back through the window. In my peripheral vision his female partner holstered her weapon.

"Miss Boone, I need you to crank this Jeep, drive directly out of Belford, and go home immediately. Do you understand?"

"Yes sir." After reaching for her license, Laurie returned her trembling hands to the steering wheel. I yearned to reach across and wipe the tears that ran down her face and fell from her chin.

The agent peered at me over the top of his sunglasses. "Why don't you let the young man in your passenger seat drive you home?"

Laurie and I exited the Jeep and moved around the front. She kept her head down as we passed. The male TBI agent removed his sunglasses and held a disapproving stare as I opened the driver's side door. He quickly moved toward me, his face stopping just a few inches from mine.

"I don't know what information Miss Laurie Boone found," the agent said coldly, "but if it contained the same details I've recently been given on this suspect, you would not allow her anywhere near this place if you cared for her. This man is extremely disturbed, extremely dangerous, and still missing. Do you understand me?"

"Yes sir."

"Now get in and crank the Jeep."

By the time I started the engine both agents had retreated to the unmarked truck. We pulled out slowly and headed home as the blue lights ceased. The man on the lawnmower studied us with an unwelcome expression as we passed.

"Laurie,...I am-"

"BC," she interrupted, still sobbing. "I'm sorry about getting you into this." Laurie reached into the back seat and retrieved Dylan's t-shirt. She wiped the tears from her face.

"We're both okay, no one is hurt," I said. "Maybe the TBI agent won't mention anything to your dad. But I'm the one who is sorry, Laurie. I'm sorry about what came out of my mouth. I hope I didn't offend you."

It was an eternity before she spoke again.

"BC…you didn't offend me. You offended the God who created you."

Even if I hadn't offended her, it was the deep disappointment in her voice that wounded me. Not much else was said on the ride back to campus.

23

Laurie,

I am not much of a letter writer, so I hope what I need to say comes out by the end of this. I need to start with another apology. I am truly sorry. I won't lie and say that I have never said such things before, and with certain people, it may have never bothered me. But it bothered me greatly with you. I never felt as disgusting and ugly as I did in the car in the moments after I said those words. Again, I am truly sorry and it pains me to know that I upset you.

I also wanted to try answering the question you asked me at the lake. What do I believe? I felt stupid for not being able to give you a response, but I'm not sure anyone has ever asked me that question. I'm really glad you had the courage to do so. It has been on my mind ever since.

I stayed for hours shooting basketball after we drove back to campus yesterday, just trying to sort out the things jumbled in my head, and trying to answer your question. I did come to one major conclusion.

I do believe in God. I am not an atheist and don't think I ever have been. There is just too much beauty and design and purpose in the world. There has to be a creator behind it all. If that is what you call God then I do believe in him, I just don't know much else about him. And I am not convinced that something, or someone, great enough to create a universe so vast and so complex really needs to know much about me.

I know you believe differently.

I know that your faith goes beyond just believing in God. You believe in Jesus and believe him to be the son of God. I have to be honest with you. I don't know enough about Jesus to have an opinion. That probably sounds absurd to hear from a guy who is in his final year of college. I've heard the Bible stories like the flood and David and Goliath, but I can't say I have ever read them myself. I know that Christians believe Jesus died and it washed away all their sins, but I don't even know how that is supposed to make any sense.

I am not trying to offend you again. I never want to offend you again. But I do want to be honest with you. I always want to be honest with you. And if I'm being honest…I hope it wasn't our last adventure.

Your friend – BC

I stood outside the student bookstore on campus, envelope in hand, facing a blue post office drop box. I still debated whether or not to send the letter. A large trashcan sat beside the mail bin tempting me to reconsider. Pulling back the metal lid, I held the envelope over the opening, but my fingers remained unconvinced and refused to turn loose.

I told myself that Laurie Boone didn't need someone like me in her life. *Just trash the letter and leave her alone.* When school started back there wouldn't even be time to think about her. At least that's what I told myself.

"Excuse me."

The loud, rough voice in the quiet afternoon startled me. As I flinched the letter slipped from my grasp and into the belly of the mail bin.

"Didn't mean to scare you," said the man. He looked out of place in his light blue work shirt, navy pants, and dirty tan boots. His hat was pulled low and he held a small package under his arm. I assumed he either worked for maintenance or he was some sort of delivery man. "But can you tell me which building is the campus library?"

As the man motioned with his hand, I noticed the tattooed head of a striking snake on his wrist. I assumed the rest of the inked serpent continued beneath the cuff of his sleeve.

"Copperhead?" I asked.

He quickly adjusted the sleeve to hide the angry snake. He put both hands in his pockets, but not before I noticed the raw, scraped knuckles on each hand. Maybe I had embarrassed the guy. Or perhaps his boss simply required that tattoos stay covered. I also decided not to ask about what appeared to be make-up covering some bruising beneath his left eye.

"You know your snakes, huh?" the man asked.

"Just the venomous ones."

"The library?"

"Sorry, yes, that building is the dining hall. The library is kind of hidden behind it. Take the sidewalk to the right of the dining hall and you can't miss it. It's a stone building…says *Nelson Hall* across the top."

"I'm actually looking for a student who may work there," said the man, nodding toward the package. "You wouldn't happen to know a Blake Cawthon would you?"

The name sounded familiar but I didn't know the student. As we parted ways my cell phone buzzed in my pocket. Two new voicemails. Neither was from Laurie. The first was from Kit and he was practically screaming into the phone.

"BC! Hey man, what's up? It's Kit. I hope you're enjoying your time with the summer school ladies. Just letting you know I'm still passing through Saturday and hoping you had a place for me to crash for the night."

I texted a reply to Kit. *"Cougar...I will inform the ladies of your arrival."*

I scrolled back through my cell to check the second message. It was from a Boone girl, just the wrong one.

"BC, this is Maggie," she stated in a hurried, whispered voice. "He knows. I've got to go, but he knows. I just wanted to give you a heads up." Click.

I replayed the message.

He knows, she had said, *he knows*. I heard other voices growing louder in the background, so I listened a third time trying to interpret what was being said. The voices sounded like Mark and Donna, but I couldn't distinguish enough words to make sense of their conversation.

Mark knew. My stomach knotted. He had spoken with the TBI agents.

If Mark knew about our secret trip to find Joe Vaughn Burrell's Belford residence, I assumed angry would be an understatement. I couldn't blame him for being upset with me or Laurie, but I was the older one, the one who should be wise enough to recognize a foolish idea and keep Mark's daughter out of danger. Laurie had said that Mark trusted me, and now I assumed, that trust was shattered. I should have told Laurie it was a bad idea, but at the time I only knew that Laurie wanted me, and only me, to accompany her to Belford. Saying "no" was never an option.

And now seeing her again probably wasn't an option either. *Mark knew about the trip. What do I do now?* I thumped the phone twice against my forehead. *Think idiot...think...*

My phone buzzed again. I checked the screen. *Private number.*

I didn't answer and hurried to my car. Before I had driven off campus and away from cell coverage, Mark called again, causing my phone to vibrate against the loose change in my console. I finally decided to just turn my phone off, which only diminished my guilt momentarily.

* * *

Ten minutes later I pulled down Eli's gravel driveway and realized my attempts to avoid Mark were futile. I parked beside the charcoal gray Explorer occupying my normal spot. Both men stood in conversation on the front porch. Eli raised a welcoming hand and grinned my way. Mark did not.

I wasted a few seconds attempting to gather my thoughts before exiting my car. I was glad Eli was present, but he retreated into the house before I ever reached the steps.

Mark remained standing. He wore a serious expression, but his initial greeting seemed friendly enough, "So BC, what have you been up to?" As always, he reached to shake my hand, which I now assumed was an interrogation trick to check for sweat on the suspect's palms.

I had a sudden desire to blurt out everything.

"Well yesterday I searched for Joe Vaughn Burrell with Private Investigator Laurie Boone and got pulled over by undercover TBI agents! How about you Mark?"

"Just working, shooting hoops, and hanging out with Eli," I responded.

Mark nodded silently. His face remained stern. Eli broke the tension by sticking his head out the screen door.

"BC," he said. "Phone call. Some girl, I tried to take a message, but she said it was urgent."

I looked toward Mark, he nodded as if giving me permission. I stepped inside and found the phone laying on a narrow, antique table in the living room. Eli had returned to the kitchen. I could hear the rattling of ice being scooped into glasses for his guests.

"Hello?"

"BC, it's Maggie, sorry to bother you, but it's important and I didn't know if you'd get the message I left on your cell."

"I got it Maggie, but I think it's too late. He is already here."

"He's at Eli's?" Panic filled her voice. "*Dylan's* over there?"

"No, *your dad* is over here, wasn't that why you called?"

"No," she replied. "I don't know why my dad is there, but Dylan knows that you were with Laurie yesterday. I heard them arguing on the phone and then Laurie took off to meet him. It sounded like he found something of yours in his Jeep."

My Cohutta College hat.

Like my Celtics hat, it also had *BC* written on the inside.

I had left it behind the driver's seat, never thinking to put it on as we passed undercover through Belford. And since I drove back to campus, it was directly behind me. Out of sight and out of mind.

A new sickness stirred in my gut. I had taken another step in adding misery to Laurie's life. Through the thin cream curtains covering the front windows I could see Mark pacing on the porch. I suddenly wished my involvement with the Boone family had ended the minute I awoke on their couch. Or better yet, Laurie and Maggie should have left my drunk rear sprawled in the parking lot of the Waffle Shack.

"Maggie," I said before hanging up. "When you see her, just tell her I'm sorry for everything." *What else was there to say?*

I glanced toward the curtains at Mark's shadowy figure beyond. But surely he knows everything. Surely the TBI contacted him. Why else would he be here?

Just get it over with…Get this over with and be done with the Boones.

I walked slowly across the living room, hesitated inside Eli's screen door, turned the latch, and stepped onto the porch to face Mark. He was gone. My heart resumed its rhythm. For a moment.

"BC!" he yelled from the driveway. Standing beside his Explorer's open door, Mark had his cell phone in one hand and his police radio in the other. "My phone is going crazy with calls, but I can't get good reception…just static."

"You have to use the rocks," I answered, which instantly sounded ridiculous.

"Do what?" Mark responded, looking puzzled, but moving my way.

"There are some large rocks on the backside of the property. It's the only spot to get any reception."

"Are you serious?"

I escorted him around the side of the house until the garden and distant rocks came into view. By the time I thought to suggest using Mr. Giles' home phone, Mark had already started jogging toward the edge of the property. Checking his cell phone as he went, Mark turned and gave a disbelieving grin. I assumed he had found a signal.

I returned to the porch thankful for whatever happened to take Mark's attention away from me, even if it only delayed the inevitable a few minutes longer. If the trip to

Belford wasn't the reason Mark was here, surely it was only a matter of time before he found out. And that would definitely be the final nail in the coffin of *BC's involvement with Laurie*.

On the small pine table between the rocking chairs sat half a glass of sweet tea and Eli's open Bible. The old man must have been reading when Mark arrived. Since Eli was still inside, probably cutting slices of pie for everyone, I picked up the worn, brown Bible.

Penciled notes and dates filled the white border around the printed scripture. Eli had one section heavily underlined.

> *Then Jesus said to those Jews which believed on him, "If ye continue in my word, then are ye my disciples indeed; And ye shall know the truth, and the truth shall make you free."*

"And the truth shall make you free," I said aloud, recognizing the phrase but unaware until reading it that it was from the Bible. Beside the verse was written *8/17/1976.* I wondered if this had been Eli's sermon topic nearly forty years ago.

The truth shall make you free…the truth shall make you free…

Suddenly, Mark came sprinting around the side of the house before my impromptu Bible study went any longer. Eli emerged just as fast through the screen door. His hands were empty of food or drinks, but his face carried plenty of concern. I assumed he had seen Mark running through the back yard.

"Everything okay?" he asked.

"Everything is fine, Pastor Giles," answered Mark between breaths. He turned his gaze toward me. "BC, I've got to go…I'll call you later, will you…," Mark stopped mid-thought as if pondering something unusual. He gave a sly grin, "BC, have you got any Friday night plans?"

"Nothing," I answered too quickly. I suddenly feared the *truth* was about to get me in deep water.

"Well, come ride with me," said the detective. "Let's go on a little adventure."

The last time a Boone made such a suggestion, a mere twenty-four hours earlier, things didn't turn out so good.

24

"Buckle up."

As I got into the Explorer, Mark's words were more of a command than a suggestion. I quickly discovered why. We pulled from Eli's driveway and accelerated along the two-lane mountain road at an uncomfortable speed. I expected Mark to flip on the siren and lights at any moment to accompany the high-speed pursuit.

"Is everything okay, Captain Boone?" I squeezed the overhead hand grip above the door like it was the only thing keeping me in the vehicle.

"Yep," Mark replied, maintaining his focus on the road. He was either ignoring me or attempting to listen to the static filled voices escaping from his police radio.

"So what brought you to Eli's?" I asked, deciding I might as well start with the questions before the detective did. No answer. Mark concentrated on the curves ahead so I kept my mouth shut. A squirrel darted onto the edge of the asphalt ahead, hesitated, and quickly decided to live another day by leaping back into the undergrowth.

"So BC, what do think about my daughter?"

The question caught me off guard, but Mark asked it as casual as if we were back on Eli's rockers instead of on the verge of flying off into a forested ravine. I stalled but the question wouldn't go away.

"Um…which one?"

"Which one do you think?"

"Laurie?"

"Yes, Laurie…the beautiful, smart, talented one about to run off to college."

"I guess I think the same as every other boy who is fortunate enough to meet her."

The corners of Mark's mouth bent upward. His eyes remained locked on the road.

Did Mark know about yesterday or not?...Wait, was he actually gauging my interest in his teenage daughter?

I held tight to the overhead handle. My heart thumped in my ears.

"Laurie and Dylan seemed to be having quite an intense argument over the phone this afternoon," Mark said. "And I heard your name come up a few times."

"Oh really…I hate that."

"Me too," replied Mark, with no attempt to hide his sarcasm. "But I was wondering what you had done to tick him off. Did you ask Laurie out?"

"No sir…I promise."

"Just wondering. Even Dylan had enough respect to get my permission first."

"Sir, I would definitely ask you before I-"

We rounded a curve and came dangerously close to the bumper of a station wagon. The bushy-haired driver was apparently at the mercy of the plodding Dodge farm truck in front of her. I put my free hand on the dash to embrace for impact.

Mark hit a switch below the dash and his siren came to life. Blue lights reflected off the back of the station wagon and I realized that Mark's lights were hidden in the Explorer's front grill, just like the truck driven by the TBI agents we had encountered in Belford.

As the station wagon and the truck edged toward the shoulder of the road, Mark accelerated past while straddling the double yellow line. The flashing lights and siren and speed sparked my adrenaline, the approaching hill hiding any signs of oncoming cars ignited my fear. It was awesome.

As we topped the hill and veered back toward the proper side of the road, Mark cut the siren and lights, but not his speed. There were no other cars in view, but the graying sky overhead appeared even darker in the direction we were heading.

"Did you see the news this morning?" Mark asked.

"No, I'm not much of a news watcher. Is it supposed to be a bad storm?"

"I asked because state authorities released the name and picture of Laurie and Maggie's attacker. We had hoped that he might pop his head out this week, but that never happened. He must have felt spooked after you grappled with him."

"After I *flopped* on him, according to Laurie's version."

"So you have spoken with Laurie?" Mark asked, reaching to turn up the volume on his police radio. I didn't answer. Sporadic drops of rain splattered across the windshield. Mark leaned toward the steering wheel and studied the clouds above. More cars appeared ahead in the distance. This time Mark turned on his blue lights and siren and left them on. We blew past pulled-over vehicles and approached the Interstate 24 connector. Mark picked up his coiled police radio receiver and chatted in cop lingo with two different individuals.

Something major was brewing and we seemed to be right in the middle of it.

We took the interstate ramp and headed eastbound toward Chattanooga. The cars on the interstate slowed as the rain intensified and Mark's blue lights reflected behind them. I still had no idea where we were headed or what we were chasing. *Were we going to Belford?*

I glanced at Mark. He seemed comfortable traveling at a high rate of speed.

"BC, I came to see you today to…to just…I guess I just came to say thanks again and to check on you. TBI agents found some disturbing things when they raided this guy's house. He is bad news, BC, and the demented scum obviously went from bad to worse in the three years he's been out of jail."

Mark took a deep breath and released it. I only listened.

"He would have killed them, BC. From what they found in his place I have no doubt his goal was to kidnap, torture, and eventually kill an innocent girl that night. And there's definitely evidence indicating the guy has had one previous victim…and maybe more." Mark blew out a heavy sigh. "And he almost got both of my girls." I met Mark's glance and could see the emotions wreaking havoc within his eyes. I looked away.

"But you saved them. You saved my family. This man has become pure evil and the good Lord put you in his path, BC. He picked you and put you smack dab in that man's path. You were simply called upon, son."

Goose-bumps ran up my arms.

"Don't you ever forget that. Do you understand me?"

"Yes sir," I managed.

I wanted to say that anybody would have done the same. I wanted to say that God had better weapons at his disposal than me. I wanted to say that it was simply coincidence, but part of me wanted what Mark said to be absolutely true. Perhaps something, or someone, *had* put me in the right place at the right time to keep Laurie and Maggie alive.

And Mark believed God chose me.

So why couldn't I believe it as strongly as he did?

"Where are we going now?" I asked, still holding the grip above with my right hand while holding back the dashboard with my left.

Mark's focus was back on the interstate. Without looking he reached for a thin binder squeezed between his seat and the middle console. He opened it in his lap and handed me a picture. A mug shot.

Wispy dark hair failed to hide a receding hairline.

A thin face and eyes that appeared more sad than violent.

Toward the bottom of the picture, on a black rectangular board, white letters read "Joe V. Burrell 063449." A date indicated the photo was nearly four years old.

"That's him," said Mark.

"Joe Vaughn Burrell," I said aloud, finally having a face to match the name. In my mind I added a cap and dark clothes and imagined him moving stealthily across the Waffle Shack parking lot.

I handed the picture back to Mark. He studied it briefly, slid it into the overhead visor, and we continued our mysterious high-speed race down the interstate.

25

B efore we reached the roadblock on the crest of the interstate bridge above Nickajack Lake, Mark became consumed with the police radio. He finally filled me in on what had caused our sudden flight from Eli's and translated what other law enforcement officers had said over the airwaves.

After Joe Vaughn Burrell's name and image were released in the press Friday morning, a flood of calls came in from all over the area. The most legit tips seemed to be from a remote wilderness area near the base of Rucker Mountain. Responding officers not only found a recently abandoned campsite, but also the charred remains of what they believed to be Burrell's van.

Hours later, about the time I was encountering Mark at Eli's, a Tennessee state trooper responded to a tip claiming someone meeting Burrell's description was sighted at a gas station just outside of Andrews. The officer pulled behind a small red truck headed south on Highway 41, flashed his lights, and the chase was on. Joe Vaughn Burrell had no intentions of making it easy. He lost the initial officer but a description of the vehicle had police swarming area roads and the interstate. Since Highway 41 runs parallel with Interstate 24 East for a distance, the consensus among law enforcement was that Burrell was either headed toward Chattanooga or back to his camping area near Rucker Mountain.

After Burrell lost the initial officer, and police and helicopters converged on the area, Mark's phone started receiving calls at Eli's. Mark only invited me along because he assumed the chase would be safely over by the time we arrived. It wasn't until we reached the interstate that Mark realized that we were destined to end up in the middle of the action.

The long-awaited call across the airwaves came from a second Tennessee state trooper who spotted the truck on Interstate 24 headed westbound. In his attempt to elude police, Burrell had found his way back to the interstate somewhere east of Nickajack Lake, but had reversed direction. He was headed our way. As the state trooper trailed the red truck at a considerable distance, the orchestrating of good law enforcement began. And the decision to block the suspect in on the concrete bridge crossing Nickajack Lake was made.

The two exits in the ten-mile span between the suspect and Nickajack were quickly sealed by local police high-tailing it from country roads to the interstate. Ahead of the fleeing truck, another state trooper, with the help of some eighteen-wheeled trucks, stopped the flow of west-bound traffic about a quarter-mile from the bridge, leaving only the emergency lane open for travel. The fleeing suspect would have only two choices: take the emergency lane or come to a stop.

As we neared Nickajack Lake, Mark found a dirt connector between the east and westbound lanes and crossed to the other side of the interstate. Due to the roadblock a few miles ahead, we blazed eastward down westbound lanes now empty of traffic. Even without the threat of approaching cars, it was unnerving traveling on the wrong side of the interstate, especially at the speed Mark was travelling.

The rain had lessened, but the pulsating blue lights on the bridge ahead contrasted sharply against the gray sky. The roadblock of police vehicles nearly stretched across the westbound bridge. Mark pulled aggressively into the last remaining gap, wedging the Explorer between a state trooper and the bridge's concrete barrier.

Mark reached under his seat and pulled out his holstered pistol.

"BC, crawl over to the back and stay down...you're not even supposed to be here." He pulled the pistol from the brown holster and stared through the windshield. I climbed over the middle console into the back seat.

"How did you know his middle name?" Mark reached again for the picture in the visor.

"Sir?"

"How did you know his middle name?" He turned the image of Joe Vaughn Burrell toward me. "You said you hadn't seen today's news, yet I never told you his name. This picture only says Joe V. Burrell, not *Vaughn*."

I stayed silent. The *truth* might set me free from the Boone family, but it was going to get Laurie into a mess of trouble.

"How did you know his name was Joe *Vaughn* Burrell?"

"Mark...I-"

Voices erupted simultaneously from the radio and from outside the vehicle. Mark shot me one last glare and squeezed out the door. I regained my breath. From the back seat I peered through the windshield. In the distance more blue lights flashed and I could see the blocked traffic. A long, barren stretch of bridge lay between the westbound vehicles and the roadblock.

And then the red truck appeared.

It squeezed along the emergency lane between the stopped cars and the concrete barrier. Oddly, the truck crept at an agonizingly slow speed. A line of flashing police lights trailed behind it. As the small truck came free of the blocked traffic it swerved back into the middle of the interstate. There was no hesitation from the driver. The truck accelerated along the open expanse of bridge toward the road block.

My heart pounded. Commands were yelled outside the Explorer. Deputies and state patrolmen took aim. The truck barreled down and I expected a barrage of gunfire before we all became a mass of flames and metal. The truck kept coming. *Shoot*, I thought, *shoot the truck!* And then, perhaps thirty yards from the roadblock, the red truck came to a screeching halt. No one fired.

A booming voice sounded. "Hold your fire! Hold your fire!" I glanced to my left. Pistols and rifles aimed at the truck. Waiting.

"Suspect is out!" the booming voice yelled.

I peeked back through the front windshield in time to see Joe Vaughn Burrell, larger than I remembered, sprinting around the back of the truck toward the side of the bridge. He held something to his ear. *A phone?* At full speed he leapt awkwardly at the bridge's waist-high retaining wall, a shiny object flew from his hand and over the side. And then he flipped. For a frozen second a pair of work boots stuck high into the air before disappearing over the edge.

Joe Vaughn Burrell had plunged into Nickajack Lake.

A horde of cops rushed to the concrete barrier.

I squirmed out the back door and joined in the sprint to the side of the bridge. Gray skies released another round of rain. Before I could stop my momentum, I skidded on the road's wet surface and plowed my knee into the concrete wall. I peered over.

It was at least a forty-foot drop to the water.

But Burrell had survived it.

Officers pointed and shouted at the figure swimming doggedly into the open waters of the lake. But there was nowhere for him to go. Two officers remained on the bridge in the intensifying rain, captivated like me by the unfolding scene, while the others fled back toward their vehicles.

Rain. Commotion. Yelling. Flashing lights. Figures moving along the shoreline. The surreal action played forth without obstruction from my high vantage point. And Joe Vaughn Burrell just swam.

He headed toward neither shore at the bridge's ends. Instead, he angled toward the lake's vast middle as if an unseen island or boat awaited his arrival. In the distance stood the historic Highway 41 bridge, but I knew the fugitive would never reach its massive pillars.

And then, finally, he began to tire.

Joe Vaughn Burrell came to a stop in the middle of Nickajack Lake. He spun back toward the bridge and I could see his mouth gasping for air. His shaved head bobbed up and down, up and down, the water rising to his nose, to his eyes…and then completely over him.

Three, four, five seconds passed.

And just as suddenly as he had disappeared, Joe Vaughn Burrell reemerged.

His arms splashed and his mouth gaped widely. He was there, engaged in a wild, futile fight against the water, and then he was gone. Ripples fled from the point of the water's disturbance before settling back into the glassy surface.

Nickajack Lake had swallowed Joe Vaughn Burrell.

26

A young state patrolman named Seaver drove me halfway back. He wasn't much of a talker and I wasn't looking for conversation, so it worked out well. After crossing the Halston County line we pulled into the first gravel connector between the eastbound and westbound interstates where a tan Crown Victoria sat parked and waiting. Although unmarked, it fooled no one. Cop car.

I pulled open the passenger side door of the waiting Crown Vic. "Hey, BC," sounded a familiar voice. Hefty detective Trent Ingle held a monster-sized soda cup in his left hand and extended his right for a greeting. Like his younger brother, he had strong, orangutan-sized hands. Unlike Dylan, Detective Ingle had apparently lost all desire for personal fitness.

Detective Ingle flooded me with questions about the events on Nickajack Lake, but I still didn't feel like talking. I kept my answers brief hoping he would take the hint, but not elaborating only caused the detective to ask more questions.

* * *

Mark had stayed behind at the scene with the dozens of other law enforcement types and the converging media. As Officer Seaver and I had pulled away, at least four news vans were stationed at various points near the interstate bridge. A news helicopter had already visited the scene and retreated northward, I presumed toward Nashville.

After witnessing the drowning of Joe Vaughn Burrell, I had stayed on the bridge long enough to get completely saturated by the rain and to see a half dozen boats reach the vicinity of where the fugitive went under for the final time.

I had been to funerals. I had seen lifeless bodies well dressed in polished caskets. But that, I suddenly realized, was only the beautified and decorated after-effects of death. Real death was ugly and mean and emotional. Real death was fierce and final. Real death was unnerving, even when it was such a man as Joe Vaughn Burrell.

At some point I had turned from the concrete barrier and moved toward Burrell's red pick-up truck left unattended on the bridge. The driver's door remained open. I had peered inside and hadn't been able to stop myself from reaching in for the familiar, thin white book that lay on the seat. I held it in front of me, rain pouring, reading the title over and over. *Cohutta College Student Directory.*

Beneath the title in black permanent marker someone had written *Property of the Joe-MAC.* In the pouring rain, standing in the middle of an interstate bridge, time had stood still.

Had he come looking for me? I had started to flip the book to my name when it was suddenly snatched from my hands. The veteran officer scolded me and pushed me away from the truck. When I finally told him I was with Captain Mark Boone, the officer escorted me off the bridge.

At the bridge's end, a muddy trail had already formed down the weeded hill leading to the lake's nearest access point. I had no desire to get any closer. Moving toward the tree line, I climbed a bank and found respite from the rain beneath a thick red oak and leaned against its dry trunk. From my shelter I still had visibility of the activity on the water, where several men stood motionless on idling boats as if expecting the submerged body to simply float to the surface in the very spot it went under.

They waited as if expecting a resurrection.

Eventually, Mark found me beneath the tree. I hadn't seen him approach, but his shoes were covered in mud and I assumed he had trekked from the water's edge.

"You okay?" he asked.

I nodded and slowly stood.

"BC, I'm going to be a while longer. We've got divers on the way and we are going to attempt to find the body if the weather will cooperate. I've got you a ride back to Eli's."

Mark nodded toward the approaching young officer.

"Officer Seaver will take care of you…but we'll talk later." Mark turned and started for the trail leading back to the lake. I knew what we had to discuss, but I was glad our conversation for the night was over. If Mark had asked me under that tree how I had known Burrell's middle name, after watching the man gasp and sink and die, I would have told him everything he wanted to know. Everything.

***

Eli had left the front porch light on.

I thanked Detective Ingle for the ride and then got directly out of the police car and into my own. I turned on the heat, grabbed a gym bag from the back seat, and watched in the rearview mirror as the tail lights of the Crown Vic disappeared down the driveway. I pulled two t-shirts from the bag and peeled off my rain-soaked one. I used one dry shirt as a towel and slipped on the second.

The digital clock on the dash read 10:49.

I had eleven minutes before the convenience stores in Halston County would stop selling alcohol. A recent county policy had passed overwhelmingly by public vote, but it had caused some grumbling with the college crowd. Now everyone had to make their final beer runs a little earlier.

I backed my car around and started toward the road. My mind returned to the bridge, to the roadblock, to the image of an evil but desperate man going over the side and eventually below the water. I thought of the student directory taken from the Joe-MAC and wondered just how close he had been to finding me. Suddenly, the beam of my headlights caught an odd movement from between the thick bushes lining the driveway.

I hit my brakes.

The lowered head of an animal appeared less than fifteen feet away. The creature hobbled from the thicket and directly into the middle of the gravel drive. She raised her glassy eyes toward my headlights and froze. The front left leg of the doe was badly broken, protruding painfully at an awkward right angle. My stomach squirmed at the sight.

If only she had come out two minutes earlier...in front of the detective...perhaps he could have done the humane thing. Why did she have to appear in front of me?

I opened my door and moved toward the front of the car. The deer remained motionless. I had no plan and no clear understanding of why I was approaching the wounded animal. Her head shifted toward my movement, and for an instant her dark eyes pierced through my own. As I stepped once more, into the beam of the headlight, the frozen doe came back to life. Her body jerked and lean muscles flashed beneath her felt. On three legs the frightened animal dashed and veered for the safety of the dark woods.

My heart raced. My insides churned.

I gagged and heaved but nothing came. I was sick of pain and suffering. I needed to sit. I turned for the car. Craving the fresh air, I left the driver's side door open and rested my forehead on the steering wheel. As my stomach slowly settled another wave of emotion arose.

I began to cry.

I couldn't fight the relentless tears nor did I even attempt to wipe away their streaks. They simply ran their natural course down my cheeks and off my lips and chin. *But why was I crying? For the doe? Because I had seen an evil criminal die?* I told myself it was for knowing that Laurie and Maggie were now safe. But my thoughts drifted to the Boone family and how they had cared for me. In truth, I didn't know the source, but as the stream continued down my face, something deep inside gradually began to feel better...to feel normal.

But why were all these strange scenes playing out in front of me?

The attack...the drowning...the deer...

God, what are you trying to-

Eli's screen door groaned loudly and slammed back against its frame. I pulled the car door shut, shifted to first gear, and accelerated toward the road. Through blurry eyes I checked the rearview mirror. Behind me shone the light of the front porch and a shadowed figure watching me exit his driveway.

* * *

It was 11:02 when I reached the first convenience store and asked the man behind the counter if they were still selling.

"Absolutely," he responded. "Anything but alcohol."

I pulled into Wimpy's as the lights turned off. Closed. I tried a third store. I put a six-pack on the counter and the lady rung it up. Perhaps she didn't know the time or perhaps she didn't know the county's new policy. Probably, she just didn't care. I reached for my wallet and realized it was still in my car. Convincing the lady I'd be right back, I left the six-pack on the counter and hurried outside. I groped the darkness beneath the driver's seat where I often tossed my wallet. My fingertips found the familiar leather.

"BC."

I straightened up and turned toward the voice. Pulled perpendicular behind my car sat an old, black pick-up with a wrinkly driver. A flannel-clad elbow jutted out the driver's side window.

"Eli?"

"You okay out here?" he asked. He had forgotten his teeth but not his familiar blue cap.

"What are *you* doing here?"

"Well, I couldn't sleep, so I decided I'd just come out and get something to munch on. I didn't have anything good at the house. Were you craving a snack too?"

I peered through the convenience store's glass front. My six-pack still sat on the counter, but the lady at the register seemed unconcerned if I was returning or not. I turned back toward Eli.

"I guess you're wondering what was going on in your driveway?"

"No, not really," Eli said. "Just needing a late night snack like I said. But Mark called the house right before you arrived. He said you had an eventful evening."

I went the majority of my life without a dad and now I seemed to have two.

"Pastor Giles, are you checking up on me?"

"I'm here for a snack."

"Oh really, a preacher wouldn't fib about such a thing would he?" I attempted to keep my tone toward my landlord respectful, but I was agitated. "Remember that part in your Bible where it mentions *the truth shall set you-*"

Eli shifted the truck into park and stepped out. He wore a red flannel pajama jacket, matching bottoms, and tall rubber boots that reminded me of a fire fighter.

"Nice boots," I commented as he walked past.

"Closest thing to the door," he snickered before strolling inside. Through the store's glass front I watched Eli meander the aisles back to the cooler. The lady at the register scooted the six-pack to the side as the crazed old preacher in his pajamas approached. I could see her wide smile. She was enjoying the scene as well.

Eli exited the store whistling. He handed me a bottled Coke and a pack of peanuts while keeping a bottle of milk and a pack of chocolate-chip cookies for himself.

"I just figured you needed a snack too. How's this?"

"This will do just fine," I answered, twisting the lid off the Coke.

"Well," said the old preacher shuffling back to his truck, "Do you want to continue that scripture challenge with me?"

"No sir, I don't."

"Good," Eli said before closing his truck door. "I'll race you home."

* * *

Before going to bed, Eli made another light-hearted comment about my attempt to quote scripture in the gas station parking lot and then he invited me to join him for breakfast in the morning. "Saturday morning pancakes are a Giles' family tradition," he said, "but I'm getting tired of up-holding the tradition alone, so how about joining me?"

I assured him that I would be there.

Upstairs in my room I feared going to sleep. I picked up the supernatural novel from my bed-side table that I had sporadically been reading and made it through a few more pages. The demons and angels were preparing for a major showdown, but even with the suspense building my eyes and body were exhausted. I dropped the book to the floor and turned off the lamp.

Today I had seen a man die.

Sleep came fast and so did the dream.

27

The billowing fog bounced across the lake's surface like a slow-motion avalanche. As I treaded the frigid waters, I once again searched the slight breaks in the tumbling whiteness for signs of shore. I listened closely for a sound suggesting the direction I needed to swim. But what frightened me more than the lack of visibility was the complete silence of the night. I knew to calm myself down, to control my breathing.

I had been here before.

I chose a direction and swam. It wasn't long before my arms and legs grew weary as my saturated clothing became heavier, and thoughts of conceding to the lake's downward pull infiltrated my mind much too soon. "Not this time," I thought. "Not this time."

I pulled against the water. I counted my strokes. At twenty I stopped to catch my breath and listen. I inhaled deeply. Under control, I told myself, stay under control.

Suddenly, a solitary point of light appeared through the fog. It was small and appeared distant, but it was there, yes, it was there, and I started in its direction.

Once again I counted my strokes...eighteen...nineteen...twenty. Breathe. I scanned the fog for my lone source of hope. Nothing. Only fog. How could a cloud of whiteness seem so evil? Hope began to crumble. After several panic-filled seconds I found the light again. Still there...in the distance...waiting. My bare hands grew numb in the frigid water. Keep going. Keep going. Must keep going.

I rested again after twelve strokes, and then ten strokes, and then after just eight. At times the rolling fog was a painted wall allowing nothing to penetrate, and at times it stretched thin like cotton allowing the flicker of brightness to be seen. But had I gotten any closer?

Breathe. Under control, under control. Keep going. Another round of pulling against the water, but after five weak strokes I was spent. I tried to breathe. My deep gasps frightened me. Calm down, calm down. Just breathe, under con-

My face fell beneath the surface and the lake entered my mouth and nostrils. I spat, coughed, and turned my face toward the sky. The view above alternated between a wispy white and an utter darkness.

Something brushed across my leg.

I screamed and more water entered my mouth. I spat out what I hadn't swallowed. Motivated by fear, I resumed my strokes through the water. Fourteen…fifteen…six-

"BC!"

My name. Who called my name? Who was there? Someone was searching! The light appeared again, this time rising and falling…as if on a boat. A boat! The water around me became choppy, disturbed. I tilted my face to the sky, trying to keep the water from reaching my mouth as I yelled.

"I'm here," I screamed, "I'm-"

I was under. I choked on the water that had spilled into my throat. I fought for the surface and coughed up the cold liquid. I spotted the light. It was closer. "Yell again," my brain instructed, "yell again!"

I took a deep breath. "I'm-"

Grabbed. Yanked fiercely. Under again. A painful grip latched upon my left leg. I kicked with my free foot and fought for the surface with my arms. The grip squeezed even tighter, pulling in its relentless desire to take me into the depths of the cold lake. I fought for the surface. I kicked at the grasp. I looked below. Pale hands, connected to serpent-like arms emerging from the dark depths, locked around my calf.

And then a face emerged. A thin face.

Wispy hair swayed in the water.

Sad eyes.

I kicked at his hands, his arms, his head. I reached down and tried to peel back his fingers. Their icy feel was evident even in the cold water. I pulled at his grasp but his strength was too much.

He would never release me. Never. And we both knew it.

Joe Vaughn Burrell was taking me to the bottom.

28

In the darkness of the pre-dawn morning, after waking from my underwater encounter with Joe Vaughn Burrell, my mind became a battleground of thoughts and worries.

I thought about my impending conversation with Mark concerning how I knew Burrell's middle name. But then again, perhaps Mark's dealings with me were over. I was six days away from leaving for the try-outs in Nashville. If selected I had planned on coming back to campus and training for the remainder of the summer, but I could always go home to Dalton and get away from this madness. Except for an appearance in my haunting dream, Burrell was dead. There would be no trial, so maybe there would be no conversation with Mark. Maybe.

As much as I tried, it was difficult to not think about Laurie. I had offended her with my careless, vulgar words and now, because of me, she was fighting with her boyfriend. Part of me tried to find enjoyment in that. But I didn't expect her to come running my way now that I had both offended her and slipped with Burrell's middle name in front of her dad. It was just a matter of time before Mark learned the reason for Laurie and Dylan's argument. He'd put the pieces together. *But should I call her? Warn her? Or just leave Laurie Boone and the whole mess alone?*

I thought about the crippled doe that had scurried into the woods. Wounded. Suffering. How long could it survive in such a condition? Perhaps it would adjust and just keep living, day by day. Perhaps.

I also thought about how I had nearly broken my word with Eli. He was a good man with only three rules. *Three rules.* A guy my age should be able to abide by three simple rules. If Eli hadn't followed me to the store I would have returned with the beer. I would have sat in the darkness on his mountain-side boulders, probably tossing finished bottles over the edge and smashing glass on God's beauty below.

At least the drinks would have helped me sleep.

I tossed and turned until a faint light appeared through the blinds. At some point I dozed again but not for long. The smell of pancakes and frying sausage swirled up the stairs, summoning my stomach. Hunger trumped weariness. Since yesterday's lunch my only nourishment had been Eli's late-night gift of Coke and peanuts. I crawled haggardly out of bed and descended the hardwood stairs.

Eli's greeting was blunt.

"Boy, you look rough." I sat at the small kitchen table against the wall, where two plates already waited. I rubbed the lingering sleep from my eyes. Eli grinned. "What did you do? Go back out on the town after we came in last night?"

I waited for my yawn to subside. "I didn't sleep well at all...bad dream and a restless mind."

"Well, maybe I should have given you the milk instead of the Coke. I slept like a rock." Eli reached above the fridge and tossed me a blue mesh hat with *Wally's Farm Supply* emblazed on the front.

"What's this?" I asked.

"Well, I don't really care for wearing hats at the table, but your hair is scaring me. So I'll take the lesser of two evils." I adjusted the back strap and slid it on. A good fit. And I was in the market for a new hat anyway. A psycho kidnapper residing at the bottom of Lake Nickajack took my favorite hat and now Dylan had the other.

Eli placed a mound of thick pancakes on the table. "Help yourself, BC." He moved to the counter and returned with a saucer of crispy sausages and a pitcher of orange juice.

"Mr. Giles, this looks delicious."

"That's because it is," he replied with a wink.

I took the top three pancakes and treated them to butter and syrup. I cut a large bite with my fork and engulfed it. "Dear Lord," Eli began. I held the tasty mush in my mouth. Head bowed, Eli continued, "...thank you for your many blessings, may this meal nourish our bodies and may our fellowship nourish our souls. Dear Lord, thank you for the fine young man you've brought to my table. Please be with him and ease his restless mind. In your glorious name I pray, Amen."

"Amen," I garbled. First Mark, and now Eli was praying for me. It couldn't hurt.

Eli forked a few pancakes onto his plate. "BC, tell me about this dream. I assume it had something to do with what you saw at Nickajack Lake?"

"Well, yes and no," I managed as I swallowed my second bite. "I've dreamt about lakes well before last night, but..." I paused, unsure of how much I wanted to confess about Joe Vaughn Burrell's appearance in my nightmare.

"How prophetic," Eli said.

"You sound like Laurie."

"Well tell me, what happens in your lake dream?"

I gave Eli the general details: the lake, the fog, the swimming to exhaustion, and the drowning. I even included last night's addition of the distant light, but I neglected mentioning that Joe Vaughn Burrell grabbed my leg and pulled me to the bottom.

Eli chewed on all that I *did* tell him.

"Drowning, huh? Like what you witnessed yesterday."

And like my father, I thought. I knew Eli was thinking it too, but he didn't mention it.

"The guy had nowhere to go," I said, stabbing a sliver of sausage with my fork and sliding it through the syrup on my plate. "He just kept swimming until he gave out. He went under, rose to the surface, then went under for good. In a strange way I knew what he was feeling." My mind replayed the scene of Burrell splashing furiously and gasping for air. *I had watched a man live the final seconds of his life.* Chills climbed my arms.

"It's not easy watching somebody take their last breaths on earth, is it?"

I knew Eli spoke from experience.

I wondered how much death he had witnessed in his days as a preacher. Surely he had been at the bedside of dying church members or summoned to be with distraught families after tragic accidents. The black and white picture of Eli's wife on the kitchen counter still caught my eye. Long skirt. White blouse. Sitting on a dock with ankles crossed. Young and glowing. I assumed he had been at her side too. I couldn't begin to imagine. Seeing the end of an evil life was gut-wrenching enough, I hadn't yet witnessed the death of someone I loved.

Eli glanced toward me and I realized I hadn't answered his question.

"No…it's not easy at all," I responded. "I'd be lying if I said it didn't shake me a little. Before yesterday, I had never seen someone die."

We continued our meal in silence. I tried to think of some other topics, but one question kept circling like a nagging vulture in my mind. And a preacher, if anyone, was the one to ask.

"Eli, the man I saw drown at Nickajack yesterday, Joe Vaughn Burrell…"

"Yes?"

"Is he in hell? Is he suffering right now for the things he has done?"

Eli sat his fork down and took a sip of orange juice. He wiped his mouth and looked directly at me. "BC, it is not for me to judge that man. All I know about him are his recent actions and what Mark Boone told me over the phone last night. And from that, I would have to assume he was not a follower of Jesus Christ."

"So you think he is in hell?"

"Well, yes." Eli's face grew somber. "And not only is he *in* hell…he ain't getting out." I imagined flames and demons and torture and screaming.

"If there is a hell," I said, more to myself than to Eli, "I wonder how terrible it really is?" Eli sat down his fork and rested his elbows on the table. *Oh great*, I thought, *I have just awakened his inner preacher*.

"BC, do you have any spiritual beliefs?"

I thought of my letter to Laurie, suddenly glad she had posed the question and made me think about such things. I wouldn't give Eli what he wanted to hear, but because of Laurie I could at least form an answer. An honest answer.

"I think so…probably. I believe in God. I think something created the universe and that we just didn't happen from some slime and lightning strikes and a million years of evolving." I pointed out the kitchen window at the mountain view that lay just beyond the backyard boulders. "I think a creator made that."

"I do too," said Eli.

I thought back to what Mark had mentioned. That God had led me to the exact place and time to save his daughters. "Pastor Giles, I do believe there is a reason and a purpose for us being here, but that is about as far as I get."

"Son, that's a step, a very important step."

"You wouldn't kick a heathen out of your house would you?"

"Not as long as he pays the rent and goes by the rules," Eli laughed. "But tell me, if you don't mind, what do you think about that guy?" He pointed to a small painting hung on the wall that I hadn't given much attention. It depicted Jesus, alone at dawn or dusk, kneeling atop a rocky hill.

"Can I plead the fifth?"

"Absolutely," answered Eli. Then he smiled and whispered, "Chicken."

"Watch it preacher man," I said playfully.

"Watch what? But BC, can you pass me that saucer of *yellow* butter?" It was early, I didn't pick up on the *cowardly* jab until I had picked up the saucer. Eli grinned. The old man was suddenly ruthless.

"Okay then, what do I think about Jesus?" I said. "I don't know. I mean I want to believe in Jesus and heaven, I do, but the system doesn't seem fair. Shouldn't a person be allowed in for living right and being a good person?"

"Well BC, are you a good person?" asked Eli.

"I hope so." My words sounded flat and unconvincing.

"So college boy," said Eli, winding up for another question. "What is the standard for being a good person and being a bad person? Most everybody thinks that they are a good person."

Eli had a point.

"I don't know, but it's too early in the morning for me to debate theology with a preacher. I just want good people to go to heaven I guess."

"Well, that's what most want...eternal happiness, heaven, but on their own terms...by standards *they* see as fair. To me that means trying to be God, and I don't think He'd like that very much."

"Probably not."

"But scripture is very clear on the subject."

"And what does scripture say?" I asked.

"That believing in Jesus and professing him as your Lord is the one and only ticket through the door."

"So, if I say that I believe in Jesus I'm in, just like that."

"Well, do you?"

I didn't have the courage to look the preacher in the eye and answer the question. I drank the last swig of juice in my glass and waited for the question to evaporate. Eli stood from the table and picked up his plate.

"You finished?" he asked. I nodded. He stacked my plate and moved to the sink. I took the juice pitcher and butter back to the fridge. The heaviness of a half-dozen pancakes made me drowsy. The bed upstairs called for my return. I'd hit the gym after a good nap.

"Eli, it was delicious. But I think I'm going to crawl back upstairs." I was nearly through the kitchen door when he spoke.

"Hey, BC?"

"Yes sir?"

"Concerning Jesus…I can promise you one thing."

"What's that?" I asked as Eli turned from the sink and grinned my way.

"I didn't devote my whole life to a fairy tale."

29

After a thousand rings I realized that Eli was not answering the phone. By the time the caller gave up I was fully awake. Still, I stayed in bed. The ceiling fan hummed hypnotically while a quilt I had placed over the blinds blackened the room. *Next time unplug the phone*, I told myself. I pushed the glow button on my Ironman watch. 1:*27 pm*.

I had never slept so late in my life.

Near my feet stood the bedpost that once held the dirty maroon hat of Joe Vaughn Burrell. I stared at it as if it held the answer to an unknown question. A feeling that something was still unresolved stirred inside me.

Two minutes later the persistent caller dialed again. I tried to wait out the eternal rings, but either Eli didn't believe in voicemail or he didn't know about it. I rolled from my comfort and staggered to the phone that Eli had just recently moved to the upstairs den. At the time I had thought adding it was a good idea.

"Hello? Eli Giles's house," I answered.

"BC! Hey man, it's Kit." Until I heard his voice it had slipped my mind that Kit had planned to be on campus. I decided to mess with him.

"Kit who?"

"How many Kits do you know?"

I gave a brief pause. "None actually."

"Ha, ha, real funny. Listen man, I'm on campus and trying to find your ugly rear. Dude, remember my message-"

"Sir, do I even know you?"

"BC, don't mess with me. I'm already mad enough to whip your tail."

"Cougar?" I asked, sounding surprised. "Is this *Cougar* Hendrix?"

"Oh, I get it. Yeah, it's *Cougar*. Whatever that is supposed to mean? And by the way, I got your letter yesterday in the mail. It sounds like Coach wrote it."

"Funny."

"Dude, I've called your cell all the way from Nashville. I guess you partied too hard last night. I had to call Coach Glynn to track you down. I hate talking to that man. And you got him calling me *Cougar* too? What's up with that?"

Besides a natural dislike of authority, Kit was still holding a grudge against Coach Glynn for being removed from the starting line-up midway through last season. The rest of the team silently praised Coach for the same decision. I had texted Coach to tell him about my plan to change Kit's name. He replied that he was willing to try anything.

"Why don't I meet you at the gym in about half an hour?" I suggested.

"It's summer BC, I'm not hanging out at the gym. And I'm hungry so I'll be at Garrison. Just come in and find me." Garrison was the main dining hall on campus. Knowing Kit, he'd have no problem finding someone to socialize with until I got there. I headed for the shower to restart my day, knowing all too well that having Cougar in town probably meant for another late night. I studied the chart tacked to the wall. Six days until I was in Nashville for the all-conference try-outs. Somehow, someway, things were still on track.

I just needed to be careful with Cougar in town.

* * *

Before leaving for campus I found Eli in his garden.

"Good," he said as I approached, "a well-rested, weed-pulling partner."

"Mr. Giles, I've got a friend in town, the *Cougar* guy I mentioned. I was wondering if, um-"

"He needs a place to stay tonight," Eli predicted. "I don't mind, just remember the rules. No girls, no drinking, and no head banging music."

Well, at least Cougar wasn't interested in head-banging music.

"You won't even know we're upstairs," I answered.

"Would you guys like for me to cook some supper or-"

My expression must have caused Eli to stop his kind offer mid-sentence. "You guys be smart," he said. "I'll leave the porch light on."

* * *

When I arrived at the campus dining hall, Cougar was nowhere in sight. His distinctive green, early-eighties Ford Bronco wasn't in the parking area, but I checked inside Garrison anyway. It was a quarter past two which made the place virtually empty of diners. A familiar looking guy on his laptop at a corner table called my name and waved me over. I knew he worked for campus security, and he always spoke when I saw him at the gym or repairing campus cameras, but I could not remember his name as I approached.

Walker?...Weaver?

I spotted his name tag on the table by his computer.

"Hey, Warner."

"You're looking for Kit, right? He just left. Said to tell you he'd be right back if I saw you. So I'm telling you." He buried his face back into his computer.

"Did he say where he was going?"

"Nope. He left with three girls. But have you heard about this?" Warner spun his laptop screen around to display the on-line article. *Fugitive Leaps, Drowns in Nickajack* read the headline. "Isn't that crazy? That lake is like right down the interstate."

"That is crazy," I answered. "Does the article say anything about the body being recovered?" Warner gave me an awkward look before putting his finger on the screen to search. Whatever the answer, I already had a second odd question waiting for Warner. A feeling of uncertainty had evolved into a lingering question during my ride to campus. And I hadn't been sure how to take the next step until seeing Warner of campus security.

"Hey Warner," I whispered, leaning in. "Would campus security cameras, like the ones in the Joe-MAC lobby, still have footage from Wednesday?"

"Absolutely...wait, why? Didn't you want to know about the body?"

I tried to think of the exact time I had encountered the Sharp family in the lobby with Coach Glynn. "How fast could you pull up footage showing the Joe-MAC front desk Wednesday, from about four thirty to five?"

Warner thought for a moment. "I don't have remote access, but I could...wait, why would I do this?"

"I need to see if I left something on the-"

"That's a lie," piped Warner, still skimming the article. "And they haven't recovered the body by the way."

I tapped on the laptop screen. "Warner, I think the man who jumped off the bridge and drowned in Nickajack may have come into the Joe-MAC on Wednesday and I want to see his face."

Warner studied my expression. "That's definitely a lie."

"I'll give you twenty bucks, Warner."

"I'll have it on a disk for you this evening."

***

I bought a Powerade from a machine in the Garrison lobby and found a bench outside in the shade. It was a hot but beautiful June day. I waited on Kit and the adventure that was sure to follow, but I was actually more eager to know what Warner would find on the security footage.

However, it didn't take long until Kit "Cougar" Hendrix's smiling face appeared in the passenger-side window of a passing blue Jeep Cherokee. The familiar car pulled into a nearby space, but a glare on the windshield kept me from seeing the driver. Eventually, Cougar's lanky, six-foot-four frame emerged from the SUV. He wore a battered Atlanta Braves cap, sunglasses, and a faded Pac Man t-shirt.

"Hey man, did Warner give you my message?" he yelled.

No one else exited the Cherokee. "Who are you riding with?" I asked, keeping my seat on the shaded bench while Cougar approached.

"That's Payne driving. Samantha Bowers is in there, your old flame Chelsea, and some Julie girl I don't know...*yet*. They were in Garrison and about to head to Lost Pond. It sounded like a plan to me, so we hit the store and loaded up a cooler."

"I'm staying away from the cooler, Cougar, I've got all-conference try-outs in less than a week."

"Well, good, you can be my chauffeur on the way back."

"Swimming at Lost Pond, huh?" I motioned toward my cargo shorts. "And Chelsea Simms is not an old flame."

"That's not what I remember, and she's already asked about you. Hey, you remember going to all those soccer games just to watch her legs?"

"Are we going to Lost Pond?"

Cougar grabbed my hand and pulled me up from the bench. "I've got shorts in my car that you can wear, and the girls brought plenty of towels. But I'm driving my Bronco out there, so leave your car and ride with me." I wasn't sure my Honda was capable of traversing the rough dirt road to Lost Pond anyway.

"Where is your Bronco?"

"By the bookstore, I walked to Garrison."

"Well, pull around and pick me up. I need to make a quick phone call."

Cougar glared at me strangely. "Like a private phone call? You got a new girl, BC?"

"No girl, I just need to make a call."

"Chelsea Simms will be jealous." Cougar smirked and jogged back to the waiting Cherokee. "BC's in," I heard him say as he opened the passenger door. As the Cherokee pulled away I scrolled through my phone to the number now listed correctly as *Laurie's Cell*. I had convinced myself that however much she might not want to hear from me, she deserved a warning before being interrogated by her father. I took a deep breath and pressed *SEND*.

As it rang I instantly second guessed my decision. I felt like a nervous seventh grader calling the class beauty. I pondered hanging up. But cell phones with caller IDs had eliminated the geek's ability to abort in mid ring.

Laurie didn't answer. My nerves settled. Her voicemail began.

"Hey, this is Laurie. Sorry you missed me, and I'm sorry I missed you, so leave a message." It was simply good to hear her voice.

"Laurie...hey...it's BC. Sorry to bother you, but I need to tell you that I messed up in front of your dad, and well...I'm afraid he may find out about the trip to Belford. I just need you to know that I'm sorry...again. Give me a call if you want."

I felt better knowing I had warned her, but I wondered if I'd ever hear her voice again. I took in my surroundings. I was a college boy getting ready for a possible trip to Europe and then my final year on campus. She had just graduated high school a month earlier and still had a boyfriend. I had one more year to enjoy college life. And she was headed to a small Christian college in Georgia where she'd no doubt meet Christian boys who did Christian things. I slid my phone in my pocket. Some things were for the best. I walked toward my car to lock it up before Cougar returned. As I reached for the door my phone rang. I quickly pulled it back out.

Laurie's Cell.

I took a deep breath and leaned against the driver-side door.

"Hey Laurie."

"No, it's not *Laurie*," said an angry male voice. "This is Dylan, and there's no need for you to be calling this phone, do you understand?"

"Listen Dylan, I need to tell Laurie-"

"The Burrell dude is dead!" he yelled, cutting me off. "So you and Laurie have nothing left to talk about. Got it?"

"Dylan, I need-"

"No, you don't need to tell her anything! If you don't understand that over the phone maybe we need to meet-"

I ended the conversation. The name I called Dylan after I hung up was a little louder than I intended.

"Dude, what is that all about?" asked Cougar, grinning through his open window. He had pulled into the space on the opposite side of my car without me noticing.

"That was nothing."

"Do we need to go jump somebody?" Cougar pounded his fist in the palm of his hand like he was ready to go a few rounds.

"No, it wouldn't be fair to unleash *the Cougar* on anybody," I replied. Kit laughed, and apparently wasn't making objections to his new nickname.

"Well then," he said, "if we're not pounding heads, let's get to Lost Pond. We've got ladies waiting."

30

Joe Vaughn Burrell, the Rattler, was dead. He hadn't known he was dead until after the family had left.

From a thicket in the woods the dead man had watched them. He waited as the father brought the last few pieces of luggage and the young mother secured her little boy in the car seat. Before pulling off with his family in their loaded-down SUV, the father checked the locked doors on his white Ford work truck parked in the grass beside the narrow driveway. Once they had left, the dead man moved across the backyard, grabbed a large rock from the home's landscaping, and broke out a pane from the back door. If anyone else was in the house, they would just have to be dealt with.

Knife extended, the man hurriedly checked all the rooms before raiding a pantry and picking up a set of Ford truck keys from the kitchen counter. He moved back to the small living room and stared at the remote control on the couch. He feared the dark television and what it knew. The Copperhead wasn't answering his cell phone, and the last message from his cousin, nearly twenty-four hours ago, was of indiscernible shouting.

They should have never split up, but the Copperhead had forced him out of the pick-up after they had *eluded the officer. And this time there had been no discussion. The Copperhead had pulled a black .40 caliber pistol and stuck the barrel against the Rattler's temple.*

"Get out, cousin," he had demanded. The Rattler had started to protest.

"We'll settle this back at the barn."

"You better be there," insisted the Rattler. "Ditch the truck and find your way back." He had slammed the door and watched the red pick-up pull away before stepping into the woods. Within seconds he heard the sound of sirens again in the distance, and somehow he had known it was the last time he would ever see the Copperhead.

Now Joe Vaughn Burrell stared at the blank screen in the empty home.

He powered on the television, and by the fourth channel saw his own face staring back. The picture was from the day of his incarceration four years earlier. He hissed and stuck his forked tongue at the image on the screen. The image was of a much weaker Joe Vaughn Burrell, he thought, not the powerful serpent he was now.

But the news told everything.

An attempted abduction of two unnamed local girls...the joint investigation of TBI agents and local law enforcement...the chase...the leap from the bridge.

Joe Vaughn Burrell was suddenly famous. And according to the red-headed reporter with the arrogance in her voice, Joe Vaughn Burrell was dead. He had plunged into Nickajack Lake from the I-24 bridge, swam a short distance, and drowned. His body, the re-

porter stated, was presumably tangled in underwater tree limbs at the bottom of the lake.

The Rattler picked a glass ash tray from the coffee table and threw it into the reporter's face. A scream of hatred and fury filled the small home.

Smashed, warped, the arrogant red-headed reporter continued to talk.

"Sources say an unidentified male Cohutta College student-athlete was not only instrumental in stopping the initial abduction, but helped investigators determine the fugitive's identity, and may have even been on scene as Joe Vaughn Burrell took his final plunge."

The Rattler moved toward the screen and drove his knife blade deep into the reporter's chest. Sparks shot from the television until the lady went silent. He would give her something to talk about. He would give them a story they couldn't possibly fathom.

31

From the rock ledge I peered down at the shimmering surface of Lost Pond. "Just quit thinking about it and jump," yelled Cougar, treading the dark green water below.

"It's not the leap I'm thinking about," I yelled down.

"The snake didn't get you, BC."

"No, but it's in the water somewhere." Which was true. The snake that had nearly struck me *was* in the water. *Somewhere*. Jumping back in made very little sense. After swimming across the pond to climb the rock face to Loser's Ledge, I had started the ascent just ahead of Cougar. My searching hand disturbed a basking snake nestled atop a shallow ledge. I reached, it reacted, I screamed. The spooked snake half slid, half tumbled down the rock face and into the water. While my heart pounded inside my chest, the laughing Cougar climbed around me to the top. I had no desire to keep climbing, but I wasn't descending back into the water either.

"That's the funniest thing I've ever seen," Cougar said once I had finally joined him at the top. So I dared him to jump and rejoin the snake, not expecting him to do so a split-second later. But like a praying mantis performing a cliff dive, the slender Cougar created an awkward sight of bony arms and legs flailing through the air.

And now he treaded and waited for me in the snake-infested water.

If only Cougar was this fearless on the basketball court.

"Show us a double flip with a twist," yelled a female voice. In the distance, all three girls stretched out on a floating wooden platform anchored near the middle of Lost Pond. The dare came from Samantha Bowers, an upcoming junior whom I barely knew. From what I had seen so far on this trip, she and Brody Payne, who were both sitting on the platform watching us with their feet in the water, had become a summertime item.

"Just wait till I climb back up and we'll do some synchronized diving," said Cougar. He swam back toward the rocks. The ascent wasn't completely vertical, and there were enough crags and protruding rocks for hand and footholds, but it was still strenuous.

"What kind of snake was that?" Payne yelled. Brody had wanted no part of the long swim or the climb and quickly volunteered to guard the girls and the cooler.

"Just a water snake," Cougar answered, still ascending the rock face.

"I think it was a water moccasin," I yelled back, "and venomous."

Across the pond Payne pulled his feet out of the water. Cougar paused to catch his breath. "So why didn't you tell me it was venomous?"

"I tried to."

"Aren't those the same as copperheads?" Cougar asked, nearly at the top. I grabbed his hand to help him finish the climb.

"Cottonmouths," I corrected. "A water moccasin is a cottonmouth. Most people say you can't find them in this part of the state, but-"

"But we just did?" asked Cougar.

"I definitely think so."

Cougar placed his hands on his knees to catch his breath and glance below for the missing snake. "Whoa," he said as he took in the view toward the water. "I didn't take a real good look before that first jump." From the water the rock ledge appeared to reach a height of around twenty feet. From the ledge down the plummet appeared no less than forty.

"Did you hear about that dude who jumped off the Nickajack Lake Bridge yesterday?" Cougar asked, still peering over.

"I heard something about it."

"It was all over the radio this morning. The crazy dude drowned trying to swim away from the cops." Cougar took a baseball-sized rock and dropped it off the cliff side. "He sunk like a stone supposedly. Anyway, let's jump, this was your idea."

"It sounded cool at the time."

I had really just wanted to keep myself busy and avoid the cooler and the girls, both of which could get me into trouble. I also figured swimming to and from the ledge would be some good cardio to take the place of my missed workout, but the snake had interrupted that plan.

Cougar backed from the ledge and got into a runner's stance. Water dripped from his trunks onto the rock surface. His concave belly moved in and out as he still tried to catch his breath from the climb. Suddenly, Cougar released a lengthy war cry, took three quick steps and jumped out above the pond. He tucked his knees into a tight cannonball position and secured his sunglasses with a free hand. A cheer rose from the floating platform as he hit the water.

My turn.

Chelsea and Julie instantly turned their liveliness in my direction with chants of "BC! BC! BC!"

"Alright dude," Cougar yelled from the water. "I've scared the snake away by now, so either jump or climb down like a lady. I backed up for a running start. But snakes and heights weren't the only cause of my anxiety. I closed my eyes, took one last breath, and then…

God, I know Joe Vaughn Burrell is not waiting at the bottom of this pond, but…

Wait…*was that a prayer that just flashed through my head?* I might have to tell Eli. *No more thinking.* I took two long steps and leapt into the sky. It was as if God hit pause and fast forward at the same time. Just when it seemed I had hung in mid-air for eternity, I shredded the water with an intense splash. The slight sting of the water didn't compare with the exhilarating rush of attempting to defy gravity. I started for the surface.

But something brushed against the toes of my left foot.

A snake?…A hand?

I gasped and water spilled into my mouth. Pulling toward the sunlight, I breached the surface of the pond coughing and spitting. Cougar laughed. The girls cheered. Payne drank. I choked.

"Dude, you okay?" Cougar asked.

"I'm good," I managed, "but I swallowed half the lake."

"You should have seen your face," said Cougar. "You ready to jump again?" I treaded water debating whether to swim back to the platform or perform a few more leaps from the ledge. I saw the cooler beside Payne. *Europe*, I reminded myself, *Europe*.

"Let's jump," I told Cougar. We climbed back up the rock face at least a half-dozen more times, resting longer and longer on the ledge between each jump.

"Hey BC," Chelsea called from the platform after Cougar and I surfaced following synchronized cannonballs. "Your cell is buzzing, new text message. It's from *Warner*, whoever that is?" I yelled for Chelsea to read it for me, but I noticed something caught Brody Payne's attention. His head turned toward the parking area. A second later, still treading water alongside Cougar, I heard the low-pitched growl of an engine. Two four-wheel-drive trucks emerged from the woods on the lone dirt road leading to Lost Pond. Older models. Massive tires. *Locals*.

One truck was shiny and black, the other the color of primer. They pulled into the parking area that lay directly in my line of sight beyond Payne and the girls on the platform.

We had kept Lost Pond to ourselves for nearly three hours. The only signs of previous visitors were flattened beer boxes, a stone fire pit, and a pair of non-matching socks hanging over a tree limb.

But now it was time to go.

"Cougar…we've got company," I said as we headed for the platform. No one had exited either of the trucks still idling beside our vehicles. From past encounters and numerous horror stories, I knew that some locals, particularly the kind that visited Lost Pond, weren't always fond of the *uppity* college crowd.

And those kind usually drove big trucks.

"We're taking this party elsewhere," said Payne as we arrived at the floating platform. The girls agreed. When Julie stood, she wobbled slightly. Cougar had commented earlier that Julie must have borrowed one of the other girl's bathing suits since she continuously held an arm across her chest to cover what the top piece couldn't. So now, needing assistance, Cougar quickly offered to be her swimming partner. I saw his devilish grin as she sank into the water and wrapped her arms around his neck from behind, pressing her chest against his back.

I treaded water beside the platform. I kept my eyes on the two trucks, from which no one had exited still, and then followed the group of beer sipping swimmers. For Payne it wasn't the straightest of swims, but he made it unassisted.

Once we reached shore the engines of both trucks shut off. We toweled quickly, trying not to make eye contact with the locals. But once it was apparent that we were leaving, a teenage couple exited each truck. My nerves relaxed. The boys were definitely local, *real local*, but too young to be the type we needed to worry about. Neither boy acknowledged our presence, but both carried two fishing rods toward the water. One of the girls, petite and no more (that) fifteen, smiled our way and gave a polite, "hello." The front of her sky blue t-shirt depicted a cross standing firm amidst a crashing ocean wave. As she turned and reached into the truck I read the back of her shirt.

'Catch the Wave at Harmony Grove – Acts 5:42'

She must know Laurie and Maggie Boone, I thought, and I started to ask the young girl until I realized how her conversation with the Boone girls might sound. *"I met this boy at Lost Pond who asked about you. He was with three bikini-clad girls and a cooler."* The young girl closed the truck door and walked toward the water to join her friends.

Payne loaded the cooler, Cougar slid a shirt over his sun burnt chest, Samantha and Chelsea discussed evening plans, but oddly, Julie was already in the back seat of the Cherokee with a towel over her head. She couldn't have dried off that fast.

"What's with her?" I asked Chelsea as she approached with my cell phone.

"One drink too many I guess," Chelsea replied. "Do you and Cougar want to join us at Holtman to cook-out…maybe watch a movie?"

"Absolutely," replied Cougar as I checked the text message on my phone. Warner had the video I asked for and he wanted his twenty bucks. I began to tell Cougar that we needed to make a pit stop on the return trip, but he had his head stuck through the Jeep Cherokee's window chatting with the suddenly reclusive Julie.

"Cougar's focus is elsewhere," laughed Chelsea. "He's got Julie on his mind." I laughed too, but mostly because in one afternoon I already had Payne and all three girls referring to Kit Hendrix as *Cougar*.

And from the looks of things, the boy's confidence seemed to be soaring higher than ever.

If only it was basketball season.

32

*A*n hour after paying Warner his twenty bucks, I sat
alone in Chelsea Simm's Holtman dorm room, the
most modern of the residential halls on campus. Most of the
suites, like the one Chelsea, Samantha and Julie shared, had a
common living area at the center of three separate bedrooms. For the summer Holtman contained three floors of
girls while the boys were housed in Parker Hall across campus.

The others had stayed outside grilling bratwursts while I
used Chelsea's computer to watch the surveillance footage
Warner had downloaded on the disk. I declined the first beer
Chelsea had brought me, but a half-hour later, after I had
found the man on the video, I gladly accepted the next one.
No more than two, I told myself, *Europe*. But I had to think this
through. Something just didn't add up.

I had definitely seen the man on the video before. Even
with a cap his face was still somewhat visible. He wore a
long-sleeved uniform shirt and dark work pants. On video,
as the Sharp family had mingled and talked with Coach
Glynn, the man had walked toward the unattended reception
desk, leaned across, and quietly lifted something from behind
it. *The student directory*, the same one I had found in Joe
Vaughn Burrell's abandoned truck. Just a few moments af-

ter the man left, I appeared on the footage being introduced by Coach Glynn to the arrogant Sharp father.

Where exactly had I seen the man from the video before?
On campus? Was this the man who I watched drown?
Was this man Joe Vaughn Burrell?

It had to be, but something wasn't right. When Chelsea came to check on me a second time, I gladly accepted another beer. *Last one*, I reminded myself, *Europe*. I heard Cougar and Julie, both loud and laughing in the living area. They were all many drinks ahead of me, especially Julie, and she didn't sound like she was holding herself together very well. I already knew I would be driving Cougar's car later in the night...once I could get him to leave.

By campus policy, no males were to be in female dorms after eleven, but it was rarely enforced, especially in the summer. Each dorm had a matron that lived in a single bedroom unit on the bottom floor, but most were retired or elderly and didn't stay up late enough to enforce the curfew.

I watched the man on the video take the student directory a half-dozen more times. I tried to remember what the man was wearing who had fled from the truck and plunged into Nickajack twenty-four hours earlier. *The boots*, I remembered the boots, the light colored work boots that seemed to freeze in mid-air before descending over the bridge. I watched the video again. It was hard to see his feet on the footage, but finally I found a frame just as he walked away and young Will Sharpe approached the counter.

Light tan work boots.

It was him.

But was this the same man I tackled at the Waffle Shack?

I needed to call Mark. I scrolled to his number just as Chelsea, Julie, and Cougar barreled into the room. "Dude," said Cougar, "what is the big deal with this video?" I didn't answer. I knew he'd be preoccupied with Julie again in a matter of seconds.

"We're just going to watch the movie in here," Chelsea said, turning off the lights, "since you can't break away from my computer."

Cougar leaned across my shoulder and pointed at the monitor. "That's Will Sharp, I know that kid. I went to high school with him. His dad is a real punk."

"That's funny," I said. "Mr. Sharp said you were like a second son to him." Cougar laughed and slid into the floor beside Julie, both reclining against Chelsea's bed. Chelsea started the movie and sat on her bed, leaving room for one more. I quickly announced that I needed to use the restroom and headed for the door.

"There's more beer in the fridge if you need one," said Chelsea as I left the room.

"Grab me one," yelled Cougar.

I shut the bathroom door and texted Mark. In case he didn't read text messages I copied the message to Laurie, at least she'd know to contact him. I wanted them both to know what I may have just discovered, just in case.

Drowned man was on campus Fri. I don't think he's same man I tackled @ Waffle Shack. May or not be JVB. 2 people involved? Call or txt when u can.

I waited a couple of minutes for a reply, but finally exited the bathroom. I walked back into Chelsea's darkened room. Light flickered from the small television screen.

Cougar and Julie were gone.

"They decided to watch a movie in her room," Chelsea said. I stood just inside her doorway. She had changed into a pair of thin pink pajama shorts and a form-fitting cotton tank top. She leaned back against her stack of pillows. My stare lingered. I looked back to the movie we were both pretending to watch.

"I forgot to get Cougar his beer," I said.

"I don't think he'll be needing it," Chelsea replied.

I don't care if Cougar needs it. I need to cool off.

"You don't look comfortable just standing there, BC. You want to sit?" Chelsea patted an area of the bed beside her. Her toes were tucked beneath the comforter that had been folded toward the bottom of the bed. "Have you seen this movie before?" she asked.

"Your roommate Julie, was she okay?"

"What do you mean?"

"She didn't seem to be much of a drinker."

Chelsea stretched her toned, athletic legs out as far as they would reach and massaged down them with her hands. "Mac is a big girl, but no, she's really not much of drinker. Samantha and I have been trying to break her out of her shell. We didn't even know her until this summer, she got placed with us."

"What name did you just call her? *Mac*?"

"She goes by *Mac* sometimes. MacDowell is her last name. Her friends that call usually ask for *Mac*, so we call her *Mac* sometimes too. You know, BC, we really haven't talked in a while-"

I pulled my cell phone from my pocket.

"Expecting a call?" Chelsea asked.

"Just need to make a quick phone call, I'll be right back." I turned, Chelsea sighed behind me. I walked into the living area, stared at Julie's closed bedroom door, and then headed toward the suite's main door. I stepped into the bright, sobering light of the dormitory's hallway. *Mac? Where had I heard that before? At Harmony Grove? With Maggie?* That was why she hid so quickly in Payne's car at Lost Pond, she had recognized the local girl wearing the Wave t-shirt.

How did a girl like Julie get caught up with us?

But my thoughts quickly turned toward another girl. The real reason I had stepped into the hallway. I stared at my phone. No text messages. No missed calls. No voicemails.

Give me a reason, God, just give me a reason to leave this dorm.

I scrolled to the number I *wanted* to call, but I knew better. If she was with Dylan it wouldn't go well. If he answered it would only be worse. Slim chance that he even told her I had called earlier. I leaned my forehead against the door. The faint sounds of music and voices escaped from behind other doors along the dorm's hallway.

Chelsea waited inside. But I thought of Julie behind her closed bedroom door with Cougar.

Smashed...reckless...vulnerable.

I knew how she'd wake up early Sunday morning.

Sick...disgusted...ashamed.

I pictured Chelsea stretched out casually in her darkened bedroom.

Attractive...single...waiting.

She had given every signal that a college boy would want, but still...

I placed my hand on the handle to go back inside but something gnawed from within. All was not well with my gut...with my heart...with my soul. I was on the rock face of Lost Pond with serpents swimming below. Stuck. Heart ramming my chest. Plummets and snakes and monsters all around. *Chelsea was not a monster*, I told myself. *No more than I was.* I had swum such waters before. Was there even a choice? Could I avoid the snake-infested waters?

Walk away. Just walk away.

But Julie…*Mac*…entangled by snakes. How could she walk away?

Snakes and monsters. I gripped the handle. *Face it, BC, you're a monster, too.*

Too much slime in my past to be with a girl like Laurie.

Go inside. Slither. Leave. Stay. Choose.

But this wasn't just about me.

Julie…slipping…

Chelsea…waiting…wanting…

And I wanted…I wanted…

I knew my answer. I turned loose of the handle. What I wanted wasn't behind that door. *She* wasn't behind that door. But that meant leaving Julie, a girl I didn't even know. A girl I had just met. A girl I shouldn't have such concern for. A sadness coated the joy of my decision…until I saw it. A revelation…right before my eyes.

I reached for the red box fastened eye level on the wall. I grabbed the clear lever and pulled. An instant high-pitched shriek like the chirping of a million metallic crickets echoed through the dorm. Too many crickets for a den of snakes to silence.

Loud…deafening…unbearable…relentless. Perfect.

I sprinted through the hallway to distance myself from the alarm.

33

The night air rushed through the open windows of the Ford F150. Joe Vaughn Burrell, the Rattler, drove the interstate like a man unencumbered by the world. Until the Copperhead's body was found, until the weak ones realized it was not him beneath those waters, he was simply a man that did not exist. Time, for now, was on his side.

And this ride was a night hunt.

Whether it led to his intended prey or to needed information, he was yet to know. But the Rattler was hunting...and planning...and being reinvigorated by the wind and the smell of his territory. The white van that had passed him only moments earlier now veered toward the same interstate exit that Burrell intended to take. Andrews.

At the stop sign at the end of the exit ramp, after his headlights illuminated the colorful Chattanooga Channel 7 News logo on the van's back doors, the answer came to the Rattler. The television reporter's words from earlier in the day still echoed in his head.

...an unidentified Cohutta College student-athlete
...instrumental in stopping the initial abduction
...helped investigators determine the identity

...may have even been on scene

...as Joe Vaughn Burrell took his final plunge.

The Rattler hissed and strangled the steering wheel. But he knew that both he and the news van were headed toward Cohutta College for the same reason. Both were seeking answers. Both were seeking the same individual. And a predator must simply follow the trail. He only had initials. Perhaps they had a name.

And just maybe, he hoped, the news van carried the same haughty, red-headed reporter from the earlier broadcast. The Rattler grinned and licked his lips with his forked tongue, hoping for the chance to meet the red head in person. Beside him on the seat lay the six-inch blade that could dissect information from anyone, especially a reporter who loved to hear herself speak.

The news van turned left onto the darkened highway toward campus.

The Rattler followed.

34

Momma Mildred was the elderly matron of Holtman. She stood in front of the dorm's entrance in her pale green robe and furry orange slippers. Arms crossed, eyes narrowed, Momma Mildred silently dared any male student to try and regain entrance to her dorm. After the fire department had given the all-clear, the girls of Holtman promptly filed back inside. Within minutes, the only students remaining on the lawn were a handful of guys grasping the realization that their Saturday night plans had been abruptly altered.

Sorry fellas.

I had been one of the first out of the building. After pulling the alarm, I had sprinted down the hallway until the first doors began to open, at which point I slowed to a brisk walk, held my cell phone to my ear, and pretended to be in a deep conversation. Outside, the sloping lawn between the dorm and the parking area had gradually filled with students. Most of the girls appeared wearing cotton shorts and t-shirts. Some had actual pajama pants. A few were still dressed for Saturday night dates or going out on the town with friends. Like a captain going down with the ship, Momma Mildred was the last out of the dorm. She had gone through all three floors banging on doors and yelling for girls to get outside.

Sitting on a wooden picnic table, I watched keenly as students exited the building. Cougar appeared before the girls. I whistled and he maneuvered through the crowd to where I sat. Chelsea appeared with Julie a few minutes later. Julie leaned on her roommate for support and rubbed her temples with her free hand. The persistent alarm obviously wasn't helping her condition, but at least she was out of that bedroom. *Away from the snakes.* Chelsea led Julie toward a cluster of girls sitting along a sidewalk and helped her to the ground. A campus fire truck arrived within minutes.

This wouldn't take long.

Cougar and I stayed on the picnic table until Momma Mildred followed the last girl back inside the dorm. She shot the remaining boys a quick, fierce look before disappearing through the door. A few moments later, the movement of blinds from the matron suite indicated that Momma Mildred was still on guard. Boys' night at Holtman was over.

We walked toward Cougar's Bronco. "Dude, can you believe that?" he asked. "Talk about bad timing. I was about to have a very good night."

"A true night to *not* remember," I said. Several cars cranked and pulled from the parking area. "It looks like several guys had their plans ruined."

"Some freshman chick was probably smoking in the wrong spot," Cougar grumbled, "and set off that stupid alarm."

We slid inside the Bronco. I pulled out my cell again. No text messages, no missed calls, no voicemails. I scrolled down through my contacts to *Laurie*, just needing to see her name. Just as I realized Cougar didn't need to be in the driver's seat, he punched the steering wheel without warning and let fly a streak of profanity.

"Dang Cougar, you're that upset about having your night with Julie cut short?" He responded with a second profanity-laced tirade that made the first seem like a nursery rhyme. Somewhere within the profanity he inserted the message that his keys were still upstairs.

But we weren't messing with Momma Mildred.

"Do you have Julie's number?" I asked.

"Dude, I don't even know her last name."

"MacDowell," I answered. Cougar peered at me strangely. "And I don't have Chelsea's number either, but I have these." I reached into Cougar's cup holder and picked up my own keys. When it simultaneously dawned on us that my car was more than two miles away, still parked at the campus cafeteria, Cougar and I bolted from the Bronco and quickly scanned the parking lot for a ride. But we were the last of Holtman's discarded males.

Whether we liked it or not, it was a good night for a walk.

* * *

Although less than twelve hundred students attended Cohutta College, the school actually owned more than ten thousand acres on the mountain. Mostly wooded and wild, the vast offering of trail systems, waterfalls, bluffs, and caves made the *Realm*, as it was called, into a nature lover's dream. While the stone academic buildings, library, dining hall, and student union were all centrally located around a series of quads, the dorms were mostly in various outlying areas. During the weekday, with parking on campus limited, the majority of students either walked or used bicycles to get around. However, most students didn't trek the campus back roads near midnight.

"Well, we couldn't have picked a better night to walk," I said. A slight breeze accompanied us along the lonely road and the lack of streetlights allowed the stars to emerge in the cloudless sky.

"Having a romantic walk with you was not exactly what I had planned for tonight," Cougar answered. But the alcohol in Cougar's system kept him chatty during our trek. We talked basketball. We discussed Coach T leaving the program and wondered if Coach Glynn would hire any former players as his new assistant. We wondered how good the team would be after losing so many seniors and another key player in Derrick Bender. Cougar was jealous of my chance to travel to Europe, but he would get his shot next summer.

And then Cougar rambled about girls and his missed chance with Julie.

I thought about a local girl I didn't mention. Nor did I mention anything concerning Joe Vaughn Burrell. Not the night I saved the girls, not the drowning, and surely not the wild theory I had that the man I prevented from abducting Laurie and Maggie Boone wasn't the same man who had drowned in front of my eyes. *It had to be a crazy theory*, I thought, *and that is why Mark hadn't answered my text…he doesn't have time right now for nonsense.*

Either that or I had been totally erased from all Boone family communication. I glanced again at my cell. No missed calls. No voicemails. No text messages.

I examined the distant stars and searched for constellations I could identify. As my eyes located a triangle of bright stars, smaller sprinkles surrounding them came into focus. I marveled at the vastness of the heavens. Cougar mumbled something about flip-flops hurting his feet.

"Do you believe in God?" I asked.

"Are you okay dude?" Cougar answered. "You've only lived with this preacher for what…two weeks?" Stopping to appreciate the night sky had put me behind a few paces. I caught up with Cougar and decided to press the issue.

"Well do you…you know…believe in God? Do you think a powerful God created all these stars?"

"No I don't," Cougar responded. "I don't at all." He pointed upward as we walked. "Look at how much is out there. We're just a very small speck in a big mess of specks."

"Maybe being just a speck is proof of God. Perhaps He created something vast and mysterious for us to know how powerful he is," I countered.

"And heaven is up there somewhere too? I don't think so, BC."

"So all these people who go to church-"

"People go to church and believe in God and Jesus most-ly because their parents did, and they are taught that if they don't, they'll roast in hell. That's why people go to church."

"So no Jesus or Satan for you, huh?"

"I'm sure Jesus was a man who taught people to be good and love one another," Cougar continued, "but the other stuff was made up later. Why are you asking?"

I told Cougar about the fiction book concerning warring angels and demons that I had almost finished reading at Eli's house. I mentioned that the book, some recent events, and a few new people in my life all had me thinking more about the spiritual world.

"So you're a *believer* now?" asked Cougar.

"I just think those concepts of good and evil came from somewhere besides the minds of people."

"Well, think about the devil," said Cougar. "If the devil is really out there causing havoc and stealing souls, don't you think he's smart enough to read?"

"I guess so, why?"

"Because of the Bible. In Revelation it says that in the end the devil is defeated and Jesus wins. If it is all true, and the devil can read the Bible, why doesn't he just give up if he knows he is going to lose?" I had never known Cougar to be opinionated on the subject, but he had me thinking.

The top of the dining hall appeared in the distance.

Not much further.

"So you don't believe any of the Bible?" I asked.

"I'm sure there is some true historical stuff in there, but think about it. You've got a world-wide flood and a boat with two of each and every animal, you've got a giant fish that swallows a man and then spits him out, and then you've got Jesus walking on water and raising people from the dead. I've read better fiction. What I can't understand is why any intelligent person would waste time believing it."

I didn't devote my whole life to a fairy tale. Eli's words from earlier ran through my mind. I desperately wanted to get Cougar at the old man's breakfast table.

Suddenly, headlights appeared behind us. We moved from the middle of the road as a second set of lights appeared further back. A white van slowed momentarily as it passed, long enough for us to read the logo and markings along its side. Following close behind was an older, white Ford truck.

"That was Channel 7 news out of Chattanooga," remarked Cougar. "What are they doing up here this late? Has anything crazy happened on campus?"

If you only knew, I thought. *But surely the van wasn't here because of...*

The van's red brake lights flashed as it slowed to pull into a darkened driveway. The truck behind the van hesitated before continuing along the road toward the main campus.

"Dude, I'm still hungry," said Cougar. "How about a trip to the Waffle Shack before we crash at the preacher's place?" I started to protest but the news van had my attention. It reversed from the driveway and aimed in our direction.

"Anywhere but the Waffle Shack," I answered, keeping my eyes on the van. "I didn't have a good experience there recently." The news van rolled slowly toward us.

"You drive and I'll pay," offered Cougar, as the news van came to a complete stop beside us. "I wonder what this is all about?"

The van's passenger side window lowered and a thickly-bearded young guy with a crooked nose and a Channel 7 News hat smiled our way. "You guys enjoying the nightlife?" he asked.

I pointed up the street toward the main campus. "Calling it quits...just heading to our car."

"Why, what's going on?" asked Cougar.

An overhead light flickered inside the van and the shadowed driver became an attractive, middle-age lady with red hair pulled back into a ponytail. "We're following a lead," she said. "But we're having difficulty tracking down a student. I was hoping you guys might be able to help us."

Cougar stepped closer. I knew what was coming.

"We're looking for a student by the name of Bradley Curran Morrow," said the bearded passenger. "He is supposedly on campus for the summer."

Cougar cut his eyes toward me.

"Sorry, but we don't know him," I said quickly.

"How about you?" the lady asked Cougar.

"Actually, I do know him. I had a class with him last year...kind of a strange, nervous acting guy." answered Cougar, holding his glare on me. I couldn't breathe.

"And do you know where we might find him?" the lady asked.

"Twenty bucks," responded Cougar.

"Do what?" said the bearded man. "We're not giving you-"

"Deal," said the lady. "Tyler, give the boy twenty bucks." The man grumbled and pulled two tens from his wallet. Cougar stepped to the window and took the cash.

"That Bradley Morrow guy is living on the second floor of Parker Hall, the guys' dorm for summer session. You'll find him there," Cougar lied. He gave the pair round-about directions to Parker Hall and informed them that most of the guys there would still be awake.

The van pulled away, but Cougar's stare remained.

"Okay, Bradley Curran Morrow, we're going to the Waffle Shack," he said, holding up his new cash. "I'm paying, but you're doing all the talking."

35

On the way to Andrews I convinced Cougar to eat at the truck stop. Highway Hank's Happy Belly Restaurant was just as greasy and fulfilling after midnight as the Waffle Shack, so Cougar didn't protest. He simply wanted to sit and hear the story of my summer. As we walked toward the entrance to Highway Hank's, I noticed a group inside sitting at a booth near the window. *A four-pack of rough looking locals.* But before I could look away one stopped eating and glared directly at me.

It was Dylan.

I froze as Cougar continued toward the door. Dylan lowered his fork but kept his eyes locked on mine. The others at the table followed his gaze.

"I change my mind," I said.

Cougar had his hand on the restaurant's door handle. "You change your mind about what?"

"About eating here. You're right. I think I'm in the mood for Waffle Shack."

Cougar released the door and spun back in my direction. "Fine with me dude. As long as I get more story time." We returned to my car, but since my recent phone conversation with Dylan didn't go so well, I kept an eye on Highway Hank's front door until we were safely out of the parking lot.

* * *

Over a ham and cheese omelet and hash browns covered in onions, I told Cougar everything about Joe Vaughn Burrell, from the dumpster to the drowning. He promised not to say a word, but just in case, I didn't divulge any information about my feelings for Laurie or the brewing hostilities with the boyfriend we had just encountered.

After leaving Highway Hank's on our way to the Waffle Shack, we had spotted the Chattanooga news van pulling in to the main motel in Andrews. It appeared they were indeed staying to search for me in the morning. I wondered who had leaked my name to the press. Not only did it make me nervous, but I knew by in the morning I would probably be answering questions from my mom, my brothers, Coach Glynn, everybody.

"Dude, Chattanooga is just an hour or so down the interstate, so you must be on your way to becoming one major news story if the reporter chick is staying just to search for you," Cougar said. He chewed his sausage, egg, and cheese sandwich. "I'm eating with a hero...a celebrity. By this time tomorrow you're going to be big time."

"Hopefully not," I mentioned, but I didn't know what to expect.

"Dude, I won't say a word until it hits the news, but then I'm texting everybody."

I had no desire to be plastered on the news, especially now that I wasn't convinced of who lay at the bottom of Nickajack Lake. I needed to speak with Mark. Perhaps he could somehow make the oncoming media attention go away. I checked my phone. Still nothing. I double checked the text message I had sent from Holtman and finally saw the small red symbol and the words *Failed to Send*.

Mark had never received my text.

It was twenty minutes after midnight, too late to call, but I resent the original text and included a second. *Need to speak with you. News crew on campus looking for me!*

"Let's just go to the motel right now and let them interview you," Cougar said. "That way I can be like those people on TV who stand in the background waving their cell phones like lunatics." Cougar mimicked his description and we both laughed a little too loud. Our outburst caught the attention of a young local sitting at the counter. I started to apologize to the scruffy-faced guy with the camouflage hat turned backwards, but he quickly spun from his stool and headed toward the door. The large cook behind the counter watched the young man leave and glanced over at me.

What was that all about?

Our waitress whisked by leaving two tickets on the edge of our table. Cougar picked up both. "Free meal courtesy of Channel 7 news," he laughed.

As he went to pay I walked toward the jukebox and peered out the Waffle Shack's large glass windows. The young guy from the counter moved across the parking lot. He came to a stop near another dark figure leaning against a car close to mine.

"You ready?" Cougar called. He popped a toothpick in his mouth and nudged the exit door open with his shoulder. I kept my focus on the pair in the parking lot. Thankfully, they seemed to be leaving. As I moved toward the door, I locked eyes with the large cook and he reminded us to drive safely.

Once outside, my attention returned to the two figures, who now seemed to be moving toward a crew-cab truck several slots beyond my car. One flicked a cigarette to the asphalt. *Perhaps I had been mistaken. Perhaps that young guy wasn't one of the locals who had been with Dylan.*

I was ready to get to Eli's. *Nothing good happens after midnight,* Coach Glynn always reminded us after Friday practices. And I had a feeling this was soon to be one of those nights he had in mind. My cell phone chimed as I pulled my keys from my pocket. A text from Mark. *Where are you?*

"So who's BC?" came a rough voice from the darkness.

"Not again," mumbled Cougar, continuing toward the passenger side of my car. But I knew it wasn't a television news crew this time.

Three figures now reappeared in the open space in front of my car. "Are you BC?" asked the same local, stepping closer, pointing at me. He spit a stream of tobacco to the ground. The other two stayed a few feet behind as if unsure what course they wanted to take. None in the group were as tall as me or Cougar, but the spokesman appeared stout and rough and experienced in the ways of parking lot brawls.

"You think you can cheat with my brother's girlfriend?" he barked.

"No one cheated on anybody," I answered. My spoken denial was the spark Dylan needed to emerge with a fury from behind the truck. He charged past the other three pointing his finger the entire way.

"You liar!" he screamed. "You liar! You know what you did! Laurie and I were fine until you came along!" As Dylan came closer I noticed Cougar in my peripheral vision heading toward my side of the car. Dylan's brother and the other two hustled to block his path.

"This ain't about you beanpole!" I heard one of the guys say. "Just stay out of it."

I backed up thinking that Dylan was going to stop before he reached me, but his face came so close that I could see the anger in his eyes and smell the alcohol on his breath. His two-handed shove to my chest sent me stumbling backwards. My cell phone clattered against the ground.

"Come on, do something!" he screamed.

"I'm not fighting you, Dylan," I yelled, holding my hands into the air. "Nothing happened between me and Laurie." He shoved me again. Cougar yelled for me to punch him, but I knew the moment I retaliated Cougar would be on the losing end of a three-man beat down.

"Come on you coward! Do something! Do something!" Dylan practically spat with each syllable. My adrenaline raced and I wasn't sure I could peacefully endure another shove.

"Dylan, you think if we fight she is going to date the winner?" I shouted. "We fight and Laurie won't give either one of us the time of day."

"I don't care you punk! I've lost her…but I'll make sure you can't have her," Dylan's voice cracked as he shouted. He shoved me a third time. I had backpedaled with each push and was approaching the glass window of the Waffle Shack. *On the next one I'm swinging.*

Dylan tensed for another rush. I balled my fist.

"Fight me you-"

"I'm calling the cops! I'm calling the cops right now!" The high-pitched voice of the Waffle Shack's weighty cook halted Dylan's charge. The cook, eyes wide and his face bright red, braced the restaurant's front door open and held a phone to his ear. "The cops are-"

The side of my face was suddenly smashed with Dylan's fist. I staggered, tripped, landed on my rear, and fell to my back. The blurry, upside-down Waffle Shack hovered above me. The bulging eyes of two late-night diners appeared behind the glass.

Cougar shouted. Sounds of a scuffle erupted near the cars. By the time I could focus Dylan was sprinting toward the commotion.

The large cook was quickly at my side. "You okay, son?" he asked, his voice seemed to echo in my head. He leaned in so close I could see the long strands of his mustache curling over his upper lip. He smelled like onions and smoke and all things fried.

Cougar.

I tried to stand, to help, but I spotted Cougar already running toward me. "BC, you okay?" he shouted.

Both Cougar and the cook grabbed an arm to lift me. A string of blood trickled from Cougar's lip. He wiped it with the back of his hand then yelled like a sailor toward the truck squealing from the parking lot and disappearing down the highway.

"Are you okay, Cougar?" I asked.

"Man that was crazy," he replied, breathing heavy. He grabbed me around the back of my neck with one hand and thumped me hard on the chest with his other.

"I really did call the police," said the cook. He dropped the cordless phone into a pocket on his apron. "They're on their way. You guys may want to stay around and speak with them, but if you want to take off I can tell them everything I saw those hooligans do. From what I saw they started everything."

209

"Then you saw it right," Cougar said, "and that punk hit BC with a cheap shot."

I needed to talk with Mark, but I didn't want to wait for Halston County officers to arrive at the Waffle Shack. I just wanted to get to Eli's and end this night.

"What do you think, Cougar?" I asked, my mind still fuzzy from Dylan's punch.

Cougar pounded his fist into his palm and grinned.

"I think I need to enroll in summer school," he responded. "This is awesome."

36

The Rattler waited in the truck, six spaces down from the news van. The pudgy, bearded man and the red-headed reporter had been in their rooms for nearly half an hour. When they had returned from the hotel's office, the Rattler was glad to see they had taken separate rooms. It would make things less messy.

The rooms were on the highway side of the building, but a small field distanced the motel parking lot from the road, which was never particularly busy this time of night. In the rearview mirror the Rattler could see the distant Waffle Shack across the highway and the parking lot where he had been so careless, where he had missed his prey, and where he had met the intruder that he now had to eliminate. Burrell sharpened the blade, growing excited that he would soon have more information to continue his hunt. No matter what, he thought, the predator must stay on the trail.

It was time.

No one had entered the parking area since the news van, and not one motel occupant had so much as pulled back a curtain. The Rattler would be quick. He would be unseen. And once he had extracted the information he needed, his strike would be fatal. Joe Vaughn Burrell opened the truck door and closed it without a sound. He rolled up his sleeves to let the Rattler's head breathe, to let it taste the night air and smell for its prey.

He rapidly flicked his own forked tongue and moved toward the motel room door, toward the lock that might slow him momentarily. He reached for the knob and inserted the metal pick. Cheap lock, he thought, this will be easy.

He was anxious to see the fear in her eyes.

He was anxious to silence the red-headed woman.

He was anxious to strike again.

He calmed his breathing.

The Rattler turned the knob slowly, silently…until a siren sounded in the distance.

Blue lights flickered against distant trees and power poles. The Rattler released the knob and slithered back toward the truck, his heart rate rising and his adrenaline pumping through his veins. He wouldn't be cornered. He wouldn't relent as easily as the Copperhead. They would feel his fangs before they cut off his head. He slid into the truck and watched the action through the rearview mirror.

The detestable siren grew louder. In the mirror, Burrell watched as a lone police car slowed and turned into the Waffle Shack. As he began to back from the motel parking space, he noticed a light from the reporter's room flicker underneath her unlocked door.

He quickly killed the truck's lights and shifted back into park. The Rattler knew it was better to blend into the surroundings at times rather than make any unnecessary movements.

The red-headed reporter pulled back her curtains and peered toward the blue lights of the distant police car.

From the darkness the Rattler watched her.

He felt the disappointment indeed, but it was not time for more carelessness. Not now. Not until he had found his prey and avenged his interrupted strike. Not until he had avenged the death of the Copperhead. No, he thought, it was not time for carelessness.

It took nearly ten minutes before the reporter finally lost interest and closed the curtains. The Rattler reversed the truck and pulled toward the highway, watching the activity taking place across the road. The responding deputy now exited the Waffle Shack door and moved toward two young men sitting on the trunk of a car. Probably drunk locals fighting over a woman, he thought.

Another car sped down the highway, crossing in front of the Rattler. The tan Crown Victoria had no markings and no activated blue lights or siren, but Joe Vaughn Burrell didn't have to watch it pull alongside the first responding deputy to know it was a cop car.

The Rattler grinned as a new plan formulated in his mind. A better plan, he thought.

The red-headed reporter would have been a gamble, but a detective would know everything. A predator must follow the trail, he thought, wherever it may lead. Even to the home of a detective.

Joe Vaughn Burrell pulled onto the road, studied the unmarked vehicle that would lead him to all the answers he sought, and disappeared down the highway, hiding in the darkness of the night.

37

BC,

> One of the Boone girls invited us to Sunday night
> singing at Harmony Grove. I'll be leaving about 5:30
> if you want to join me. Bring the Cougar if you want.
>
> Eli

I draped my head over the edge of my bed, wiggled my
sore jaw back and forth, and stared at the note that lay in the
floor below. The room was cool and silent and I had little
desire to crawl from beneath my covers. I reread the note.
Cougar had actually read it first. When we had finally arrived
at Eli's, well past one o'clock in the morning, the patrol car's
headlights illuminated the front door and waited on us to get
safely inside. Cougar had lumbered up the porch ahead of
me and pulled the taped piece of paper from the screen
door. After laughing that I now even had "the preacher-
man" calling him *Cougar*, he read the note aloud and then
sarcastically sang two verses of *Jesus Loves Me* as we headed
upstairs.

I reached from the bed, plucked the paper from the floor
and examined it as if it contained some secret message.

"One of the Boone girls…"

I assumed it was Maggie, but I sure hoped it was Laurie.
Perhaps she had already received the apology letter I sent.

But hadn't I mailed it just two days ago? With everything that had happened since then it seemed like it had been weeks. But just before last night's punch, the enraged Dylan clearly said that he had "lost her."

Maybe things were different now. Maybe Laurie did invite me. *Maggie.* It had to be Maggie. Up to her tricks again, I thought, just like she had put Laurie's number in my cell under Mark's name. But it really didn't matter who invited us, I still planned on joining Eli.

I sat up on the bed. Laurie's relationship status wasn't the only piece of information I had learned in the Waffle Shack parking lot. It wasn't the only revelation that had altered my world. Not by a long shot.

The old floor creaked as I struggled toward the dresser. Cougar slept soundly across the hall in the upstairs den and Eli, I knew, was at church. I wandered downstairs to the kitchen. On the back of a chair hung the Wally's Farm Supply hat Eli had given me. I slid it on and opened the fridge.

I poured a glass of orange juice and moved to the small kitchen table, sitting where I could see out the back windows, in the same chair where I had eaten Eli's pancakes the previous morning. *Things had been so much different twenty-four hours earlier.*

I rubbed my sore cheekbone where Dylan had smashed my face and tried to rewind the past twenty-four hours in my head.

Speaking with the police officers…Dylan and his gang…the news van…pulling the fire alarm at Holtman…Julie…Cougar…leaping from the ledge at Lost Pond…sitting in this very seat discussing religion with Eli.

Yes, things had been very different twenty-four hours earlier…back before I believed in resurrections.

* * *

After Dylan pounded my face, the first officer on the scene at the Waffle Shack had been a patrolman named Vickers. He quickly took our names and brief statements, radioed in some information, then went inside and talked at length with the cook and two customers sitting near the large glass windows. Several minutes later, as I waited on the back of my Honda listening to Cougar's version of the brawl, a familiar tan Crown Vic pulled into the parking lot.

"Cop car," said Cougar.

Detective Trent Ingle parked in a nearby space and emerged from his car just as Officer Vickers finished with the witnesses and exited the Waffle Shack. Detective Ingle wore a strange expression, which I assumed was due to being called to a fight started by two of his brothers. *Punks.*

Officer Vickers passed by us without speaking and met with the detective for a private conversation. I whispered to Cougar. "Remember the guy who punched me?"

"Yeah."

"And the guy with the dip who did all the talking?"

"Yeah, I punched him."

"Well, that detective is their older brother."

"Great," Cougar replied sarcastically.

The officers turned in our direction. Detective Ingle stayed a few steps behind. Vickers cleared his throat. "Mr. Morrow, Detective Ingle needs to speak with you after I'm finished."

"I bet he does," Cougar said boldly. "Don't want charges pressed against the little brothers, huh?"

"I'm not here concerning the altercation," Detective Ingle said, stepping toward Cougar. But the odd expression still clinched to his face worried me. "I heard Officer Vickers call in BC's name over the radio, I just now learned that my brothers were involved. Officer Vickers will handle the altercation and any charges you want to file. And then he's escorting you boys home."

Detective Ingle abruptly turned toward his vehicle.

"Okay fellas," said Officer Vickers. "All three witnesses inside corroborate your story. I have two names at this point. Dylan Ingle, age twenty. Colby Ingle, age twenty-three. Detective Ingle is quite sure he knows who the other two individuals are, and he is going to assist me in verifying that information. But you two need to decide whether or not you plan to press charges."

"Absolutely not," Cougar said.

His instant response surprised the officer.

Cougar, I learned while Vickers checked our story inside, had about a ten-second slug fest with the rest of Dylan's crew. When Dylan had decked me and all eyes were fixed on us, Cougar assumed that he was next, so he quickly jabbed the largest of the three, Dylan's brother Colby, square in the nose. The other two immediately rushed him. Cougar described the ensuing few seconds as chaos and survival, but the only evidence of his bout was a red mark running under his right ear and a slightly busted lip, which had already stopped bleeding.

Cougar. No fear of venomous snakes. Fighting three locals at once. Perhaps he *was* living up to his new name.

But I had no idea why Cougar was so set against pressing charges. I had a feeling my dealings with Dylan weren't over and I debated if involving the legal system would end things or make it all worse. But internal debates following a blast to the head, especially after midnight, are difficult to settle.

"How about you?" Vickers asked.

"I don't know," I answered.

"You don't have to make your decision now. I'll be filling out a report. If you decide to press charges just contact the Halston County-"

"Can I just tell Mark Boone?"

"You can contact *Captain* Boone." Vickers responded. I nodded. "He can explain what you'll need to do." Officer Vickers turned toward Detective Ingle who leaned against the side of his Crown Vic. "I'm done here Detective. They are all yours."

"I just need BC."

I walked toward the detective, who waited to speak until Officer Vickers had returned to his patrol car. "Have you spoken with Captain Boone in the last few hours?" His tone and worried eyes caused my heart to sink.

"I haven't spoken with him all day. Is everyone okay?"

"Then I assume you don't know about the body."

"The body?" I asked. "Did they find Burrell's body?"

"You college folks don't follow the news much do you?" I shook my head. The detective continued. "BC, they pulled the body from the lake late this evening. That part has been all over the news. Mark took off to Nickajack as soon as he heard, but he called me an hour ago…and there seems to be a problem."

I knew where the detective was headed, I knew my theory that I had texted Mark wasn't so crazy sounding anymore, but I asked anyway. "What kind of problem with the body?"

Detective Ingle exhaled a long breath and raised his eyebrows. "Well, for starters, it was the wrong body."

38

Cougar staggered into Eli's kitchen a half hour after me carrying his shoes and yawning. His Pac-Man t-shirt was draped across his shoulder. Adjusting his eyes to the light of mid-morning, Cougar leaned against the frame of the kitchen doorway as I finished the last of my orange juice.

"Did you call your girlfriend this morning?" Cougar asked.

"She's not my girlfriend."

"Oh, that's right, she's that Dylan dude's girlfriend. He just knocked your head off because you hooked up-"

"I told you Cougar, I didn't touch her."

"Just tell me the details, BC."

"Nothing happened. That's the details."

"You're no fun. Let's go get my keys," Cougar mumbled. He turned and walked barefooted toward the front door. "There's a cop car at the end of the drive way," I heard him yell as the screen door creaked open.

On the ride to campus Cougar said very little for the first few miles. I rolled down my window and wondered if I smelled as much like the Waffle Shack as he did. Cougar re-adjusted the rearview mirror to find the patrol car following us. "So that detective was really the brother of those other two goons?" he finally asked.

"Yep, I explained all of that."

"You told me what you wanted me to know."

"Yep. But you never told me why you were so quick not to press charges."

"You never asked." Cougar was right. With my mind bouncing between what Laurie would think of my late-night clash with Dylan and then trying to comprehend the resurrection of Joe Vaughn Burrell, everything else just seemed insignificant.

"I just wanted it over with," Cougar said. "I don't know them and they don't know me, and by not pressing charges I can leave it that way. Unfortunately for you, you know the whole clan. And besides, I punched that ugly dude first, so I wasn't pressing my luck once the officer seemed to be on our side."

Officer Vickers should have been on our side, I thought, we didn't follow Dylan's crew to the Waffle Shack and wait to start a brawl. Detective Ingle, however, was the one who had surprised me. Never once did he try to talk me out of pressing charges against his brothers, not even a subtle hint or threat. I actually wished that he had, because after sleeping on it, I still didn't know if pressing charges was the right course to take.

Cougar interrupted my thoughts. "So who took the Nickajack plunge instead of that Burrell dude?"

"I'm not exactly sure." And according to Detective Ingle, neither was law enforcement. From what Mark Boone had told Detective Ingle over the phone, the body had no identification, was similar in appearance to Joe Vaughn Burrell, but just wasn't him.

Detective Ingle had reached into his Crown Vic in the Waffle Shack parking lot and handed me a sheet of paper, a photocopied page from the Cohutta College student directory. The detective explained it was from the same directory I had pulled from the truck above Nickajack Lake.

The drowned man had indeed been the same man from the Joe-MAC surveillance video. And the photocopied paper proved he had indeed been searching for me. But with no clue that my last name was Morrow, the unknown man had been going down the list of male students with the initials *BC*. Fortunately, most of them were off campus for summer and the ones on campus weren't harmed. While I had assumed Joe Vaughn Burrell had fled the area, he had an accomplice hunting for me.

And now no one knew Burrell's whereabouts. Whether he was on the hunt or on the run was unknown. But he was indeed out there...somewhere.

When I saw that the last name checked off the directory list was *Blake Cawthon*, I remembered exactly where I had met Burrell's accomplice just hours before he found the bottom of Nickajack Lake. I thought back to my encounter at a campus mail bin with the delivery man with the scraped knuckles and the snake tattoo. I had spoken face to face with the very man attempting to hunt me down. I had stood arm's length from a man I could only assume wanted to kill me.

Detective Ingle looked stunned in the Waffle Shack parking lot when I asked if the drowned man had a copperhead tattoo starting at the left wrist and running up his arm. I then told him of the chance encounter on campus. According to Detective Ingle, Mark had mentioned an impressive snake tattoo on the dead man's body. While Detective Ingle thought the body may have been in the water too long to distinguish the exact type of tattooed snake, he would pass my information along to Captain Boone.

Before we left, I informed Detective Ingle that a news van parked at the motel across the highway was searching for me. Initially, the detective shrugged his shoulders and didn't appear interested in that part of my problem.

But I needed him interested.

"Look Detective Ingle," I had said. "Someone has obviously leaked my name to the media. What if they do a story and Burrell learns who I am? Or what if Laurie and Maggie Boone's names have also been leaked? Are you willing to let them be put in danger again? How do you think Captain Boone would feel about his daughters being plastered on the news with their attacker still on the loose?"

Detective Ingle had perked up at the mention of Mark's name. He then puffed out his chest, nodded confidently, and said he would stop by the motel and attempt to resolve the issue. Sure enough, when we all pulled onto the main highway after leaving the Waffle Shack, Detective Ingle turned into the motel. Cougar and I ascended the mountain highway toward Eli's, Officer Vickers close behind.

* * *

Without my sunglasses, I shielded my eyes from the bright sun that waited at the crest of the approaching hill. My cell phone chimed as the mountain highway split the twin stone pillars marking the entrance to Cohutta College. The trailing patrolman stayed close behind. I checked my phone. Eleven new voicemails and dozens of text messages. Detective Ingle had apparently failed to keep my name from the media and I had a bad feeling about what I'd find in the morning newspaper or hear on the local radio. I kept a CD playing in the car just to keep Cougar from scanning through the stations. My gut felt queasy knowing a media whirlwind was about to begin.

I turned off my phone and slid it in the side pocket of my cargo shorts. I decided to wait until I had dropped Cougar off before I listened to the messages or read the texts. I needed to think this through.

We pulled into Holtman. As Cougar snapped the reclined seat forward and yawned excessively loud, Brody Payne emerged through the dorm's front doors.

"That's a good sign," said Cougar, exiting the car. "Hopefully that means the girls are home." Payne carried a large apple in one hand, a water bottle in the other, and a Frisbee under his armpit. He headed our way, keeping an eye on the deputy's car that parked several slots over.

"What's up guys?" he yelled.

"Left my keys here last night," answered Cougar as he met Payne on the sidewalk. I stayed in the car, window down and radio off.

"Bummer. Hey, you guys up for some ultimate Frisbee at the intramural fields?" Payne asked. He chomped a large bite of apple. Besides the Frisbee, Payne's frayed khaki pants and flip-flops didn't give the impression the game would start anytime soon.

"I'm headed to Chattanooga," answered Cougar.

"How about you, BC? Frisbee?"

Before I offered a good excuse Cougar chimed in. "BC can't, he's got choir practice at church this afternoon." He chuckled over his little joke as he jogged on toward the dorm.

Payne tilted his head in thought. "So no Frisbee, BC?"

"No Frisbee." I said. Cougar disappeared through Holtman's doors and I hoped Payne would soon vanish as well. I needed to check my voicemails and contact Mark. During our late-night drive back to Eli's, following our encounter the Ingle brothers, Mark had sent one final text. It read: *Fighting Dylan? Really? Get to Eli's, stay at Eli's.*

Instead of leaving, Brody Payne settled back against a nearby bike rack.

"Are any of the girls home so Cougar can get his keys?" I asked.

"They're all up there trying to wake up. I just dropped Samantha off. Julie was on the couch. Man, that girl looked a little rough this morning." Payne took another large bite of apple but kept talking. "She told us about the fire alarm being pulled. Said it cleared the whole dorm and that Momma Mildred was irate."

"Did she say who-"

"So how did you guys get home last night?" Payne asked. He peered past my car, his forehead scrunched in deep thought. I followed his gaze to Cougar's Bronco. I told Payne about our late night campus hike, our trip to Waffle Shack, and the short version of our scuffle with the locals. Just as I mentioned that the foursome sped off in their jacked-up truck, Cougar reemerged through Holtman's front doors. I wondered if he had encountered Julie upstairs and how that awkward conversation may have sounded.

"Hey slugger," said Payne as Cougar neared. "BC says you took on three locals."

Cougar held two balled fists into the air. "It wasn't a fair fight, they needed three more to have a chance." Cougar filled the air with a ridiculous combination of punches. After a final upper cut and a knee to an imaginary groin, Cougar turned his glare in my direction. "But you'll never guess which fire alarm got pulled last night?"

"Which one?" I replied nonchalantly.

"The one just outside the girls' room," Payne answered. "Probably one of the *nuns* living across the hall. Chelsea's goody-goody neighbors have already reported them twice for being loud and having me over. They're always trying to shut down the fun."

"Yeah, it was probably one of them," said Cougar. He nodded but left his eyes on me. It appeared he had formed his own theory.

39

The Crown Vic idled for a few seconds at the end of the driveway, causing Joe Vaughn Burrell to wonder if he had been spotted. But even from a distance Burrell could see the detective adjusting some items on the dashboard and taking several sips of coffee. Eventually, the detective backed into the road. Joe Vaughn Burrell quickly leaned down in the truck cab as the detective passed, and then watched in the rear-view mirror until the Crown Vic completely disappeared.

Burrell cranked the F150, pulled down the road, and entered the detective's driveway. He parked behind the white sedan with "Trish" on the license plate. Later, Burrell knew, he would need to relocate the truck behind the house or in some nearby woods, but for now he needed to appear as if he belonged.

Burrell tucked the knife into his belt and walked up to the front porch. He tested the knob. It gave no resistance. Joe Vaughn Burrell, the Rattler, stood at the doorstep of Detective Trent Ingle's unlocked home. Eyes shut, focusing, he calmly exhaled a long, deep breath.

All strikes are quick, he thought.

The Rattler entered the house, his senses firing rapidly as he scanned the small living room. Old hardwood boards creaked beneath his boots.

"Trent, is that you?"

He followed the voice. Gaining speed, he crossed the living area and rounded a corner, encountering his prey as she stood, items in hand, beside a small kitchen table. His hand found her throat, silencing her scream and sending a glass of cranberry juice and a newspaper to the floor. He pushed her backwards until she collided forcefully against the refrigerator.

Her eyes begged, but he clutched her soft throat. Her hands pulled at his wrists, but her strength was no match for his and they both knew it.

"Scream and I will kill you," he whispered in her ear. Her knees gave way and he allowed her panic-stricken body to slide to the floor. With his free hand Burrell removed the knife and held it in front of her fearful eyes. He relaxed the grip on her neck and knelt beside her.

"I have questions for you, mam," he said, sliding the blade against her face, "and all I want to hear is a yes or a no. Do you understand?"

She nodded, tears beginning their way down her cheeks.

"Is there anyone else in the house?"

"No," she managed.

"Are you expecting any visitors today?"

"No," she said once again, tears flowing harder.

"Do you have a digital camera?" he asked, extending his own serpent-like tongue toward her face.

Confusion and fear swirled in her eyes, exciting the Rattler. He slammed the point of the knife into the floor just inches from her head.

"Do you have a digital camera?" he asked again.

"Yes," she said in a defeated whisper. Wonderful, just like it was meant to be, he thought. Burrell felt the juice from the spilled glass against his knee. He watched the deep red liquid darken the newspaper that lay on the floor beside his prey. He read the large head-line. 'Cohutta Hoopster a Hero.'

And below those words was the picture of the one he sought. The one who would feel the full venom of the Rattler. His heart raced.

"Yes, just like it was meant to be," he said to Trish Ingle, admiring the confusion and futile pleading with-in her eyes.

Joe Vaughn Burrell calmly removed his shirt, letting the rattlesnake breathe, letting it smell the fear growing in the air.

I assumed Eli didn't wear his t-shirt, overalls, and blue *Cougars* hat to church, but that was how I found him on the front porch once I returned from campus.

"You might want to read the paper," were his first words as I neared the steps.

"I've heard," I said, trying to sound confident. I had listened to most of my cell phone messages after Cougar had left, but the only person I had called back was Mark. And he was furious. He vowed to find out who had leaked my name to the media, even if it meant pursuing the termination of one of his fellow officers. And after giving me the gist of the article that had been printed in the *Chattanooga Daily Tribune*, Mark assured me that Laurie and Maggie's names had not been mentioned.

Just mine. Along with my picture.

Mark couldn't talk long. He was headed to Nashville with a TBI agent when we spoke, but he did say that he and I needed to have a longer discussion later that evening. He still expected answers from our Joe Vaughn Burrell conversation on the bridge. In the meantime, Mark suggested that I return to Eli's and stay away from campus.

Eli Giles held the front page of the Chattanooga paper toward me. '*Cohutta Hoopster a Hero*' read the large headline.

My junior picture from the Cohutta College basketball guide accompanied the article. In the headshot I wore a navy coat, red tie, a crooked grin, and soaring, gel-spiked hair.

Eli folded the paper and handed it to me. "I like the hair."

"It was a phase," I joked, or at least tried, hoping to mask the fear growing within. Joe Vaughn Burrell was among the living and my name and face were front page news. With the news van prowling near campus, I had to assume my face was already plastered on the television as well. I hoped that Burrell was a fleeing fugitive and nowhere near the area, but my gut said otherwise.

"Where's your buddy?" asked Eli. "I don't get to meet *the Cougar*?"

"It's probably for the best." I fell into a vacant rocker, glanced restlessly through the article, then folded the paper and stuck it under my arm. I assumed the newspaper could legally print my name and picture without my consent, but the article still angered me, even if it did make me out to be the hero.

Eli squinted intently at my face. "Did the visit with your buddy end badly? Looks like somebody put a bruise on your cheek." The pain from Dylan's surprise punch had faded, but a bluish mark remained as proof of his fist's vicious collision with my face.

"That's nothing, Mr. Giles," I answered, rubbing my cheekbone. "How was church?"

"You changing the subject?"

"Absolutely."

Eli laughed. "Church was good, this young pup of a preacher gets me fired up. I like the way the Holy Spirit uses him." Eli summarized the sermon while my mind pictured a twenty-five-year-old foot stomper with a cheap dark suite and short tie, holding the Bible high in one hand and pointing accusingly toward his congregants with the other.

"How old is the *young pup*?" I asked.

"Probably in his forties," Eli grinned. "But he acts more mature, he…"

As Eli continued on about the preacher, my mind drifted back to the article tucked under my arm and its unnamed sources revealing me as the savior of two local girls. Based on the missed calls on my cell phone, my family was well aware of the article. I needed to return some calls and let them know I was okay, but I dreaded the exhausting conversations. I pulled out my phone. The note Eli had left on the door concerning the singing at Harmony Grove clung to my cell. "So tell me about this singing we've been invited to tonight?" I asked.

"Tell me more about that newspaper article, *Hero*."

"You first."

"Deal. I haven't visited Harmony Grove in years, but lots of churches like to devote one Sunday night a month to singing, so I assume that's what it will be. No sermon…just a choir and church folks praising with their voices."

Mark had said that his girls often performed at church. Perhaps Laurie wouldn't just be in attendance, maybe she'd be on stage as well. *To hear her play, to hear her sing…I couldn't pass up such a chance.*

"Which of the Boone's invited us?" I asked.

"It was the daughter that called, said her family would sure like to have us there. I thought that was awfully sweet."

"Which daughter? Laurie or Maggie?"

Eli shrugged. "I don't recall, but it was definitely one of 'em."

As much as I now feared Joe Vaughn Burrell, I simply needed to see Laurie Boone. Mark had warned me to stay away from campus, but he never mentioned anything about avoiding church. Surely Mark would be in favor of me attending church. *Surely.*

* * *

I leaned against one of Eli's backyard boulders and twirled a much smaller stone in my hand. Walking through the backyard I had picked up two flat, palm-sized rocks lying alongside Eli's garden. Perfect skipping rocks, I thought, but I had no lake. From the edge of the preacher's property I launched the first stone as far as I could from the receding mountain. Part of me wanted to do the same with my cell phone.

I knew who to call first. I knew who I *had* to call first. I took out my cell and scrolled to the M's. Without hesitation I hit SEND. My mom answered on the second ring.

41

E li pulled his pick-up into a space midway between Harmony Grove's old brick sanctuary and its newer, larger counterpart. He stared open-jawed at the sight of the glass and stone structure. "I guess it has been a while since I've been here," he said, pointing to the older building. "I hope they are still using that for something other than storage. God used some good preachers in that place over the years, but I can't believe how small it looks now."

A Halston County deputy pulled into the open space outside my door. I nodded to the officer who had trailed us all the way from Eli's. According to Mark, I would be seeing a deputy everywhere I went until Joe Vaughn Burrell was apprehended. And I was sure the officer did his duty by reporting our current location to Captain Boone.

I studied the older sanctuary that Eli was describing and that I had recently visited. "They've turned it into their youth building," I said. "I brought Maggie Boone here last Sunday and stayed to hear her sing. The place was actually crowded."

"Well good," said Eli. He leaned toward the steering wheel and squinted. "What does that banner say hanging between those columns?"

"*Wave 5:42*. Their youth service starts at exactly 5:42." I checked my watch. It was nearly ten minutes until six, but

233

only one car, a green Camry, was parked in front of the youth building. "Last Sunday there were a few more cars."

"Well, they may not have a youth service when they have Sunday singing," Eli said. "But why the 5:42 start, did she say?"

"Maggie said it was from a certain verse...in the Book of...Ash?"

"The Book of *Acts*," Eli clarified. "Acts 5:42. A good verse. It says *And daily in the temple, and in every house, they ceased not to teach and preach Jesus Christ.*"

Amazing. I wondered if the retired preacher had the entire Bible stored in his brain. I shook my head in disbelief at the old man.

Eli grinned. "That is actually one of my favorite verses. And they start their youth service at 5:42...clever. I tell you BC, these youth ministers today are some creative folks."

The Toyota sitting alone in front of the youth building was the same green Camry from when I had dropped Maggie off the previous week. *That's Mac's*, Maggie had said, *She goes to the college...you probably know her.* I didn't then but I sure did now. Mac was Julie. Julie was Mac. She had jumped in the vehicle quickly at Lost Pond to avoid the local girl wearing the *Wave* shirt, but I was impressed to see that she was still helping the youth. However, I wondered if seeing me again would be a bad reminder of a rough night that was only a fire alarm away from being much worse.

We exited the truck and headed toward the front doors of the new sanctuary. The deputy who had parked behind us, my guardian, now followed on foot. Two middle-age couples walked ahead of us. One couple held hands, the other couple both texted on cell phones.

"Do you think they're texting each other?" Eli laughed. He reminded me to turn my cell off before we entered, but I had left it in the truck. Thirty-three unheard voicemails and countless unreturned text messages waited on my phone. After speaking to my mom and assuring her I was safe, I had sent text replies to both my brothers, but after that I had just given up and turned the phone off. I looked forward to entering Harmony Grove and getting away from the madness for a couple of hours.

Atop the new sanctuary's stone steps, in front of large white doors, waited two greeters and Detective Trent Ingle. Jeans. Sunglasses. Untucked collared shirt. I assumed the detective was the undercover guardian of the Boone girls.

The elder greeter, by at least five decades, immediately recognized Eli. "Hey preacher," he said, extending his hand and a genuine smile. Beside him, the plain clothed detective nodded toward me then met his law enforcement colleague at the bottom of the steps for a quick word. *Small-town secret service*, I thought. As Eli finished his chat with the elder gentleman, the younger greeter, maybe a year away from needing his first razor, pulled open one of the massive doors for us to enter.

"Welcome to Harm-"

Suddenly a familiar voice escaped from inside.

"Excuse me...excuse me...sorry, sorry...excuse me!"

Maggie. She barreled through the small crowd in the foyer area and shot between me and Eli before realizing who we were. Halfway down the steps, she turned abruptly and her enormous smile appeared.

"BC! You made it. Oh, hello Pastor Giles, nice to meet you!"

She grabbed Eli's hand and nearly shook it from his wrist.

"You okay Maggie?" I asked.

"Oh, yeah, I'm fine. I left my guitar in the car and we're about to start. My dad is somewhere between here and Nashville, said he'd be here as soon as possible. See ya!" She turned and bounded down the remaining steps and toward the parking lot. Her secret service detail in the jeans and untucked shirt trailed along, but without the skipping and singing and smiling.

I followed Eli inside, through an open foyer, and into a beautiful, octagonal sanctuary. Five sections of pews radiated at a slight curve from an elevated stage. Eli chose a pew near the back in the middle section. I sat beside him and scanned the crowd. It wasn't packed, but I guessed there were more than a hundred individuals milling about, chatting, or finding their seats. A few made final preparations on the stage. Besides the traditional piano and risers for the choir, the stage also contained various guitars, a keyboard, and a drum set behind an arching shield of Plexiglas.

But I saw no sign of Laurie.

"Do you sing?" asked Eli.

"Not when I can help it," I replied. He handed me a piece of gum.

"Well, when we stand, just chew real slow with your mouth open and it might look like you're singing. That is what my son Joseph used to say."

Maggie caught my attention as she reentered the sanctuary and walked briskly down the aisle toward the front. She carried her guitar on stage and placed it in a small stand behind the piano. She appeared to be her usual, vibrant self. I wondered if Mark had even told her that Joe Vaughn Burrell, the man who nearly abducted her, was still alive. But it was all over the news and Detective Ingle was standing post in front of the church, so surely she had to know. *Surely*.

Maggie jogged down the stage's carpeted steps and hurried toward the first pew in our section. Between the numerous heads sitting in front of me I could see her talking animatedly to a small group of youth. One appeared to be the same polite girl from Lost Pond and beside her, I was nearly certain, was the same skinny boy who had toted their fishing poles. We had left that day because we were initially worried about them, while they had sat in their trucks probably intimidated by a group of college students. I smiled at the thought.

Maggie knelt in the pew and spoke with someone sitting behind her friends. Her mouth moved full speed, her eyes full of excitement. I leaned forward for a better view.

Laurie.

The Boone's oldest daughter sat with her mom a few pews behind the youth. Laurie shifted and slowly scanned the vast room behind her. Her dark, curly hair was shorter than when I had last seen her. Her gentle smile made me wonder what Maggie had said. *Was she looking for me?*

Laurie continued her slow gaze around the sanctuary. Just as I raised my hand to catch her attention, a wide, slow-moving woman shuffled herself directly in front of me. After a long sigh and several attempts at getting her garments adjusted, the woman finally eased down into the pew.

"Hello fellas," came a familiar voice. "Mind if I sit with you?" Mark stood at the end of our pew. Our much needed conversation would apparently take place at the church.

"Please join us, Captain Boone," said Eli.

We made room. Mark reached across me to shake Eli's hand. My hands grew damp and I wiped them on my pants. *Don't be nice Mark, don't...*but he spoke my name and reached for my palm. *It is all part of his training*, I thought. Find the guy with the sweaty palms and find the guilty man.

"We'll talk after the service," he said quietly. I nodded.

As I pondered what all Mark might know, what all we had to discuss, the worship band struck its first notes and everyone began to stand. We turned our attention toward the stage and to lyrics projected onto two mounted screens. I stood between my holy landlord and the captain of the Halston County detectives and slowly chewed my gum.

I knew we'd discuss the resurrection of Joe Vaughn Burrell.

...and if I, and the Boone girls, were currently in any danger.
...and we'd discuss how I knew the fugitive's middle name
...and perhaps we'd conclude with a chat about a trip to Belford
...and a roadside meeting with the TBI.
And then...

Well then I wondered why Dylan, dressed nicely, hair styled, his biceps stretching the band of a thin, short-sleeved Polo, was moving down the aisle of the church and sliding into a pew several rows in front of me. Perhaps Mark had invited him to discuss last night's Waffle Shack drama as well. I wiped my hands on my pants and chewed my gum a little slower, not quite ready for the evening's music to end.

Not quite ready for the interrogation to begin.

42

After the worship band's third consecutive song, the pastor of Harmony Grove took the stage from his seat in the front pew. *Pastor Russ*, as I later learned he was called, didn't fit my mental image of a small-town Baptist preacher. Perhaps in his late thirties, his short hair was casually spiked and he peered through trendy, dark-rimmed eyeglasses. He wore a collared shirt with no tie, khaki pants, and what appeared to be hiking or rock climbing shoes. I wondered if he sported the same trendy attire on Sunday mornings. I also wondered what Eli thought of this "young pup" on stage.

Pastor Russ accepted a microphone from the worship band's lead singer, led the congregation in a brief prayer, and then invited everyone to be seated. "Good evening again," said Pastor Russ. "I would just like to welcome everyone to our Sunday night singing. Big crowd tonight, and I know we want to hear more of that wonderful music, but I need to bore you first with a few announcements."

A polite laugh rose from the congregation.

"First of all, we're a week away from our Constructor's for Christ Mission Trip to White Creek, Missouri. We currently have thirty-four men, women, and youth signed up to go. If anyone feels led to join or assist in anyway with that ministry, please call the church office on Monday. The church we're helping build in White Creek is still on schedule, so we should be doing some roofing and sheet rock work for the week we're there."

"And cooking!" yelled a female voice from the crowd, bringing another round of laughter.

"And our kitchen ladies will do some *mighty fine* cooking," echoed Pastor Russ. He nodded and rubbed his belly for emphasis before glancing back at his notes. "Also, we'll be having a deacon ordination on Wednesday night for Mark Boone. I see the Boone ladies, is Mark here tonight?"

Mark raised his hand until Pastor Russ spotted him. Heads throughout the sanctuary turned our direction. As Pastor Russ continued a few glares lingered on me. I wondered if they recognized me from the newspaper or were just checking out an unfamiliar face in their sanctuary.

"We usually do our deacon ordinations on Sunday evenings," said Pastor Russ. "But since Mark is taking part in the mission trip and will be leaving Friday evening, he'll be ordained during a special Wednesday night service. So please come out to hear Mark Boone deliver his testimony and to celebrate as a church family. Also, we'll be having a…"

Mark's going out of town?

As Pastor Russ rattled through more announcements I wanted to ask Mark about this church-building trip. Surely with everything going on he wouldn't leave. Or maybe Mark was taking Laurie and Maggie as well, getting them out of town and hiding them in Missouri for a week. But what did the preacher say Mark was doing on Wednesday night? Giving his *testimony*? I thought about asking Eli exactly what that meant before the next song began, but I'd learned from numerous hushings at movie theaters that I was a terrible whisperer. If I remembered, I'd ask Eli on the drive home.

As Pastor Russ stepped down, the Boone girls emerged from the audience and replaced him on stage. Laurie strode toward the piano wearing a knee-length green skirt and a white sleeveless top. I felt awkward admiring her nicely tanned arms and legs while sitting in a church...*and* while sitting beside her dad. Laurie pulled a microphone stand closer to the piano and lowered it. Maggie adjusted her guitar strap and checked the (mic) in front of her with two quick taps, while Donna waited patiently near center stage holding a cordless microphone.

Maggie strummed the guitar once, exchanged glances with Laurie, and both began to play. Donna swayed gently to the sounds her daughters created, closed her eyes, and began.

> *"I stand amazed in the presence*
> *Of Jesus the Nazarene,*
> *And wonder how He could love me,*
> *A sinner, condemned, unclean."*

Laurie and Maggie's voices joined Donna's.

> *"How marvelous! How wonderful!*
> *And my song shall ever be:*
> *How marvelous! How wonderful*
> *Is my Savior's love for me!"*

Mark leaned forward and rested his elbows on the pew in front of him, his eyes transfixed on the stage. I was in the presence of a proud husband and father.

Laurie's lone voice suddenly seized my attention. She closed her eyes as the soft lyrics flowed through her lips, the slight sway of her body with the rhythm of the music barely perceivable, but I noticed. And I was mesmerized.

> *"He took my sins and my sorrows,*
> *He made them His very own;*
> *He bore the burden to Calvary,*
> *And suffered and died alone."*

Beautiful. I could listen to her sing and play the piano every day. As the three Boone girls combined vocals once again for the chorus, Eli and others in the congregation gradually joined in.

> *"How marvelous! How wonderful!*
> *And my song shall ever be:*
> *How marvelous! How wonderful*
> *Is my Savior's love for me!"*

It was apparent that the final stanza was for Maggie. As she leaned toward the mic to sing she pushed the guitar to her side. Laurie let up on the piano. The only sound in the entire room was Maggie's voice rising through the silence as if it was going directly to God. My skin tingled. Maggie's voice was simply a gift. She sang:

> *"When with the ransomed in glory*
> *His face I at last shall see,*
> *'Twill be my joy through the ages*
> *To sing of his love for me."*

Several people around me joined in again for the final chorus. As the voices of the Boone girls subsided, I started to clap before realizing it might not be proper church etiquette. Thankfully, the entire congregation followed my lead.

"He is a great God indeed," said Donna from the stage.

The Boone girls, who treated the congregation to two more impressive songs, were followed by a surprisingly good male quartet, an older lady with seriously powerful pipes, and the worship band who returned on stage to end the night. As pews emptied and aisles filled, we waited. Dylan, however, did not. As Mark shook the hands of passing church members and fielded congratulations on both his deaconship and his talented family, I watched Dylan move aggressively toward the front like a salmon fighting upstream. He was obviously headed for Laurie. Spotting him, Laurie stood between pews, facing his direction, waiting.

But Dylan never made it.

Donna Boone stepped in his path, halting his advance. The slender lady stood calmly, but with eyes that reminded me of a mother bear defending her cub. Then she placed her hand on his shoulder. I couldn't be sure, but from a distance it appeared she simply said, "Not tonight Dylan, not here."

Whatever the exact words, he turned and made his way back up the aisle. I tried to look away. I tried to not make eye contact. But the sight of me sitting beside Mark briefly halted the big boy in his tracks. He hadn't noticed me on his way in. But now, fists balled, face tense, he huffed past the last couple speaking to Mark and through the sanctuary doors. *Great*, I thought. *Round two, coming up. Ding, ding.*

"There goes your buddy," said Mark with a grin.

"Yep."

Mark leaned forward to peer around me. "Reverend Giles, would you mind letting me and BC have a few minutes to speak?"

"No problem, Captain Boone," said Eli. "I spotted a few old-timers that I haven't seen in years. They don't move too fast, maybe I can still catch one in the foyer." Eli pulled himself up and headed for the opposite end of the pew.

Before our conversation began, Mark and I both realized the Boone girls were now headed up the aisle. Maggie was well in the lead. She hugged Mark as he told her how beautiful she sang. Donna and Laurie followed a few steps behind.

"Hey BC, it's nice to see you again," Donna said, a protectiveness still lingering in her eyes.

"You all sounded amazing," I offered.

"Thanks for coming, BC," said Maggie. Laurie stayed silent.

Mark patted his wife's hand. "Donna, if you and Maggie don't mind, I need to have a discussion with BC and Laurie. It shouldn't take long, would you two wait for us out in the foyer? You might find Reverend Giles out there looking for company."

"He will talk your ear off," I warned.

"Maggie and I can handle Reverend Giles," Donna replied.

And you might find Dylan out there waiting for me as well, I thought. But from what I had just seen, she could handle him too.

43

Detective Trent Ingle found the house key and jiggled it in the lock until the stubborn mechanism gave in. He had told his wife that he would replace it, and now he thought she locked it just to prove a point. Agitated by the lock, exhausted from putting in a full work day on a Sunday, all that melted away as he opened the door to the smell of hamburger meat frying in the kitchen.

"I'm home, babe," he called, "it took longer than expected for Mark to get back from Nashville." He followed the smell, stopping midway in the living area to remove his gun, keys, and cell phone. He placed them inside the drawer of the sofa table. When they had kids, Trish had told him, the gun would have to be stored somewhere safer.

"You didn't tell me it was a burger night," he said again, expecting a response. Perhaps she was on the phone, he thought, or upset with him again for failing to call and check in with her during the day. He knew how much she worried about the dangers of his job.

"Sorry I didn't get to call, babe, just a busy day."

As the detective rounded the corner toward the kitchen, his forward momentum came to an abrupt halt

245

as he nearly collided with the gun pointed directly at his face. Panicked, startled, he stumbled a few steps backward as his mind raced to make sense of the scene.

The shirtless man holding the pistol grinned. In the other hand he held a spatula. The tattoo that decorated the man's body looked eerily similar to one the detective had recently seen in a dead man's photo.

Trent Ingle knew who was standing in his kitchen.

"Where's my wife, Burrell?" he asked hesitantly.

"Hello detective, your wife showed me where you kept this revolver…and some other items." Joe Vaughn Burrell slid the spatula beneath a thick roll of gray duct tape on the table and flicked it toward the detective. "Fine lady you got there, very helpful. I need you to-"

"Where is Trish?" the young detective demanded, tears and anger forming in his eyes.

"And as I was saying, Trent, you need to take that duct tape and start wrapping your wrists-"

"And I said where is my wife?" yelled the hefty detective.

Joe Vaughn Burrell grinned. "Trent," he said as if they were old friends, "as you can so obviously see, you are not in charge of this situation. I'll answer your questions as soon as you take that duct tape and-"

Trent Ingle lunged for the man standing in his kitchen, but the distance between them was too great. The bullet slammed into the detective, spinning and crashing him to the floor. Pain and then blood saturated his right shoulder. The gasping detective lay on his back staring at the ceiling. His chest rose and fell rapidly. Tears of pain and anger welled in his eyes. He knew his wife was dead and that he would soon join her.

Joe Vaughn Burrell moved to the stove, scooping the frying hamburger from the skillet and laying it on a plate. He kept an eye on the detective as he prepared his food. Finally, Burrell took a seat at the small kitchen table and placed the revolver beside his meal.

"Well, Trent, you just don't seem to be as hospitable as your wife. She's a good host, did exactly what I said and that is why she is still alive...for now." Burrell took a bite of the hamburger and briefly held the portion in his mouth, savoring its flavor. He settled back in the kitchen chair, unfolded a newspaper, and chewed slowly. The wounded detective bled and moaned from the floor as Burrell enjoyed his meal.

Ketchup dripped from Burrell's mouth and onto his chin. He wiped his face with his fingers and used his forked tongue to lick the red sauce from his skin.

"Trent, your wife answered everything I asked except for one question, but I know for her sake you'll be able to produce the correct answer."

Detective Ingle hung no hope on the false words of the psychopath in his kitchen. He knew his wife was dead, no matter what this evil serpent said. He stared at the ceiling waiting on death and whatever came after it. Joe Vaughn Burrell leaned from the table and dropped a small red camera on the detective's chest. Trent Ingle recognized it immediately.

"You may want to look at the first few pics. You may become more cooperative."

As Burrell turned back to his paper, the detective picked up the camera with his left hand and scrolled through only two images before dropping the camera against the kitchen floor. Trent Ingle glared with a fu-

tile hatred at the tattooed man sitting at his kitchen table.

"What do you want to know?" Trent Ingle managed
through clinched teeth, the disturbing images forever
burned into his memory.

Joe Vaughn Burrell casually took another large bite
of his hamburger and then held the front page of the
Chattanooga newspaper toward the detective.

"For starters," Burrell said through a mouthful of
food, "where do I find BC Morrow?"

44

Laurie sat sideways in the pew in front of us. She ran her long, tanned arm along the top of the pew. A small cross dangled from a silver bracelet on her slender wrist. Reaching forward, Mark gently squeezed the back of her neck and commented on how well she had played and sang.

"Thank you daddy," Laurie said. Then Mark got straight to the point.

"BC, let's begin by learning how you knew Joe Vaughn Burrell's middle name. We have already established that you didn't get it from the news. And please be honest, we both have people waiting."

Laurie lowered her head. I hoped she was praying for me because I wasn't sure where this tale was about to go. I cleared my throat in an attempt to activate my hesitant voice.

"Well, I was on the phone with Laurie and she mentioned a file that you had left out...on your desk or on the counter maybe. Anyway, I talked her into peeking into it and she found the name and the address of your suspect, Joe Vaughn Burrell. We didn't have any way of knowing that he was actually *the guy*."

Mark folded his arms and adjusted back in the pew. "Go on," he said. "Tell me about the trip to Belford. You know, where the two of you ended up driving by the home of our suspect multiple times?"

Mark knew about our trip. But was it from the agents who pulled us over or had he gotten the information out of Laurie? If it was from the TBI, he may not know everything.

I hoped my courage to face him eye to eye might make me sound more convincing, but my voice began to quiver as I spoke. "Well…Laurie gave me the address and I asked if she was up for an adventure. I knew there was the slight possibility of Joe Vaughn Burrell recognizing our cars from that night in the parking lot, so I talked her into borrowing Dylan's."

Mark, silent and stoic, appeared to study my face more than my words.

"Mark, it was a dumb idea and it was completely my fault. I should have never put Laurie in danger like that. I am truly sorry."

Mark softly placed his hand on Laurie's shoulder. She raised her head and looked toward him. The wetness in her eyes belied her soft smile.

"Laurie, BC and I are going to be just a little longer, go ahead and take off with mom. You and I can speak later."

"Okay," she said just above a whisper. Laurie wiped her eyes with the back of her hand and spun toward the aisle. As she passed our pew I realized that she and I hadn't spoken one word to each other. And still, somehow, I seemed to have upset her.

"You sounded awesome tonight," I said before she left the sanctuary.

Laurie looked back. "Thank you BC,…thank you," she answered, followed by a smile that would have convinced me to drive back to Belford right then if she'd asked.

The door closed behind her. Only Mark and I remained. He crossed his right leg and interlaced his fingers across his bent knee. Somehow, the vast sanctuary suddenly felt like a stuffy interrogation room.

"BC, I accept your apology, but tell me something." Mark paused for several seconds. Surely he could hear my heart slamming inside my chest. "Do you really think you can lie to a veteran detective while sitting in a church?"

"Not at all," I said. "Not at all."

* * *

Mark knew everything. Everything. He had already confronted Laurie and she had filled in the gaps that he hadn't pieced together. I apologized again, this time for being untruthful, but when I expected the venting of Mark's anger, he dropped his right arm behind me along the back of the pew and then said very simply, very genuinely, that he forgave me.

Forgiveness. I didn't know what to do with that.

Somehow saying "thank you" didn't seem sufficient, but I said it anyway.

Then Mark slapped me lightly on the back of the head and pointed toward the thick wooden cross mounted beyond the stage. "But you just lied in church college boy, so you may have bigger issues to worry about than me."

That was true. And I thought of one major issue in particular.

"How worried should I be about Joe Vaughn Burrell?" I asked.

Mark's stoic expression returned. "BC, we haven't received the first tip since before the drowning. Everyone thinks he used the diversion of presumably being dead to flee the area. I want to agree, but my gut keeps gnawing at me. Maybe it's just because my girls were involved. That's why I ordered more police protection today, which we really don't have the manpower to do. Thankfully, Detective Ingle offered to keep an eye on my family all day until I could get back from Nashville."

"So do you know yet who *did* go over the side of the bridge?"

"Not yet, but I think the TBI will know something soon. Whoever he was, he not only resembled Burrell, but he obviously had a strong desire not to be arrested."

"Detective Ingle told me about the snake tattoo."

"Even with the body being in the water for nearly twenty-four hours, it was quite an impressive tattoo. Just a long, hideous-looking snake. And yes, it appears to be the very guy you spoke with on campus."

Chills crept up my arm. My thoughts swirled back to the newspaper article and the fugitive.

"What should I do now after being plastered all over the news?"

"Avoid campus and stay at Eli's like I told you on the phone. We'll patrol that area as much as possible without giving away your location." Mark's eyes narrowed and he studied the side of my face.

"Tell me, BC, why didn't you fight back against Dylan?"

"I just didn't."

"He's a big guy, but I can't see you being intimidated. I think you had another reason."

"I guess I wasn't looking for more trouble."

"Maybe, but I think it had to do with the same reason you tried to take the blame for Laurie a few minutes ago.

You just lied to me trying to keep her out of trouble. I think you didn't fight Dylan because you knew it wouldn't sit well with Laurie."

I didn't answer.

"And I think you have strong feelings for my daughter." I fidgeted with the Baptist hymnal sitting in a wooden slot on the back of the pew in front of me. "BC, if you do, I only ask that you pursue her slowly. Laurie hides it well, but she's a little wounded right now. And wounded daughters make for very protective parents." I thought back to Donna, after the singing, standing fiery eyed in front of Dylan.

"Do you understand?" Mark asked.

I understood. I understood completely.

Or in other words, tread carefully college boy. Daddy carries a gun and Mama Bear can bite.

45

I felt like a good 'ole country boy driving Eli's truck. No automatic windows, no CD player, no carpet on the floorboard. Just a long bench seat, a skinny black steering wheel, two knobs on a radio, and over a quarter of a million miles on the odometer. Like its owner, the truck was simple but well preserved.

After leaving the sanctuary, and scanning the parking lot for signs of Dylan's jeep, I had found Eli walking back from the youth building with a stern-faced, bald gentleman. As I met them near the truck, Eli tossed me his keys and joked to the other man that he had hired a chauffeur for the summer. My pleasant greeting didn't receive much response from the other gentleman.

We finally settled into the front seat of Eli's truck. "Some people," he muttered.

"What about 'em?" I asked. Either the truck or Eli was causing me to talk country.

"Some old folks just tire me out with their bickering," he continued. "He took me over to the old sanctuary and showed me all the youth had built and the fish they had painted on the walls. The way he spoke about it, you'd a thought that Satan himself had set up headquarters in there."

We pulled through the parking lot toward the highway. "Well, what *did* you think about it?"

"I loved it. A building doesn't need to waste away if it can be used to bring in the unchurched. And some of what us old folks like don't appeal to the young crowd. But I liked that big wooden stage. And I loved those painted fish with the dates of when those kids were saved. That youth minister is doing good work. I may have to come to one of those *Wave 5:42s*."

The thought of Eli surrounded by teens jamming for Jesus made me laugh.

"I'm serious," he said.

"I know you are, that's why it's funny."

Eli pulled his seat belt across his lap. "Did you and Mark get everything straightened out in there?" The mentioning of Mark's name reminded me of what I had wanted to ask Eli.

"I think so. But what does it mean to *give your testimony*? Like what the pastor said Mark was doing Wednesday night."

"It means that Mark is going to tell his story. He'll share publicly how he accepted Jesus Christ as the Lord of his life. Why, you interested in coming back?"

"Maybe."

"That Harmony Grove would be a good place for a young guy like you to get involved. And from the way you watched that oldest Boone girl sing, I'd say you already have some motivation." The preacher shot me a mischievous grin.

"I might go back Wednesday night," I said.

"Well, if the devil don't fill your schedule I'll join you."

"The *devil*...," I snickered. "Do you really believe that there is a devil out there keeping people out of church and doing evil deeds?"

"Yes I do, BC. And he is as real as Joe Vaughn Burrell." Eli knew how to get my attention. "I believe in scripture, BC, so I believe in Satan…and his demons."

My mind formed the comical image of a mischievous red devil holding a pitchfork, and suddenly, I remembered Cougar's question from our late-night trek through campus. I wondered if I could stump the preacher.

"If the devil, or Satan, is so clever and smart, do you think he is able to read?"

"I would think he can read every language," answered Eli.

"And if the Bible is from an all-knowing God, and tells us that Satan is going to lose in the end, why doesn't Satan just give up? You know…if it's pointless for him."

"Because it's not pointless for Satan."

"What do you mean?"

"Well, BC, Satan won't give up because of *pride*. Pride is his greatest sin and the reason for his downfall. I think Satan is so arrogant and full of self-pride that he actually thinks he can change the words of Revelation. And even if he does know that he can't defeat Jesus Christ, which he can't, he'll continue just out of spite."

"Out of spite?"

"Satan *will* go to an everlasting hell and he'll gladly take as many souls as he possibly can just to keep them from everlasting joy with Jesus. So, keeping souls from heaven is not pointless work for Satan."

I needed Eli for my next religious discussion with Cougar.

"You know, BC, they probably go over these issues at Harmony Grove."

Harmony Grove. I thought back to the wooden cross hanging in the sanctuary, the one Mark pointed to after I lied to him. Even in church, trying to be good, trying not to hunger for the beautiful girl playing the piano, trying not to wish harm against her ex-boyfriend sitting a few pews in front of me, I had sinned. How had a man lived into adulthood without ever sinning? If it was true then he *wasn't* a mortal. If it was true then he had to be God. I imagined Jesus hanging from that very cross inside Harmony Grove and streaks of blood dripping from his pierced hands and feet to the carpeted stage below.

Could I believe the son of God really came to earth just to die? Could I believe that?

We continued down the two-lane road.

"Eli, when Jesus was dying on the cross, did Satan think that he had won?"

"That's a deep question, son. But I think humble sacrifice is something Satan can't understand. I believe Satan was utterly confused by what Jesus was doing on the cross. Perhaps he did think he had won. But three days later he wasn't confused. Three days later Satan knew he was in serious trouble."

"Because of the resurrection?"

"Absolutely, BC...because of the resurrection."

Rising from the dead. Coming back to life. How was such a thing even possible?

Eli read my mind in the silence. "I'm not talking about a Joe Vaughn Burrell case-of-mistaken-identity type of resurrection," he said. "I'm talking about a nailed on a cross, pierced with a spear, sealed in a tomb *dead* kind of resurrection. Now how cool is that?"

"Did you just use the word *cool?*"

"Why?" Eli asked. "Have you young folks already changed words on me again?"

"No, *cool* still works," I answered. Maybe I really could picture the old man jamming for Jesus at the next Wave 5:42.

46

"*Y*ou have reached Captain Mark Boone of the Halston County Sheriff's Department, please leave a message and I'll get back with you when time allows.*"*

Kneeling in his bedroom, holding a small notepad in his trembling hand, Detective Trent Ingle could feel the steel pressing into the back of his head. He studied the words Burrell had written and tried to catch his breath as he waited for the beep of Captain Mark Boone's voicemail.

"Hey Captain, this is Trent," the detective said. "Sorry to leave this message so late...but I won't be in tomorrow, got some sort of stomach bug...been throwing up most of the night. Trish has it too. I'll get back in touch with you when I can."

As the phone went silent, Detective Ingle felt the steel tip of the revolver lift from his head, but a swift kick to the back of his wounded, gunshot shoulder sent pain coursing through his fatigued body. He braced his fall against the floor with wrists latched together with duct tape. The detective's shirt had been pulled over the shoulder, bunched around his neck, and a hornet's nest of duct tape covered the wound.

"Now detective, let's see if you can be a little more cooperative this time. You will not want to see the next

259

round of pictures I take with your wife. I promise you that."

Joe Vaughn Burrell slammed the heel of his boot against the detective's shoulder, and then waited for Trent Ingle's scream to subside before getting back to his interrogation.

47

Joe Vaughn Burrell found me.

I had tried to fight him from my mind as I tossed and turned until well past midnight, but once again he found me in my dream. But this time, after kicking his clutching grip from my leg and swimming for the surface, I heard the splash of Burrell breaching the water behind me. I swam for my life. I swam through the fog for an unseen shore while his arrogant laugh grew closer and closer. *Swim faster. Wake up. Swim faster. Wake-*

I willed myself awake, but there he was. A figure of black in my doorway. He came forward. Dark. Looming. Real. Silhouetted by the stairwell light.

My heart jumped, my mind fired shock waves to alert my arms and legs. *Get up, go, move.* I spun off the bed. The sheets clung to my legs as I twisted, snatching my feet like a cowboy's lasso. An awkward grunt escaped as I tried to get my hands extended before my face met the floor.

"Whoa, BC, it's me...Coach Glynn."

A blinding light flashed from above as Coach Glynn pulled the chain on the ceiling fan light. I lay on the floor, boxers only, a thin sheet wrapped around my lower legs. Above me, Coach Glynn wore black athletic pants, a solid black form-fitting athletic shirt, and black Adidas running shoes. He tossed some folded newspapers on the edge of the bed and reached down to lend me a hand.

"I didn't mean to startle you, BC."

"Good grief, Coach, you're only dressed like the grim reaper. What are you doing here?"

"Looking for the *Cohutta Hoopster Hero*. What else?"

As far I could remember, Coach Glynn had never stepped foot in any of my dorm rooms, much less my bedroom. I untangled my feet from the twisted sheet and looked for a shirt.

"I've called your cell about ten times."

"You and everybody else," I answered, not realizing how rude I sounded until seeing Coach's expression.

"I really didn't expect to find you here. The rumor on campus is that you're hiding out of town with a friend. I looked up Eli's address in the phone book and came by just to check."

"It's a good spot to hide out. No one from campus knows I'm here."

"Besides me."

"Right...besides you. But what's the deal with the black? You about gave me a heart attack."

Coach Glynn turned and held in his slight pudge of a mid-section. "My wife says black has a slimming effect." I filed that Coach Glynn quote in my memory to share with the guys later. Cougar especially.

I slid on a pair of basketball shorts and rubbed my eyes. "So what brings you out here so early?"

Coach Glynn walked to the window and removed the blanket hanging over the blinds. More light poured into the room. "It's nearly eleven BC, no wonder you struggle with those early morning practices during the season. But I came by for a couple reasons. First, I just wanted to check on you and see if I could help in anyway."

"Thanks Coach, but I'm just going to lay low and avoid campus. You can tell the guys at the athletic department I won't be at work for a few days, maybe longer."

"I'll tell them, but I don't think you can totally avoid campus. That's the other reason I came out. Dean McAllister has called me repeatedly. He wants you in his office as soon as possible."

"Can't I just call-"

"No, I asked about you calling him. Dean McAllister was very adamant about you being there in person. He wouldn't give me any details. But there are several news crews on campus, so I suppose he wants to discuss how the college wants to deal with the media situation. I've already turned down about five interview requests myself."

Dean McAllister. I had no desire to ever enter Dean McAllister's office again. He had interrogated me, broke me, and threatened me after a momentary lapse of judgment during my junior year, the same poor decision which led to my three-game suspension in basketball.

Coach Glynn moved toward the doorway. "So you really saved two girls from being abducted?" he asked.

Sitting on the bed, I picked up the newspapers Coach had brought. "Yep."

"And the guy you stopped is still on the loose?"

"Back from the dead," I said.

"And you're sure you're okay?"

The phone rang across the hallway. It quit after one ring. "Was Eli down there?" I asked.

"He sent me right up when I asked about you. But he didn't mention that you were still asleep." *Did the closed door and total darkness not give it away, Coach?* The man in black turned toward my training calendar pinned to the wall. "Four days until try-outs, huh?"

"Yes sir, hopefully this will all be over by then."

Footsteps sounded on the stair case outside the door. "BC, phone call, it's your mom!" Eli yelled.

Coach grinned and pointed to the newspapers I held. "Just some more articles about you in today's papers. And when I asked you to step up and be a leader, I didn't mean you had to become a famous crime fighter. But I'm proud of you, BC, just let me know if I can do anything."

"Thanks Coach."

"BC!" Eli yelled again. I followed Coach Glynn through the bedroom doorway and found Eli on the third step from the bottom holding a phone, its cord stretched as far and tight as possible. He held his hand over the mouthpiece. Coach patted Eli on the shoulder as he passed.

"Nice to meet you, Coach Glynn."

"Take care, Mr. Giles," replied Coach before letting himself out.

I lowered my voice. "Eli, tell her I'll call her back."

"Nope, house rule number four, I just added it. Worried mommas always get what they want, and she doesn't sound happy." *Which was why I wanted to call her later.*

I moved to the upstairs den, picked up the phone, and waited until I heard the click of Eli hanging up downstairs.

"Hey, Mom."

"Mothers get what they want, and I've decided I want my son at home. Got it?"

"So you heard Eli?"

"I did. But why didn't I hear from my son last night?"

"We went to church and-"

"Church? That's a new one."

"Sorry, Mom, but I'm safe here. And I know I promised to call, but-"

"BC, that's not the only reason I'm calling. Do you know a Dean McAllister? He's already called here twice this morning. He is one loud and persistent individual. Will you-"

"Go to his office so he'll quit calling you."

"Exactly…then get your tail home to Dalton."

* * *

After a quick shower I headed down to Eli's living room to slide on my shoes. Eli held the Nashville paper, apparently given to him by Coach Glynn, and was reading in his recliner. I didn't expect him to do so aloud.

"The initial break in discovering the identity of Joe Vaughn Burrell appears to have taken place because of the late-night hunger of a Cohutta College senior," read Eli, shooting me a grin before getting back to the paper.

"According to a source affiliated with area law enforcement, in the early morning hours of Saturday, June 1, Joe Vaughn Burrell's attempt to abduct two females from the Waffle Shack parking lot in Andrews was spoiled by the heroic actions of Bradley 'BC' Morrow, a rising senior at Cohutta College.

According to the school's athletic website, Morrow, 21, is a Dalton, Georgia native and plays on the Cohutta College men's basketball team. According to the source, after witnessing Burrell's attack on the two unsuspecting victims, Morrow rushed across the restaurant parking area and a scuffle ensued, allowing both females to escape. Before the suspect fled, the source also credits Morrow for obtaining the license plate number of the vehicle. It is believed that the two unidentified females, as well as Morrow, suffered only minor scrapes and bruises during the encounter. Morrow has not been available for comment on the incident.

Burrell, 37, whose body was originally thought to have been pulled from Nickajack Lake on Saturday afternoon, is now the prime suspect in another unsolved abduction and may be linked to two others. The source did not divulge the names of the victims in those abductions, citing the cases were currently under intense investigation.

The body of the fleeing suspect who leapt from the I-24 bridge over Nickajack Lake during a stand-off with police has yet to be identified. That individual's connection to Joe Vaughn Burrell has not been…"

*Abduction…murder…*the words created more emotion now that I actually knew and cared for Laurie and Maggie Boone. Images from that fateful night flashed back into my memory. *What if I hadn't been there? What if Burrell had taken them?* The thoughts angered me and I suddenly wished more than ever that Joe Vaughn Burrell had indeed found the bottom of that lake.

"So who did they pull from Nickajack?" asked Eli, taking a break from the article.

"I wish I knew." I started for the door.

"Son, you're in the midst of one strange story," Eli said. "Murder, abduction, folks jumping off bridges, a fugitive on the loose…these reporters are loving you."

"Well, it's time to find out what Dean McAllister thinks about it. I've been summoned to campus, Eli. I just hope Captain Boone doesn't get too upset with me."

"Hold on," said Eli. He popped out of his recliner and scurried down the hallway to the kitchen. He returned with the Wally's Farm Supply hat and the keys to his truck. "Everybody on campus is looking for you and your little car, so if you're going to chance it-"

"Do it undercover," I finished.

48

I parked Eli's truck along the curb in front of the white Victorian style house with the black shutters and the wide front porch. Across the street, in the college's main quad, a camera man and reporter used the stone academic buildings as a backdrop as a curious group of students looked on from a distance. I pulled my hat lower and exited the truck. My police escort pulled along the curb several spaces behind me.

From my freshman orientation I still remembered that the historic three-story home, nestled among a mixture of cherry and dogwood trees, had served many uses for the college for more than a century. But during my time on campus it had always functioned as the administrative annex.

And this was my second trip to see the dean.

After crossing the sidewalk I followed the narrow brick path which divided an immaculate lawn. Flashbacks of my previous trip to Dean McAllister's office emerged as I climbed the steps to the porch. *But this time*, I reminded myself, *I was being summoned as a hero. Perhaps the college wanted to market me and put me on display as an example of its values.*

I turned the knob of the thick, solid oak front door. Inside, behind an L-shaped antique desk, an attractive brunette receptionist turned her attention from her computer monitor and the Solitaire rows that lined the screen.

"I'm here to see-"

"Hey, BC," she said. I studied her face more closely.

"Hey, Julie, I didn't recognize you with your hair down."

"And not falling on my face," she added, obviously a little embarrassed. "Hopefully I look better than I did the last time you saw me, but I actually saw you at Harmony Grove last night. Are you going to church there now?"

"Um, I don't know...I was summoned to see Dean McAllister."

Julie held up a copy of the same Nashville newspaper Coach Glynn had brought to Eli's. "I know, I've read all about it." She laid the paper back on the desk and motioned toward the vacant seats of the small waiting area. "You're obviously next, but you'll never guess who he's meeting with right now."

Before I could respond a figure appeared in the old home's main hallway.

"Hey, superstar! I thought you were in hiding?" rang Brody Payne's voice.

"You were meeting with McAllister?" I asked.

"Yeah, it seems somebody left a flask with my initials on it in the dining hall yesterday. Odd, huh?" Payne grinned, shrugged, and then slapped me on the shoulder. I started to ask how his meeting with the dean ended, but he was moving unusually quick.

"Gotta run guys...take care *superstar*...I'll get your autograph later. See ya, Julie," said Payne, looking at the receptionist. "And tell your new roommates to keep the noise down." The last line dripped with sarcasm.

"New roommates?" I asked as the front door closed behind Payne.

"The two girls across the hall had an open room and I asked if I could move in." Again she lowered her eyes as if embarrassed.

"Not going well with Chelsea and Samantha?" I asked.

"It was me, not them. I just needed a different environment, not that they took it very well when I tried to explain. But I've got to pass my summer classes, and I'm not really much of a party girl-"

"Mr. Morrow!" roared a voice from the hallway. Dean McAllister's head tilted from his office door. "I will see you now."

* * *

Someone once told me that as a person ages the nose and ears never stop growing. I remember this each time I encounter Dean McAllister.

But even with his elongated lobes and thick beak, it is Dean McAllister's dominating voice that is truly unforgettable. It booms. It echoes. It tests the eardrums. For Dean McAllister there is little difference between yelling and casually conversing. And unfortunately, he seems oblivious to his abnormal volume, even with his monstrous ears.

"Shut that door and take a seat," the dean thundered as I entered his office. He remained behind his desk and kept his focus on a large stack of papers. Dean McAllister seemed in no hurry to deal with me and there was no comfort to be found in the wooden chairs arranged too close to his desk. I studied his ears and hoped he wasn't able to hear my thoughts.

Dean McAllister lowered his pen, straightened himself in his high-back chair, and furrowed his brow. "Tell me all about it, Mr. Morrow," he roared.

"Well, sir, I was at the Waffle Shack and I noticed this guy-"

"Not that," Dean McAllister bellowed. "If I want to know all about that I'll read the paper or search the Internet. Tell me about the fire alarm you pulled Saturday night at Holtman. That is what I want to hear about."

I froze. A half minute passed. I was well beyond the point of denying it with any credibility and I knew it. Dean McAllister knew it too. He returned to his papers and left me drowning in silence.

Start with something simple, I told myself. *But who had told? Julie?...Payne?*

Without looking up, Dean McAllister resumed his interrogation.

"Do you remember our last conversation in here?" he asked. "I do. It was about six months ago. You told me the most incredulous story and wanted me to be naïve enough to believe it. So, after you tell me why you pulled the fire alarm, which is a felony to do so in a public building, and had a fire unit unnecessarily deployed to one of our dormitories, try and give me one reason why you should not be expelled from Cohutta College. Because I can't think of one."

Expelled? What happened to being summoned to the dean for my heroic medal of honor? For my "we're proud of you son" slap on the back? Expelled meant no senior year, no basketball,...and no Europe.

Dean McAllister held his glare a bit longer before reaching to pull out a bottom drawer. He lifted a red folder, slid out a stapled packet containing several pages, and dropped it on the desk. He lifted his pen and leaned in to write.

He thinks I did this just to be a punk…a nuisance…

"Mr. Morrow, 'BC' does stand for *Bradley Curran*, correct?"

He has no idea I did it for the girl just right down the hallway.

"Mr. Morrow," he repeated. "I can fill out these forms with or without you."

And what were the chances that I would see Julie again…right before meeting the dean? Does this mean she had told? Or does this mean that I should-

"BC, I assume your silence confirms your guilt. I will make a decision and get back with you. At the very least you should expect a fine and a one-year loss of all athletic eligibility. But you know where the door is, and I'm sure you have reporters outside to speak with."

The truth shall set you free…The truth shall set you free…The truth shall…

"I pulled it," I announced. "Just me. I was with some friends and we were at Holtman after hours. We had spent the day at Lost Pond and then went back to Holtman to grill and hang out. It got late and my friend was with a girl who had drunk entirely too much. She was in bad shape, they both were, but she didn't know what she was doing. And then they disappeared into a bedroom. She didn't need to be back there with him but she was. I *had* to do something. I was with her roommate and I didn't need to be around her either. It wasn't right, nothing was right, and I didn't know what to do. I couldn't barge into the bedroom and tell them to quit. So I went into the hallway to think…and then I just pulled the alarm. I'm sorry it caused a hassle with the fire department. I'm sorry that it was illegal. But I can't say that I'll ever be sorry that I found a way to get that girl out of that situation. She didn't need to be in that bedroom."

My rant had gotten Dean McAllister's full attention, but I had obviously forgotten to breathe. My chest rose and fell in its search for oxygen. I lowered my eyes. I didn't want him to speak. I didn't want him to say anything. I knew the heartless man wouldn't care one bit what my reason had been. He lived in the world of black and white rules and I was guilty.

How could I have put myself in this situation? Why had I gotten involved in Cougar and Julie's business?

I debated which punishment would be worse, being expelled from Cohutta College or being allowed to stay while stripped of all athletic eligibility and losing the opportunity to play basketball on campus and in Europe. I knew that Dean McAllister's decision could be appealed to the Student Disciplinary Council, but that group of intellectual overachievers, social innocents, and power pleasers never went against the dean, and especially not for a good-timing jock.

"BC."

I raised my eyes for the verdict.

Dean McAllister clasped his hands and rested his chin on his knuckles. "You told me the absolute truth, didn't you?"

"Yes sir, I did. And I would like to keep the names of the others out of this."

"And if I ask you for their names?"

"I'd prefer you didn't, sir, but I'll tell you if you ask me."

Dean McAllister readjusted in his chair. He took the packet of papers in front of him and slid them back into the red file folder. He picked up his pen and tapped it repeatedly on his desk.

"BC Morrow, you have changed," he finally stated. "I don't think I am speaking with the same individual that I spoke with before. And the individual sitting before me now should not be held accountable for offenses committed by the former individual. This, to me, seems to be your first offense. There will no doubt be a consequence to this illegal and potentially dangerous action that took place in Holtman. But since this is the first offense of the honest young man sitting before me, neither expulsion nor extra-curricular suspension will be considered."

It took several seconds for his verdict to sink in.

"Thank you, Dean McAllister," I said, rising from my chair. He half-swiveled his chair and leaned awkwardly to reach an elegant wooden table behind his desk. He righted himself and spun back to face me holding the day's newspaper. He held it up so I could see my own picture.

"And now I would like to hear about this," requested the dean.

"It's a long story, Dean McAllister."

"I'm all ears," he stated.

Yes, you are, I thought. *Yes, you are.*

49

T he Rattler smiled.

"Admit it, Detective Ingle, it is a beautiful plan. Would you like to hear it again?"

Trent Ingle didn't respond. With duct tape covering his mouth he couldn't respond. But the detective, wounded, beaten, sitting on a concrete floor and hand-cuffed to a metal pipe running out of the wall, kept his eyes transfixed on his wife's face across the darkened basement. Even from a distance, even in the dim light, the torture and hopelessness in her eyes was obvious.

Joe Vaughn Burrell squatted beside the detective and whispered. "Trent, beautiful plans are comprised of many elements. Opportunity, timing, resources, and most importantly..."

Burrell stood, removed the knife from his belt, and moved across the small basement toward the detective's wife. Trish Ingle, shaking, bound similarly as her husband, flinched as Burrell ran his hand along the side of her head and slowly stroked her hair. Suddenly, he yanked her blonde hair and sliced off a large portion with his blade. He brought the blonde clump up to his lips, tasting it with the tips of his tongue.

"Motivation, Trent. The most important part of a beautiful plan is motivation. I know I have mine, but what is going to be your motivation tonight?"

The detective hung his head.

"Don't fret Trent, all is not lost," Burrell said as he moved back toward the detective. "You should be honored to have such a prominent role in my plan. You and I finding each other was simply fate, simply destiny."

Joe Vaughn Burrell squatted once again in front of the detective, then took the clump of Trish Ingle's hair and brushed it up and down the detective's face. Trent Ingle kept his eyes downward toward the concrete floor.

"But Trent," the Rattler whispered, dropping the clump of blonde hair into the detective's lap, "just in case you don't see yourself cooperating fully, I want you to think about your motivation. It would be a pity if you didn't cooperate, since she has so much life left in her."

The detective turned his face toward the wall.

Joe Vaughn Burrell hissed and laughed and sat on the concrete floor. "Oh yes, Detective Ingle, let's go over our plan once again. You see, beautiful and successful plans are made up of several elements, such as opportunity, timing, resources, and…"

275

The flashing blue lights startled me.

I pulled Eli's truck to the side of the road and wondered if I had missed a stop sign or failed to use my blinker. The aging pick-up was obviously not capable of speeding, but it was somewhat nerve-wracking being trailed at every turn by a patrolman. The officer only gave the siren a short blast, and after trailing me to the shoulder of the road, turned off the flashing blue lights.

I checked my rearview mirror. Behind me sat a charcoal gray Ford Explorer.

Mark. Smooth as always, I hadn't even noticed him take the place of my patrolman escort.

I exited the truck and raised my arms high in the air like a criminal at gunpoint. As I approached the Explorer, Mark lowered his darkly tinted window.

"We heard you were headed back to Eli's." he said.

We?

I peered past Mark to find Laurie waving from the passenger seat. "Hey BC," she said. "You look like a local boy driving that old truck."

"That was my intention," I shot back, pointing up to my *Wally's* hat.

"We'll follow you over to Eli's. We've got some news for you," said Mark.

"Can I get a blue light escort?" I asked.

"I don't think so."

I started back toward Eli's truck when another idea struck me. I turned back toward the Explorer and Mark again rolled his window down. After my meeting with Dean McAllister I was feeling quite brave. And honest.

"Captain Boone," I said respectfully, but loud enough for both of the Explorer's occupants to hear. "If you don't mind, I would like to ask your permission for Laurie Boone to ride with me the rest of the way."

Mark looked toward Laurie for her answer.

She grinned and opened the passenger side door.

* * *

I pulled Eli's truck from the roadside with Laurie Boone sitting across the seat. She wore lengthy, form-fitting white shorts, cuffed at the bottom, and a navy t-shirt with *Toccoa Falls College* written across the front. She held a light blue envelope in her hand.

"What's that?" I asked.

"Just a letter to a boy," she answered.

"What boy might that be?"

"Just a boy who thinks he can write a letter apologizing for his stupidity and all will be forgiven."

"A *stupid* boy, huh?"

"Yep."

"So he doesn't have a chance of having his apology accepted?"

"He'll just have to read the letter."

"Does the letter happen to mention anything about a fight with the girl's ex-boyfriend?"

"No, it doesn't. But I'm told it wasn't much of a fight."

Low blow Laurie.

"Would you have rather I-"

"I'm just kidding with you, BC," interrupted Laurie. "I'm glad you didn't start that mess with Dylan. If you remember, I already know that you'll fight when needed…when it's right. I know all about what happened with Dylan." Laurie pointed back toward the Explorer following us closely. "After church last night dad spoke again with the officer who worked it…and I also spoke with Dylan."

"And what did he have to say?"

"That you were too scared to fight him and that he knocked your head off."

"And what did you say to him?"

"Goodbye."

I liked Laurie's answer, and I was done thinking about Dylan as well. I just wondered if the big lad with the solid right punch was done thinking about me.

"Is that what your dad wants to discuss?...Dylan?"

"No," said Laurie, turning her stare toward the passenger side window. "He wants to talk about the body pulled from Nickajack Lake…they know who it is now."

"And?"

Laurie looked back my direction. "Even dead, the man is definitely someone we need to worry about."

* * *

A strange vehicle was parked in front of Eli's house when we arrived. The dark, older model BMW with Georgia plates had come to a stop more in the grass than in the driveway.

As I waited beside the truck for Mark to arrive, Laurie head-ed down Eli's long gravel driveway.

"Where are you going?" I asked.

"To put a letter in the mailbox," she responded, keeping her back to me while holding the envelope overhead. "You can read it after we leave." Mark, slowly pulling down the driveway behind us, gave his daughter a strange look as he passed her. He lowered his window as he parked beside me.

"And what did you say to tick her off this time?" Mark asked, smiling.

"She's putting a letter in the mailbox, says I can't read it until you guys leave. Is that good or bad?"

"I'm afraid I can't help you on that one," replied Mark, studying the car parked oddly in the grass. "We can stay on the porch and not bother Eli and his company."

"He didn't mention having company. I'm not sure whose car that is."

Mark reached for some papers in his car and I headed for the porch. I hesitated as loud, muffled voices came from inside the house. Seconds later, the escaping murmurs be-came louder, angrier. Someone shouted from within. I sprinted for the front door and attempted to clear all the steps on one leap.

My left shoe caught the edge of the last step, sending my body forward. I landed face down on the stone porch. By the time I recovered back to my feet, Mark had passed me and was entering the house. I noticed that his right hand gripped the handle of his holstered pistol. Catching the screen door before it closed, I followed the detective into the house.

"Whoa Mark!" yelled Eli as we barreled into the living room. The unknown, dark-headed figure standing beside the red-faced Eli instinctively stepped back and raised his hands. The stranger's eyes were locked on Mark's pistol.

"Mark...BC...," said Eli, obviously trying to calm everyone down, including himself. "I'd like for you two to meet my son Joseph."

51

According to Captain Mark Boone, Randall "Copperhead" Gore had several things in common with his cousin Joe Vaughn Burrell. Both stood over six-feet tall. Both had tattooed serpents stretching from wrist to wrist. Both were in their late thirties and had spent time behind bars. And like Joe Vaughn Burrell, Randy Gore had a desire to abduct young girls.

Mark pulled a piece of paper from a file and laid it on Eli's kitchen table. Mug shots of both men were aligned side by side. Laurie examined the paper and then slid it toward me. It was easy to see the resemblance in the two men, and it was strange to think I had encountered both of these deranged individuals.

The TBI had searched Randy Gore's home shortly after they identified his body. And according to Mark, what they had found filled in many missing pieces.

Gore took his first victim thirteen months before his own death. Karen Vickers had spent a May evening enjoying a graduation party along with thirty or forty others near the University of Tennessee campus in Knoxville, but according to witnesses, after an argument with her boyfriend, Karen made the decision to walk back to her apartment alone.

Until the search of Randy Gore's house, no one knew why she had never made it home.

The picture of Claire Beasley that appeared in the papers after New Year's depicted an attractive and innocent face, but the articles told of a life filled with issues. During her first week of work at Lowery's, a more bar than restaurant establishment twenty-five miles east of Chattanooga, Claire became Gore's second victim.

Following her parents' divorce, two miserable academic semesters at the University of Tennessee at Chattanooga, and another half-year of wasting her father's money at a nearby junior college, Claire Beasley disappeared. Perhaps, many had theorized, the troubled girl fled town to start fresh somewhere new. The pictures in the photo album beneath Randy Gore's bed proved otherwise.

"Have the relatives of the two girls been told?" I asked.

"I am sure they were informed today," replied Mark.

Laurie closed her eyes and lowered her head as if saying a quick prayer. The kitchen became strangely quiet and I could hear Eli and Joseph still talking on the back porch. The tone of their conversation had changed drastically since we arrived.

"Do you want to hear the rest?" Mark asked, rubbing the top of Laurie's hand. She nodded for him to continue.

Besides being young and attractive, Karen Vickers and Claire Beasley shared one last common bond. Both had spent their final days in a windowless backroom of a small brick home on Randy Gore's eight rugged, secluded acres near Dunlap, twenty miles north of Chattanooga.

In the home, TBI agents found everything needed to incriminate Randy Gore except the bodies of the two girls. According to Mark, had Gore not sunk to the bottom of

Nickajack Lake, he would have taken his last breath from the electric chair.

Besides various pictures of their time in captivity, the album contained headlines and articles from regional newspapers concerning the abductions. It also contained two thick locks of hair. The hair of each victim was twisted and taped to form a number. Karen Vickers dark hair formed a *1* and Claire Beasley's auburn strands were fashioned into a *2*.

Except for the last page, the remaining pages of the photo album were blank, eerily waiting to be filled.

It was the final page that clarified much for investigators and produced another link to Joe Vaughn Burrell. A three-by-five picture of thin, dark wrists bound with a black cord was taped oddly in the back. No news clippings or strands of hair accompanied it. The wrists in the photo were crossed, exposing the palms and slender, curled fingers. Inside one palm, written in what appeared to be paint or blood, was again written the number *1*.

But the skin's complexion, appearing almost of Asian descent, did not belong to Karen Vickers. This victim was a different number one. This was Joe Vaughn Burrell's number one. This was the Rattler's first abduction.

And Laurie and Maggie Boone would have been numbers two and three.

A distinct healed scar between the left thumb and forefinger helped identify the girl in Burrell's picture from a missing person's database. Her name was Susan Kim, and her clothes had already been found, folded neatly, in the basement of Joe Vaughn Burrell's Belford home. The same home Laurie and I had seen with our own eyes. The picture explained another mystery for law enforcement. In bold red on a basement wall, Joe Vaughn Burrell had chalked an odd set of large letters and numbers.

R-1 C-2 had made little sense at the time, but agents now understood. It was Joe Vaughn Burrell's scoreboard, and he was losing.

The Rattler: 1 abduction. The Copperhead: 2.

The same pictures of hair twisted into numbers from Randall Gore's album were also found during the raid of Joe Vaughn Burrell's home. The cousins were boasting to each other of their conquests, and the game had become competitive. By snatching both Laurie and Maggie Boone, Joe Vaughn Burrell had intended to take the lead.

* * *

Mark tapped on the paper displaying the two cousins. "These two competed with each other in a very sickening way. And BC, you not only messed up Burrell's big night and kept him from taking the lead, but you are also responsible for the break in the case that put Burrell on the run and resulted in his cousin's death."

"So what are you saying?"

"I guess there's a chance Joe Vaughn Burrell could be happy knowing his opponent is dead, but I don't think so. I would think he's even angrier now that the Copperhead is out of the game, and thanks to the media, Burrell now has a name and face for his rage."

"What do you want BC to do?" asked Laurie.

"My mom wants me at home," I answered.

"Yes, she does," answered Mark surprisingly. "I called her earlier, but Dalton is not where I want you to go. I'm sending Laurie and Maggie with Donna to White Creek, Missouri tomorrow morning. Our church-building mission group doesn't leave until Friday evening, but there is already another church group working in Missouri who they can stay with, so they are just going early. I'm staying here until Joe Vaughn Burrell is located, but I'd feel better if you'd consider going with my family to Missouri and getting out of this area."

"On the mission trip?"

"It is the safest place I can think-"

"Mark," I interrupted. "In just four days…Friday morning…I'm leaving for the all-conference try-outs in Nashville. I plan to be in Europe playing basketball this August. I can't go to Missouri and-"

"BC, my goal is to make sure that you're still alive in August."

"Mark, I understand that. But I can't pass up the opportunity to play in Europe. I've trained for months and I'll never have a chance like this again."

"I know that, BC, but this situation is slipping out my hands. The TBI has completely taken over the case, and I assume federal agents will also be involved."

"And you want me in the church version of the witness relocation program? Mark, I just can't do it."

"That is what your mom knew you would say, so I made her a second offer."

"And what is that?"

"*Boone house arrest*," Mark answered. "Starting tomorrow, once my family leaves, you'll be staying with me until Joe Vaughn Burrell is in custody."

.

52

I didn't realize that Eli and Joseph Giles were waiting to speak with me until after I had waved goodbye to Laurie and Mark from the front porch. As I reentered the house both men stood in the living room. Joseph was thin like his father but taller, and by my guess was in his early-forties. His curly, dark hair stood several inches off his forehead and his slim, black eyeglasses gave him the look of an intellectual. Joseph's balding, overall-clad father decided to cut through the pleasantries.

"BC, my Joseph here is worried about that maniac coming here to look for you."

"My intentions were to discuss this with my dad in private," stated Joseph. "I apologize for losing my temper in front of you and Captain Boone earlier."

"I can step back outside Eli, it's no problem," I offered.

"Nonsense," responded Eli. Joseph kept silent but protested with his eyes. Eli moved across the room and dropped into his recliner. He pulled the handle and popped his feet off the floor. Joseph took the couch while I stood.

"Well, go ahead," said Eli toward his son. Joseph shifted to the front edge of the cushion.

"This isn't against you personally," began Joseph. "Like everybody else I've seen the news, and I've talked with dad, so I know what you did to help those girls. That was awesome…truly heroic, and it tells me a lot about you. But now I'm just concerned for my dad. With this Burrell guy still alive, I'm just afraid you being here puts my dad in danger." I gave an understanding nod and Joseph continued. "BC, I just want my dad to be safe, you understand that don't you?"

Selfishly, I hadn't once thought about my presence putting Eli at risk.

"I understand completely, Joseph, and I don't blame you for being worried. In my mind this house is the safest place I know. But if it makes you feel better, I'll be-"

"Staying right here where you're safe," interjected Eli.

Joseph lowered his gaze and grinded his palms together. "BC, my dad likes you. You obviously listen to his stories and he thinks you keep life entertaining."

"Real entertaining," smiled Eli, holding up a newspaper with my picture on the front.

"BC, I just can't be in Atlanta worrying-"

"I'll be leaving tomorrow, Joseph," I finally interjected. Both men looked in my direction.

"And where are you going?" demanded Eli.

"I'll be staying with Captain Boone. He's sending the rest of his family to the mission trip in Missouri tomorrow."

"And what about that Europe try-out?" asked Eli.

"I leave Friday morning if I can escape from Mark's."

The old man grinned and patted the arms of his recliner. "Well, I'll be right here if you need me," stated Eli.

"Dad, I need you to come with me to Atlanta. BC leaving actually makes me worry even more," said Joseph. "I know it's unlikely that this Burrell guy could track BC down, but what if he finds the house with no one here but you?"

"That won't happen," answered Eli.

"Why?" asked Joseph, "Are you going to invite some of your old deacons over for protection? Have a gathering of old men with shotguns on the porch?"

"What do you want me to do?" asked Eli.

"Come to Atlanta for a couple of weeks like I've already asked."

"Nope, I think I'm going on that mission trip to Missouri."

"Dad, you are not," Joseph barked, his brow furrowed. "You don't need to be climbing ladders and working in the heat. You've done enough mission-"

"I'm just messing with you Joe," said Eli, winking in my direction. "But son, I'll tell you what I do need. I need you to take me and my grandson to an Atlanta Braves game in that fancy stadium and I need some of those chili burgers and onion rings from that greasy place we use to visit."

"The *Varsity*? So you'll come back to Atlanta with me?"

"If you can meet those conditions."

I couldn't help but laugh at the serious expression Eli held while waiting on Joseph's answer. Joseph shook his head and then looked toward me. "How do you live with this guy?" he asked.

How could I not? I thought.

* * *

Eli and Joseph left for Atlanta after eight that evening.

Before walking out the door, Eli had offered to leave his ancient brown Bible for me to use. According to him, I could take it Wednesday night to Harmony Grove and also read it while I was under house arrest. Joseph, who warmed up to me after I agreed with his concerns, announced that he had something even better. He jogged to his car and returned with a box roughly the size of a small textbook.

"How about your very own?" Joseph asked, handing me the dense box as he came back inside the house. I pulled the top lid off and studied the navy blue cover of the holy book inside.

"Joseph, that is a very nice Bible," Eli commented.

"Are you sure?" I asked. I assumed thick Bibles, like college text books, weren't cheap.

"I'm involved in our Bible ministry at church," Joseph answered. "We found that the pocket-sized Bibles are hard to read and eventually get lost. And we wanted to show others that we were serious about them reading God's word." He pointed at Eli's ancient, battered Bible. "Why don't I give you one too, dad? The apostle Paul might want that one back."

I was waiting on the Giles boys to leave before I went to the mailbox to fetch Laurie's letter. Once we finally shook hands and said goodbyes, I didn't make it off the front porch before the phone rang. I headed back inside the house.

"Giles' residence," I answered.

"It's me dude," said a familiar voice. *Cougar.*

"How's Chattanooga?"

"I'm actually on the interstate. Are you partying tonight at the preacher's house?"

"Not exactly."

"I would stop and pick up some ladies but I'd hate for any fire alarms to get pulled," Cougar stated coldly. I walked toward the door, as far as the cord would reach, and peered down the driveway. *So what if Cougar knew?*

"Dean McAllister wasn't too happy about it either," I responded.

"Well, McAllister didn't miss the opportunity that I did," Cougar countered before the line went silent. He either hung up on me or drove through a dead spot. Maybe he really was that mad, but we were friends...we were teammates, and he'd get over it. I hung up Eli's phone and pulled out my cell to find Cougar's number, preferring to just call him back from the house rather than venturing out toward the rocks for reception.

Before I realized I still had Cougar listed under *Kit*, Eli's phone rang again.

"Hey Coug', are you seriously hanging up on me over a girl?" There was a moment of hesitation from the person breathing heavily on the other end.

"Hello? BC Morrow?" boomed Dean McAllister's voice. I readjusted the phone a few inches from my ear.

"Yes sir, Dean McAllister, this is BC. I didn't expect to hear from you today."

"Well, BC, sorry to contact you so late, but I was still in my office and had reached my decision. After reviewing all information and referring to past incidents of a similar nature for precedence, my ruling is that you will be suspended from all college dormitories for one year."

It took a moment for the implications of the dean's statement to filter through my brain.

"So I lose my dorm room for next year?" I asked.

"Correct, nor are you allowed to enter any dormitory on campus without administrative approval. Failure to comply with this directive will result in a more severe disciplinary action. Do you understand?"

"Yes sir, I think so. I have to live off campus, but I can still enter the other college buildings?"

"Correct."

"And play basketball?"

"That is correct. I will send a document concerning the suspension to your school mailbox and to your home, as well as paperwork concerning your right to appeal the decision to the Student Disciplinary Council."

"That won't be necessary Dean McAllister, I accept your ruling." It could have been worse, much worse, and I knew it.

"Son, just to make it clear. You will need to find your own accommodations off campus for your senior year at Cohutta College. Off campus housing is very limited in our area, so you need to begin searching as soon as possible."

I glanced around Eli Giles' home. Perhaps I *would* be spending a little more time with the preacher man.

53

*A*fter hanging up with Dean McAllister, I called my mom to let her know about the dorm suspension. I told her most of the story, but mainly I wanted it off my conscience and I wanted her to hear the story from me before she received the dean's letters. The conversation took longer than expected, and by the end I had tuned out my mom's lecture as my mind drifted back toward the distant mailbox.

As darkness pushed the final sliver of sun beneath the mountain and Laurie's letter beckoned me, my stroll down the driveway quickly picked up speed. Crickets cheered and mosquitoes chased me to the finish line. *But what had Laurie written? Would it simply be an acceptance of my apology? Or would it hint at something more?* I lowered the lid to Eli's oversized black mailbox and the remaining evening light revealed the light blue letter and a red digital camera.

Strange, I thought, *I hadn't seen Laurie with the camera.*

I took both items and closed the lid. I slapped a mosquito that attacked behind my knee and jogged back toward the house. Within minutes I was underneath the light of a living room lamp. I studied the light blue envelope with *BC* written in smooth purple ink, anxious to know its contents.

But the small red camera intrigued me.

I laid Laurie's unopened letter on top of the Bible Joseph had given me. I powered on the camera. The battery symbol flashed indicating it was still half-charged. I pushed the play button and a picture of Eli Giles' house emerged. It was taken from the end of the driveway. My car, Eli's truck, and Joseph's car were all distinctly visible. I scrolled to the next picture. It took several seconds for my mind to comprehend what I was seeing. My hands trembled.

This couldn't be.

I scrolled to the next picture...then the next.

How could he...

I dropped the camera to the ground, grabbed the Bible and Laurie's letter, and sprinted up the stairs. I slammed the door to the upstairs den behind me, locked it, and slid the couch against it. I grabbed the den phone and dialed.

"9-1-1 Emergency," answered a female voice.

"I need you to contact Captain Mark Boone!"

"Excuse me sir, can you please give me the address from where you-"

"I need Captain Mark Boone at Eli's! Tell him BC-"

"Sir, I need the address from which-"

"Burning Maple...333 Burning Maple," I yelled. "This is BC Morrow and-"

"Sir, can you calmly explain..."

I could explain everything, even with the camera still laying downstairs on the floor. Female hands bound together with a black cord. Fingernails painted pink. Across one pale palm ran a deep cut from which blood trickled.

The second picture was of a female's bare back with a large, black knife placed ominously against her skin.

The third picture showed a close-up of her eyes. Scared and pleading, but alive.

No envelope. No package. The camera had simply been placed in the mailbox.

Joe Vaughn Burrell had delivered it himself.

54

"There's the patrol car that follows me?" I demanded of the 911 operator. Hearing the sound of an approaching vehicle on the gravel drive, I crawled across the darkened upstairs den and peeked through the blinds hoping my security detail had returned.

"Sir, law enforcement is in route to your location. I'm not aware of any such patrol from earlier-"

"There are headlights coming down the driveway right now," I whispered to the female 911 dispatcher. "Is that an officer?"

"Sir, can you see blue lights activated on the vehicle?" she asked in reply, her tone professional, yet worried.

"No...no blue lights, it's just creeping slowly down the driveway."

"BC, just stay in the room and keep the light off," she instructed. When she spoke again it was hurried and obviously not directed toward me. "Unit seven, be advised, caller reports that an unknown vehicle is approaching the house. What is your ETA?"

I didn't hear the response but unit seven must have answered.

"BC, the deputies are a few minutes away. Stay on the line and keep me informed on the vehicle in the driveway. I have someone contacting Captain Boone."

The headlights continued to approach, turning off as they neared my parked Honda. I strained to see through the darkness. *Why hadn't I turned on the porch light when I ran out to get Laurie's letter?*

A single small light suddenly flickered behind the windshield.

"I think he's smoking," I told her.

"Can you see the driver?"

"It's dark…and there's a tree limb in the way, but he's just sitting in the car."

I spoke too soon. The car's interior light flashed as the driver opened the door. Peering through the blinds and the obstructing tree branches outside the window, all I could see was a blur of color and movement before the light vanished. The lit cigarette seemingly floated in the darkness beside the car before being dropped to the ground. A second later it disappeared, I assumed crushed beneath the foot of Joe Vaughn Burrell.

Darkness. Silence. My heart pounded. *Where had he gone?*

"BC!" he yelled.

Faint footsteps sounded below on the stone steps and then onto the porch.

I hadn't locked the front door behind me.

"He's on the porch," I whispered to the 911 operator as distant blue lights finally pulsated through the thicket of trees near the main road. The first police car hesitated to make the turn, but then picked up speed again as it raced down Eli's driveway. A second set of flashing lights followed close behind.

"The officers are here," I relayed into the phone. Sirens wailed. Tires slid to a halt in the gravel drive. Clattering noises, like rocking chairs being knocked over, echoed from the porch below. I expected to hear gunfire at any moment.

"BC, you need to move away from the windows," instructed the 911 operator.

"Police! Show your hands! Show your hands!" I heard from below. I released the bent blind and lay flat on the floor. Shouts continued from outside. *"On the ground! Get on the ground!"*

"Don't shoot! Don't shoot!"

More heavy steps sounded on the porch, more clattering, and then a thud, like something, or someone, being knocked up against the house.

"I think they've got him," I whispered to the dispatcher.

"Stay in the room until you hear from an officer," she responded. It didn't take long. Shouts from inside the house quickly announced the presence of Halston County deputies, and I yelled my location in return. Footsteps raced up the stairs. I dropped the phone and slid the couch away from the door. A gray-haired officer with gun drawn waited for me at the top of the stairwell.

"BC Morrow?" he asked. As I answered he grabbed my shoulder and led me quickly down the stairs. At the bottom, straddling the threshold of the front door, a second officer held his left hand out signaling for us to stop. His right hand aimed a black 9mm toward the ground. I had seen his face before.

Officer Vickers…from the Waffle Shack.

"Do you know a *Cougar*?" he asked.

"Do what?"

"I'm *Cougar*, tell him it's *Cougar*," grunted a familiar voice from the porch. A thud and a "*shut up*" sounded from outside. I nodded affirmatively toward Officer Vickers.

"That's my friend Kit...from the Waffle Shack," I reminded the officer, "from the fight with the Ingles."

"Bring him inside," the officer instructed, shaking his head and holstering his weapon. Two officers roughly escorted Cougar through the doorway. Off balance, hands cuffed behind his back, Cougar fell to his knees inside the living room. Fear seeped from his eyes. Blood trickled from his nose.

* * *

Captain Mark Boone wanted us out of the house.

He entered Eli's with concern and purpose, but as he studied the pictures on the camera I could see the confusion in his face. I answered all of Mark's questions, assuring him that I hadn't heard anything or seen anyone. He quickly found the phone in the kitchen and I could hear him asking if everyone was okay. And then I heard him ask for Laurie. "Yes, BC is okay," I heard him say. "Listen Laurie, when you put the letter in Eli's mailbox was there a camera in there as well? Did you notice any cars near the road?"

Officers continued to assemble in Eli Giles' living room. Some that arrived late weren't in uniform and others were wearing TBI vests. When Mark stepped back into the room the buzzing and chattering ceased. He had the attention and respect of all of the men, even the agents.

"Joe Vaughn Burrell is close, very close, maybe even watching," announced Captain Boone. "That camera was put in the mailbox within the past two hours. Joe Vaughn Burrell has sent a message that he's very much in the game. And we need to win this one quickly."

Mark tossed the camera to one of the agents. "We need to figure out who the female is on that camera. According to the camera's time stamp she was alive four hours ago. We need to find her." The agent nodded and headed out the doorway. Mark looked at Cougar and me sitting on Eli's couch. Cougar had tissues packed inside his busted nose.

"BC, get your keys," Mark ordered, "and drive you and your friend directly to my house." He then turned to the officer nearest me.

"Officer Vickers, follow them to my house. Officer Wilson is already there, but you two need to check my house, check the perimeter, and then stay there until you hear from me."

"10-4 Captain," replied Officer Vickers.

"The rest of you need to get your vests, check your weapons, and get yourselves focused. Tonight we're hunting for Joe Vaughn Burrell."

* * *

Officer Vickers approached me and Cougar underneath the glow of a flood light in Mark Boone's back yard. Ignoring the officer, Cougar picked up a nearby basketball and took a shot on the Boone family goal. Cougar was too wired from the night's events to stay inside. And Cougar, I knew, was still angry that the officers had manhandled him and busted his nose on Eli's front porch.

I had decided to stay outside because of the orange Jeep parked in the Boone family driveway. *Dylan's Jeep.* I had never gotten to open Laurie's letter, which was still at Eli's, and the orange Jeep in front of the Boone home suddenly made me second guess what was written. Perhaps Laurie had given Dylan a second chance after all. Perhaps the letter was her way of letting me know that *we'd always be friends, but…*

"Are you sure you two don't want to go inside?" asked Officer Vickers.

"I'm good out here," I answered. Cougar didn't respond.

"Well, I need to speak with Mrs. Boone again, but then I'm coming back out. Don't leave this backyard," Vickers ordered.

"Or what, you'll bust our nose?" replied Cougar.

Officer Vickers stopped halfway up the back deck's stairs, obviously not finding the humor in Cougar's remark. "Or I'll hide you somewhere much safer, like a cramped cell in the Halston County jail," the officer responded before going inside.

Cougar threw the ball against my back. "Quit thinking about you-know-who and her boyfriend inside and let's play."

"I thought you didn't play basketball during the summer," I answered, forcing the ball back at Cougar.

"After those cops harassed me I need to take some aggression out."

As did I.

Five minutes later Cougar and I were both intently locked in a fierce one-on-one battle in the Boone family backyard. He was taller, more athletic, and highly motivated to talk trash, but I could shoot from distance and was quicker than him when he came too far from the basket. Tied at four baskets apiece, Cougar fouled me hard with a forearm to the head as I drove by him to the goal.

"That was for the fire alarm," he remarked, giving the ball back to me.

"It needed to be pulled," I fired back, starting the next possession. I dribbled low, switching the ball from hand to hand, trying to get Cougar leaning so I could make a move to the basket. Cougar used his long arm to shove my hip and knock me off balance. But as I kept dribbling, he kept talking trash.

"*BC Morrow*, defender of all women, from the Waffle Shack to the dorm room," he said sarcastically.

"I did what needed to be done," I answered. I drove at Cougar, lowering my shoulder into his midsection before quickly pulling back to create some space. I took a quick shot. The ball circled the rim and rolled off. I beat Cougar to the rebound but he was instantly against my side, daring me to shoot over his long, skinny arms. Holding the ball firm with both hands, elbows extended, I tried to clear space against the taller Cougar. He kept talking.

"Too bad you can't pull the Boone's fire alarm and get Dylan away from Laurie-"

I pivoted hard, my right elbow catching too much of Cougar's face. He yelled and covered his nose with both hands, but even in the dim light I could see the stream of blood splattering against the concrete court. Bent over, Cougar yelled again and added several profanities to let me know what he thought of me at the moment.

"Cougar, I'm sorry-"

The Boone's sliding glass door opened on the deck above and Officer Vicker's appeared, gun drawn. He looked down at the two of us and shook his head.

"I'm supposed to be protecting you two…get inside now! That's an order."

55

I scooped ice into a plastic grocery bag. If Cougar's busted nose wasn't broken, it was at least going to be badly swollen. As I headed for the bathroom where Donna was tending to Cougar, the phone began to ring.

"Maggie, will you get that?" Donna shouted. I laid the bag of ice on the bathroom sink. Donna scolded me with her eyes and held a towel against Cougar's face. The phone continued to ring.

"BC, can you answer that please?" said Donna. I followed the ring and found the cordless phone in the living room on the arm of the couch. Cougar moaned from the bathroom.

"Boone residence."

"BC?" asked a male voice. It sounded like Dylan, but I knew he was outside. As the wounded Cougar and I had entered the back door, Officer Vickers had escorted Laurie and Dylan out the front.

"Yes?" I answered.

"This is..." The voice trailed off. "BC, this is Detective Ingle. Are Laurie and Maggie there with you?"

"They're here, why? Aren't you with Mark? Have you found Burrell?"

My questions went unanswered for a few seconds. I could hear the detective breathing heavily on the other end.

"Detective Ingle, are you-"

"BC, we've discovered a bag of evidence stashed in the woods. It contains Burrell's clothes...and your hat...from the night he attacked Laurie and Maggie. Mark wants to know if you three can identify the items."

"I'm not sure I remember what-"

"He just gave me the order and told me to hurry," said the detective. The front door opened and Laurie entered. The beautiful Boone daughter moved quickly toward the hallway without a word.

"Okay, just let me-"

"Listen. Meet me out front, I'm almost at the house," said Detective Ingle before he hung up. I met Laurie and Maggie in the hallway. They stood outside the bathroom, checking on Cougar. Maggie held another empty plastic grocery bag, I assumed for Cougar's bloody shirt. Both Boone daughters shot me disapproving glances. I had suddenly become the bad guy, but I had news that was more important.

And so did Laurie.

"Both officers just left," she said. "They got a call while I was outside with them. Burrell was spotted near campus and the whole force is headed that way."

"Thank the Lord," said Donna from the bathroom. "We need to pray that his ends peacefully."

"That was Detective Ingle on the phone," I said. "He wants us three to meet him in the driveway to try and identify the clothing Burrell was wearing from the night of the attack."

"Now?" asked Maggie.

"Yes, and he said he's in a hurry."

Cougar groaned again. Donna reached from the bathroom and took the plastic bag from Maggie. "Maggie, before you go out to meet Trent, get a clean shirt for Cougar from your dad's drawer." Maggie moved quickly, Laurie silently slipped past me on her way to the front door. I followed her outside and onto the front porch. "Laurie, I really didn't mean to bust Cougar's nose-"

"Just boys being boys, huh?"

I started to answer, but headlights appeared down the neighborhood street. We hurried down the steps, but the Crown Vic hesitated in the road and turned awkwardly into the driveway, as if the detective was having difficulty steering. By the time Detective Ingle finally parked, parallel to my own vehicle, Laurie and I stood beside his window.

But something wasn't right. Even with only a nearby streetlamp to help see, it was obvious the driver had no intentions of speaking with us. Detective Ingle stared forward as if we weren't even there. He lowered his head dejectedly. His hand never left the side of the steering wheel.

"Trent?" Laurie called loudly, trying to be heard through the glass.

The passenger side door opened causing the car's interior light to come on. And I saw immediately why the detective's hand had never moved. His left wrist was fastened to the steering wheel with a set of handcuffs. His right arm lay awkwardly in his lap as if injured. A piece of duct taped covered his mouth.

The passenger stood and peered at us across the roof of the car. The streetlight lit the man's face...his smile...and the green Boston Celtics hat he wore.

"Hello BC...hello Laurie, now shouldn't there be a third?" He aimed a black pistol directly at Laurie. "What were the odds that we'd ever meet again?"

* * *

There was a quiet evil in Joe Vaughn Burrell's voice and I hated him more, feared him more, each time he spoke. He had quickly ordered Laurie around to his side of the car. I grabbed her arm and pulled her behind me.

"Be smart son, your hero days are over," Burrell said calmly. "There's still several lives in your hands, but there will be one less in two seconds if you don't-"

"My dad will hunt you down," Laurie said.

"So be it. Now tell Detective Ingle goodbye," Burrell responded coldly. He lowered the weapon from Laurie and aimed it inside the car at Trent.

"No," Laurie yelled. She broke from behind me and moved around the back of the car, stopping just out of arm's reach from Burrell. The monster tossed Laurie a thick role of duct tape. "Miss Laurie, just follow orders quickly and things won't get so messy. He winked at Laurie just before the front screen door creaked. *Maggie.*

'No Mag-" Laurie began, but Burrell's free arm quickly wrapped around Laurie's head, his hand covering her mouth. He pulled her toward him and placed the barrel of the gun against her temple. He whispered in her ear as his eyes remained locked on me. Maggie's quick footsteps sounded on the porch, then on the sidewalk behind me. Even with the patrol car's headlights illuminating her descent to where we stood, I knew she would be too close before she realized the danger.

"Don't let it get messy," Burrell said quietly.

I lunged for Maggie as she approached, covering her mouth before she could see the situation. I had no idea how Burrell would react if Maggie screamed, but I had to keep him from pulling that trigger. Maggie's eyes were wide with fright and she tried to push away from me. "Don't scream Mag," I said, "Just don't scream."

"Hello Miss Maggie," came the calm voice I longed to silence. Her eyes shifted to Burrell. "I need you to listen carefully or I'm going to squeeze this trigger, do you understand?" Maggie nodded, her whole body trembled and tears streaked down her face. "I need you to open the door of BC's car...BC, where are your keys by the way?" I wanted to lie, but I couldn't risk angering Burrell.

"They're in the floor board in front of the driver's seat," I responded.

"Miss Maggie," Burrell continued, "check the gas gauge for me, pop the trunk, then get in the back seat. Can you remember all that, dear? Good, do it now." Maggie moved slowly toward my car.

"There's a half tank left," I said. "Just let them go and keep-"

"Perfect...BC, it's like we planned this together. And now we don't have to ride in this hideous cop car. Now shut up and stand by your trunk," Burrell ordered.

I didn't see what choice I had. As I moved behind my car, Burrell led Laurie around the front of the detective's Crown Vic, keeping her pulled close and the gun leveled against her head. I could hear Maggie sobbing in my backseat. I could see Trent Ingle with his head still down, either too ashamed to look up or already in complete acceptance of what was to come. I knew he could reach the car's horn with his forehead, but I felt like the moment he did Burrell would start pulling the trigger. Maybe the detective knew that too.

But I also knew getting in the trunk of my own car was a death trap.

Burrell stopped beside the detective's door, placed his gun on the top of the car, and reached for the handle. I saw my chance and broke for Burrell as he opened the car's door, betting that I could cover the distance before he could reach back for the gun, aim, and fire. But he didn't have to.

Before I made it halfway to Burrell he produced a knife, which I could only assume had been attached to his belt, and brought the point directly under Laurie's chin. I started to backpedal.

Please don't, I thought, *Oh Lord, please don't let him...*

"BC...it appears I'm going to have to make a believer out of you. So which one will it be?" He pressed the knife point harder under Laurie's chin. Fear filled her eyes.

"Don't please, I'm sorry. I believe you...I'll do whatever you say, just-"

"I'm in a hurry son. Which one?" he repeated. I sunk to one knee in the driveway and pleaded.

"BC, I hate indecisive people." With one quick motion he drove several inches of the blade into the detective's left shoulder. A muffled scream escaped from behind the duct tape covering Trent Ingle's mouth. He thrashed and twisted in pain, his left wrist still secured to the steering wheel. Burrell pulled the blade from the detective's shoulder and quickly placed its edge back against Laurie's throat.

"Turn around Mr. Hero," Burrell said, pushing Laurie toward me and retrieving his gun off the car's roof. He now held a weapon in each hand. Burrell instructed Laurie to tape my wrists together behind my back. My thoughts went to Donna and Cougar in the house, oblivious to what was taking place in the driveway. Maybe they had seen through the windows, I thought. Maybe Donna was calling 911 right now. *Just don't walk out that door, please God, don't let them walk outside.* Tears welled in my eyes. Wrists bound, I had no choice but to duck my head and twist awkwardly into my open trunk. Laurie's hand stayed on my back until I was completely on my side. I brought my knees up toward my chest, my eyes found Laurie's for a brief moment. Tears. Fear. Defeat. There was so much I wanted to tell her.

"It's going to be all-"

Burrell slammed the trunk and all went dark before I could finish. I saw nothing, but sounds found their way into the darkness. The closing of car doors. The cranking of the engine. The muffled orders of Joe Vaughn Burrell.

And as the car began to move and my head bounced against the edge of a tire jack, I heard Maggie praying in the backseat.

* * *

Over the next several minutes I was able to determine that Burrell was in the backseat with Maggie. Laurie drove as Burrell gave instructions, knowing she wasn't in a position to try anything foolish. At some point Maggie's prayers and crying had stopped, I assumed by threat or by duct tape. Joe Vaughn Burrell had won. The resurrected monster had found the very girls he had once let slip away and the punk college boy who had spoiled his plans. My mind began accepting the fate that was surely to come.

But Burrell had left a bleeding officer in the Boone's driveway. He had to know it was only a matter of time before every law enforcement agency in Tennessee and beyond would be searching for us. He had to know they had the description of my car and would have roadblocks and patrols everywhere. Perhaps he simply knew this would all end tonight, for him and for us.

We picked up speed. There had been no stops in the last few minutes. The tires of my Honda hummed loudly and I knew we had reached the interstate. I could hear sounds of large transfer trucks beside us. But there were no sirens to be heard. No one was pursuing. No one had a clue where we were.

But where was he taking us? Back to the bridge? To Nickajack?

In the darkness I thought about Trent Ingle and hoped Donna or Cougar found him before he suffered long. I thought about the panic that must have ensued once they finally stepped outside to look for the girls. I thought about my mother and my brothers and things I should have said, things I would say right now if I could just see them one more time. I thought about Laurie and Maggie and questioned why their lives would have to end this way. I cursed and cried and knew that there was nothing I could do. There was nothing *I* could do. There was nothing...

God, save those girls, I pleaded. *God please save those girls.* Words and anger and truth spilled from my gut. *God...I don't care how...make us wreck...send Mark...take me instead...but please God....save Laurie and Maggie, please take Laurie and Maggie, don't make them endure what is to come. Lord, please.*

I cried and panted and yelled in frustration. The car slowed from the interstate and I knew we had exited an off ramp and stopped. I twisted my wrists back and forth trying to loosen the duct tape. I kicked at the inside of the trunk in anger, scraping my knee against metal. My head banged once more against the tire jack. *God please-*

I heard Burrell's muffled words in the car. More orders. Muffled directions to the place where I assumed it was all going to end. But I heard other words, murmurs, coming from somewhere else. *Someone else.*

We continued on.

God please save Laurie and Maggie, I begged.

At some point the car turned onto a long gravel road. When the sound of crunching rock finally faded, the road grew even worse. My Honda's tires slowly bounced with the divots and ruts of the rough terrain. And around me the words murmured again. I thought it was Maggie praying, but the quiet, calm words soon became as clear as any voice I had ever heard.

Take him with you, I heard. *Take him with you.* The voice was with me, inside the trunk, inside the darkness. The message made no sense but the voice was so familiar, like Eli's, or Mark's, or perhaps...but it was so very calm and so very clear. The car slowed, crept, and I sensed that we were drawing closer to the end.

Jesus, please be with Laurie and Maggie, I said to the darkness. *Save them please. Please take them away from this Lord...just please don't let them suffer...they worship you...take them quickly if you have to, just don't let them suffer-*

The car stopped abruptly. My head slammed against the car jack once again. Joe Vaughn Burrell gave more muffled orders and the engine to my Honda finally shut off.

I made one final, desperate prayer from the darkness.

And then I waited...and waited...on death to begin.

56

When the trunk finally opened, its interior light shown on Burrell. His shirt was off and the trunk light illuminated the rattlesnake inked forever into the man's arms and chest. He held a basketball that had been in my backseat.

"Hello BC," he said. "How was the ride?" I made eye contact with the monster. He grinned and reared back with the basketball, but I had nowhere to go. As I flinched the ball ricocheted off the side of my face. "Nice catch superstar, now get out of the trunk." I lifted my left leg and rolled onto my right shoulder, trying to work my way out of the small trunk. As I balanced on my right knee and reached for the ground with my opposite foot, Burrell grabbed a handful of my hair.

"Let me help you, son," he said. Burrell yanked my head fiercely and my body followed. I spilled from the trunk trying to take the impact with my shoulder, but my face smashed against dirt and rock. I rolled onto my back, my arms still fastened tightly behind me. Trees reached into the darkened sky. Fear and adrenaline mixed with the pain emanating from my head and face. A boot quickly landed in my gut, taking the wind from my lungs. I rolled onto my side, gasping for air.

And then I saw them. Laurie and Maggie.

Light from the trunk illuminated their forms. Each girl was only several yards away. Burrell had their backs against separate pine trees, their wrists fastened behind them around the trunk, their mouths covered with tape. They faced each other, separated by the rugged forest road that ran back into the night. Joe Vaughn Burrell knelt down beside me and whispered in my ear.

"After my *discussions* with Detective Ingle," he said. "I had a gut feeling that other detective would take you to the safety of his home tonight. Ever since you saved his precious daughters it sounds like you've just become part of the family. But BC, you only delayed the inevitable, and I've got something very special planned for you." As he stood he kicked the back of my head with the toe of his boot. The world spun, my vision became foggy. I sensed the girls' reaction and heard their muffled cries. He kicked my head once more and the world became a blur.

My hands were suddenly cut loose. Another object fell against the side of my face. My eyes could barely focus on the duct tape that rolled a couple feet along the dirt road before tipping to its side. I rolled onto all fours and searched for Burrell. He stood several yards away, in front of Laurie, the gun aimed directly into her forehead.

"Get up BC, now," he ordered. "And pick up the tape."

I staggered to my feet. The ground wobbled as I took a step and reached back down for the roll of duct tape.

"Just let them go-"

Burrell fired a shot. Wood splintered a foot above Laurie's head. More muffled cries. The fear of death in both girls' eyes.

"Please-"

"Get in the driver's seat and tape your left hand to the steering wheel," Burrell ordered. I looked Laurie in the eyes, knowing it would be the last time. Tears flowed down her face.

"I'm sorry Laurie, I'm sorry," I said, before turning away. I slid into the open driver's seat and placed my left hand on the steering wheel. I had no choice. The monster had won. With my right hand I wrapped the tape around my left, over the remnants of tape that Burrell had cut but still clung to my wrist. I lifted my left hand ever so slightly from the steering wheel, hoping to keep what slack I could. *Dear Lord, please-*

The passenger side door opened.

"Tape please," Burrell said, hand extended. I threw the roll onto the dashboard. "Hand on the gear shift please." Burrell placed his pistol on the dash and made four or five loops with the tape, locking my fingers and hand painfully to the round gear shift. Then he relaxed, casually sitting in the passenger seat as if we were good friends about to take my car out for a spin. He produced a large, black knife from his hip and gently ran the blade against his open palm as he spoke.

"BC, you are going to die now."

I didn't respond, Burrell continued. "I wanted to give you the opportunity to be a real man...to take your own life...the same way you took my cousin's." Burrell reached across me and turned on the car's bright headlights, illuminating more of the dirt road. I expected more forest, but only one large tree was visible ahead. The dirt road before me ascended slightly, and widened, like a place once used for vehicles to turn around. Beyond that was only a dark emptiness. *A cliff?*

"BC, you're going to drive this car straight ahead. Nick-ajack Lake awaits you. And if you don't…I'm going to make you watch the Boone girls slowly suffer as they take their final breaths." He leaned toward me.

"Do you understand me?" he screamed. I spat in his face.

Burrell raised the knife, rage in his eyes. I yelled and leaned away as he brought it down into the center of the steering wheel, causing the horn to sound. He punched the side of my face twice and cursed me. As I tried to regain my senses, Burrell cranked the engine. When my eyes finally focused I saw the pistol from the dash now aimed directly at my face. The horn continued to sound with Burrell's knife planted firmly inside it.

Take him with you, whispered the calm voice.

"I need that horn and you to go away. Drive off the edge or you'll have a front row seat to a horror show you'll never forget," Burrell said. He leaned to get out of the car.

Take him with you, ordered the clear voice again.

I obeyed.

I instantly shifted into first gear and floored the gas, slamming Burrell back into his seat. His foot kept the passenger door open. I aimed for the thick tree along the right side of the road, hoping to slam into it head on and take my chances. Burrell cursed and raised the pistol. I ducked to my left, turning my face, pulling the steering wheel with my duct-taped hand. The car bounced over a rock or root. A deafening gunshot splintered the glass of my window, followed instantly by the sound of the passenger-side door crunching against the tree. Burrell screamed, the instant pain causing him to fire a random second shot into the dashboard. I held the accelerator down and shifted into second gear.

Take him with you.

Burrell raised the pistol toward my head. "I'll kill you…"

And then the sound of dirt and rock beneath the tires disappeared. We were falling, twisting…*how far to the bottom?* Another gunshot…fire ripped beneath my chin…

And the water met us like a wall.

My shoulder rammed against the driver's side door and crunched the remaining glass in the window, the left side of my head slammed against the car's roof. Water was everywhere. Fog and darkness filled my vision. *Don't stop*, I thought, *keep moving*. I coughed out a mouthful of lake and twisted and turned my head to find air. I yanked and pulled at my wrists still duct taped to the steering wheel and gear shift. The car seemed to roll and twist in the lake. I couldn't focus. I needed to orient myself. For the moment I only knew that I was still alive, I could breathe, and that water was everywhere. *And rising.* I took in a deep breath but strangled as water spilled into my throat. I coughed and spat out more of the lake.

Where was Burrell?

I pulled savagely against the tape. My right wrist shifted and became loose…very loose. I pushed off the console with my foot, yanking my arm with all the force my adrenaline could provide. My hand popped free of the gear shift knob, but my left hand seemed to tighten the more I pulled and twisted.

And then I felt another shifting of the car. I took one last breath before everything was completely under water. I used my free hand to tear at the tape, but it was too thick and wet and wouldn't release. I pulled harder…my free hand slipped from the tape and struck something solid in front of me…the knife…still plunged into the horn.

Burrell's knife. But where was Burrell?

I yanked the knife from the steering wheel and attacked the tape on my left wrist. Adrenaline gave way to panic. I needed air. I frantically sawed back and forth not caring if it was tape or skin, just needing to get loose…just needing to breathe.

And then my hand came free. *Get out…keep moving.* My head and shoulders were quickly through the shattered window, my hip caught a shard of glass, the shock more exhilarating than painful.

And then my leg was caught within the car…

Not caught…grabbed. *Burrell.*

Like in my dream, my always fatal dream, the monster was taking me to my death. I kicked at the hands that held my ankle. *Let go…let go…*

But his grip grew stronger, tighter.

I knew he would never let go. We would die together.

I reached down for the car in the underwater darkness and pulled my body back toward the window. I needed to breathe, I needed to be free of Burrell. My mind was growing dim. I still held the knife. I reached into the dark and furiously jabbed the blade at his hands…his arm…anything.

I felt the release of one hand as Burrell fought my attack. I slashed frantically. The blade tip caught something solid and the handle tore from my fingers.

Burrell's remaining grip released.

I pulled my legs through the window and aimed for the surface.

How far…how far? Somewhere…above me…darkness.
Can't judge the distance…I wouldn't make it.
Pull…kick…can't breathe…just one more.
Gasping…swallowing more of the lake…one…more…pull.

I broke the surface and coughed out the water that I hadn't swallowed. I inhaled the life-giving air and filled my lungs, keeping my face toward the heavens.

I gasped repeatedly. Treading, searching through blurred and battered eyes, the night simply appearing as shades of gray and white blended together, like fog and smoke. I listened for the shore...*it had to be close...it had to be*...light broke the darkness above me...and then a voice.

"BC!...BC!" With new hope I swam, battling the pain and the water toward the one who kept calling.

57

My bag was packed.

My excitement for the trip to Nashville could not have been any higher, and I was ready for the chance of a lifetime. Since my car had become a submarine on the bottom of Nickajack Lake, I was at the mercy of Captain Mark Boone for a Friday morning ride. I left my heavy, *Cohutta College Basketball* travel bag on Eli's front porch and limped my way across the yard to the shady spot under the poplar tree. I aimed for the very spot where the retired preacher often relaxed. I plopped into his chair which faced the house, and maybe, I thought, I had found why Eli Giles liked that very spot. Besides offering some shade, it created a pleasant view of the house with just enough of the back yard showing to reveal the garden and gorgeous view beyond.

Eli had helped build this place with his father. One of the greatest memories of his life he had told me, and I assumed that was what he reminisced about while sitting near the poplar. He was still in Atlanta visiting Joseph and his grandson, but I planned to visit him at his home when I returned from my trip. I also planned to ask the preacher if he'd rent his upstairs to a former good-timing party boy who had been suspended from the dormitories for his senior year. I couldn't think of anywhere else I'd rather stay.

I put my feet up on the over-turned half barrel and pulled the letter from the light blue envelope. I read Laurie's letter for perhaps the hundredth time, never growing old of its brief message, never growing old of studying her handwriting and how she wrote my name. I thought about all that had transpired since I first encountered the Boone girls and Joe Vaughn Burrell in a dark parking lot two weeks earlier. In some ways, the last two weeks now felt like the first weeks I had ever lived. Things were different now. I was different now.

The voice I heard calling from the small cliff four nights ago had been Mark's. During the time Mark was having me followed around town, he had the TBI secretly attach a magnetic GPS transmitter to the underside of my car. It obviously proved beneficial once he learned we had been abducted by Burrell. Mark and several others arrived at the scene just moments after I drove Joe Vaughn Burrell and myself into Nickajack Lake.

Mark admitted that he had mixed feelings about closing in on the GPS beacon. He had no choice but to pursue the car and his kidnapped daughters, but he was worried about what he would find. And his greatest fear was encountering Burrell with us three as his hostages. He knew law enforcement would have no time to create any element of surprise. Those woods were Burrell's domain and the Rattler would not be captured alive. Mark feared the maniac would quickly turn his gun on the three of us if cornered.

I think Mark would have been right on that assumption.

But Mark had discovered his girls, still bound to the trees, and they had quickly informed him that I was in the car that had just plunged into Nickajack. Mark admitted later that he thought he would never see me alive again. But he ran to the cliff's edge, with the headlights of several police cars shining behind him and into the darkness above the lake.

I had swum toward those lights.

I had fought the water to reach Mark's calling voice.

Captain Mark Boone had managed his way down the cliff face and met me at the shoreline. He pulled me from the water and hugged me like I was his son. I don't remember much else, only that he stayed with me on that muddy lakeside in the darkness until the paramedics arrived. I remember him telling me that Laurie and Maggie were okay. I remember being hoisted up the cliff side. And I remember Laurie Boone taking my face in her hands and kissing me just before they loaded me into the back of an ambulance.

Trent Ingle had also survived. Donna had called 911 while Cougar did everything he could to stop the bleeding shoulder, including putting some of the duct tape from the gunshot shoulder over the knife wound. Detective Ingle's wife Trish was later found tied up in the unfinished basement of their home. She was very bruised, beyond frightened, and had a deep knife cut across her palm. Physically she was okay, but the psychological recovery from her encounter with Joe Vaughn Burrell was going to take much, much longer.

Joe Vaughn Burrell, however, was dead.

And this time there would be no resurrection. Divers went for the body that night, and there was no discussion from law enforcement about waiting until morning. According to Mark, everyone just needed to know. Burrell's body was found inside my sunken car. His lower right leg was badly broken and wedged against the passenger door that had been caved in. I guess the tree I hit had done its job.

* * *

I stood from my shady rest under Eli's poplar once I heard Mark Boone's car slowing and turning onto the gravel drive. He was alone. Even with Burrell dead, Donna had taken the girls the next afternoon and left for the mission trip in Missouri. She and Mark wanted Laurie and Maggie far away from the media storm descending upon Andrews. The Boone family had visited earlier that morning with me and my mom in my small hospital room, but I didn't get any time to speak with Laurie alone. That had been Tuesday, and the doctor kept me in the hospital for further observation until late Wednesday evening. After being released, I had finally gotten to read Laurie's letter once my mother took me back to Eli's house. It simply read:

> *BC,*
> *I do forgive you. And I too hope*
> *it wasn't the last of our adventures.*
> *You can save me anytime,*
> > *Laurie.*

Dylan had made one last effort for Laurie that night at the Boones, but he didn't get the answer he wanted before Officer Vickers, aware of the history between Dylan and me, escorted him out.

I limped slightly toward Eli's porch to get my travel bag as Mark parked his Explorer.

"You need help?" he asked, walking my way.

"Sure, if you're offering." I handed him the heavy bag and picked up my Bible.

"You seem to be moving better, BC, but are you sure you're still up for this?" Mark asked.

"Chance of a lifetime, Mark, I can't pass this up. Bruises and cuts will be the last thing stopping me," I groaned.

Mark laughed. "Well, you've got the ride to Nashville to think about it. But I'm not sure you understand how physically demanding this may be on your body."

"I've made up my mind."

"So you're giving up a chance to try-out for the all-conference team, *a chance to play in Europe*, just to go help build a church in Missouri?"

"Mark, like I've told you, I don't have a choice. After hearing that voice in the trunk of my car, and having my prayer answered, I just don't have a choice. Europe will always be there."

"And you think flying from Nashville to Missouri in a little four-seater with a TBI agent is the chance of a lifetime?"

"Absolutely. I've never flown before, so I'm excited."

"I still can't believe you had the nerve to ask the TBI for a free plane ride," Mark laughed, "but they felt like they owed you since you pretty much handled the entire case for them...and for me."

"Well, it was the least I could do," I shot back. "But I've got a few questions you can help me with on the ride." I held up my new Bible with Laurie's letter folded inside.

"BC, I'm no preacher but I'll answer what I can."

I sat in the passenger seat of the Explorer and grinned at the detective still holding my travel bag just outside my door. "Captain Boone, not all my questions are biblical. I have a few concerning a dark headed girl with a gorgeous smile that I plan to ask on a date once I get to Missouri."

Before the detective could respond, I closed the door, and for a brief moment at least, I had finally gotten the last word with Mark Boone. I was ready for the ride.

And I was so looking forward to the journey.

*In my distress I **called upon** the LORD,*
and cried unto my God: he heard my voice out of his temple,
and my cry came before him, even into his ears.

Psalm 18:6

THANK YOU FOR READING

CALLED UPON

BY JASON SWINEY

For more information on this novel please visit:
www.calledupon.com

Or contact the author, Jason Swiney, at:
calleduponnovel@gmail.com